BLOOD TIES

THE WITCHES OF WHEELER PARK: BOOK 6

CHRISTINE POPE

BLOOD TIES

Copyright © 2021 by Christine Pope

ISBN: 978-1-946435-40-8

Published by Dark Valentine Press

Cover design by Lou Harper

Ebook formatting by Indie Author Services

JOANNA WILCOX GLARED AT THE COLLAPSED section of the split-rail fence that enclosed one of her alpaca pastures and held back a curse. It seemed as though she'd spent the last year fixing one spot, only to have another come falling down. Most likely, she needed to have the whole thing replaced, but she didn't really want to think about how much that would cost. She had a rainy day fund for those sorts of things, true, and yet she didn't know whether an amount that had once seemed like a comfortable cushion would cover installing brand-new fencing to enclose her five-plus acres on the northeast edge of Flagstaff.

And she had a feeling that the unusually snowy winter they'd all just lived through hadn't helped matters, either. Not that the winter had started out that way, but once Addie Grant had managed to break down the blocking spell a couple of witches up in the Seattle area had cast, storms had filed into northern Arizona one after the other, like jets coming in for a landing at Phoenix International Airport.

In a way, that was a good thing; Flagstaff needed the tourist dollars a good winter skiing and snowboarding season would bring. On the other hand, though, near record high amounts of snow had given the city's infrastructure a beating.

Including her fences.

Since there was no one around to hear it except Daisy and Lola, two of her alpacas who munched on the hay she'd scattered in the next pasture, Joanna allowed herself a sigh. But that was all she'd allow herself. There was work to be done.

Repairing the fence was a bigger job than she could manage on her own. Several times over the winter, her cousin Jasper had come over to help her whack things more or less into shape, and so she figured she'd give him a call now. While no one in the Wilcox family was exactly hurting for cash, thanks to the monthly stipend they all received from a general fund, Jasper didn't have a regular job, unlike most of the other Wilcox clan members. He was usually up for making a couple hundred bucks here and there in exchange for taking on the occasional odd task.

His phone rang several times, and she worried that either he was somewhere out of range or maybe had a bad connection. He lived on the west side of the San Francisco Peaks, in a small cabin on Forest Service land, and his phone service could be pretty spotty.

But then he picked up. "Hey, Joanna."

"Hey, Jasper," she replied. "It looks like another chunk of my fence has decided to give up the ghost. Any chance you could come by to lend me a hand with it?"

A pause. Then he said, "I wish I could. But I already promised Connor that I'd go down to his place and do the monthly inspection there."

Damn it. Connor, the clan's *primus,* didn't live in Flagstaff full-time, and generally spent the winter months—except for a chunk of Christmas week—down in Jerome, where his wife Angela had grown up. In a little more than a month, they'd be back in Flag to spend the summer in their house at that city's more comfortable elevation, but in the meantime, Jasper had the task of going by their home in Forest Highlands every month to make sure everything was still safe, secure, and running smoothly.

"That's okay," she replied, even as she mentally ran through a list of other people in the Wilcox clan who might be able to give her a hand. Problem was, there weren't many of them, since it was a Wednesday morning, and most able-bodied people with the right skill set were at work.

Maybe she could manage the project by herself. The poles were heavy, and trying to leverage them into place on her own wouldn't be easy, but better that than cramming all her alpacas into one pasture while she tried to get this one in order. And Elspeth and Polly were due to drop their babies any day now....

Before she could continue, however, Jasper said, "I think I know someone I can send over. Let me give him a call. And if he's not available, I can try to come by late this afternoon. We wouldn't be able to get it all done, but we'd be able to make a start."

"Sounds good," Joanna told him, even as she wondered who he planned to send as a replacement. She opened her mouth to ask the question, but then the call ended.

Scowling, she stared down at the phone, not sure whether Jasper had hung up or whether the connection had simply dropped out. With Jasper, it was hard to say. He could have taken her response as a signal that it was all settled, and therefore they didn't need to hash out anything else.

Or, because he lived in the back of beyond, Verizon could have hiccupped at exactly the wrong moment.

Since her phone remained silent, she guessed it was probably the former.

At least he was sending someone over.

Which meant she might as well get as much prepped as she could. She'd already moved the alpacas out of the pasture with the damaged fence, but she knew she could save some time by transferring a bunch of replacement rails out of the shed where they'd been stored all winter and over to the spot where the repairs needed to be made. At least her fences were made with eight-foot lengths rather than the more unwieldy eleven-footers, and so she hoped she could manage them on their own.

A frown pulling at her brow, she made her way down the muddy path to the shed. Inside was the trailer and little Polaris Ranger she used for most of the lighter hauling jobs on her ranch. She had a vintage Chevy Silverado for the heavier stuff, but since the weather had finally warmed up, melting snow had turned most of the lanes on her property into veritable mud baths, and so she liked to use the Polaris for getting around.

Loading up the replacement rails took her about twenty minutes. By the time she was done, she'd gotten hot enough to take off the down vest she'd been wearing over her flannel shirt. She tossed it onto the passenger seat of the Polaris and carefully pulled out of the shed, towing the trailer back to the spot where the damaged fence waited for her.

A man stood by the fence, apparently inspecting it more closely. Since his back was to her, she couldn't tell who it might be. He didn't seem familiar, though; even from the back, she could see his hair was medium brown, not the usual near-black of most Wilcox family members.

Who the heck had Jasper sent over to give her a hand?

At the sound of the Polaris approaching, the stranger turned. Piercing, pale blue eyes met hers, and she realized at once who the man must be, even though she hadn't actually met him before this.

Randall Lenz, former Homeland Security agent, given refuge with the Wilcox clan because he'd sabotaged his own project in order to free the witches and warlocks who'd been held at a government facility for testing.

Joanna didn't know why their paths hadn't crossed before this. Then again, she didn't get out much—and neither did he, from what she'd heard. He tended to keep to himself. Her cousin Lorelei had rented him a cottage on the south side of Flagstaff's historic downtown section, and he kept a pretty low profile by most accounts.

"Hello," he said as she climbed out of the

Polaris and came toward him. "You're Joanna? I'm Randall Lenz."

He had a nice voice, not overly deep, but mellow, smooth. Supposedly, he'd grown up in Manhattan, but he didn't have a trace of a New York accent.

"Hi, Randall," she replied. "It's nice to meet you. And yes, I'm Joanna. Jasper sent you over?"

Randall nodded. Like her, he was dressed for rough labor, in faded jeans and a flannel shirt, although he wore heavy work boots instead of the worn cowboy boots that tended to be on her feet no matter what the season. "I've never fixed a fence before, but I should be okay if you tell me what to do."

Joanna had to repress a smile. That was probably the first time she'd ever had a man actually request that she order him around.

All right, that wasn't exactly what he'd said. Still, she was a little impressed that he was okay with letting her take the lead. Too many men she'd known wanted to act as though they were the expert, no matter what the subject at hand.

"It's really not that hard," she said. "Mostly, we just need to lift these new rails into place to replace the ones that got cracked or broken over the winter. In a few spots, we'll need to install new posts, too, but at least the footings are already there and we won't need to pour cement or anything."

Randall looked a little relieved at that explanation. Although he appeared lean and fit—and a quick glance at his hands told her they weren't the soft hands of a guy who'd spent his entire life at a desk—Joanna guessed he'd never had to do much in the way of manual labor. Why would he, when he'd spent years and years working for Homeland Security? It wasn't like he'd been a ranch hand before he showed up in Flagstaff.

All the same, she was a little surprised by how good a worker he turned out to be. He followed her lead and lifted rails and held posts without comment, never asking to take a break, never even seeming to break a sweat. In fact, he was so quietly efficient that she began to wonder if maybe he had done this sort of thing before, as implausible as that notion might seem.

When she asked, though, he shook his head. They'd taken a break to have some water, and he allowed himself a large swallow before saying with a faint smile, "No, I was a city kid. I had the obligatory summers at camp—my parents didn't want me staying in New York for my entire summer breaks—but I don't think canoeing or learning to build a campfire exactly qualified me to rebuild split-rail fences."

His words made her realize how completely different his upbringing must have been from hers. True, as the adopted child of civilian—nonmagical —parents, he hadn't even known about the powers that lay hidden within him, whereas Joanna had been raised by a witch and a warlock, well aware of her place in the Wilcox clan.

She wondered if he would be troubled by the realization that most of the Wilcox clan knew his personal business. Connor wasn't the type to gossip, but he'd relayed a few details about Randall Lenz's background, just so people would have a better idea as to why he'd come to live in their family's territory.

And Joanna had to admit that she'd thought she knew where she fit in with her own witch clan…until her weather-working powers began to surface, and her parents feared that the clan's former *primus,* Connor's older brother Damon, might use those powers for ill. They made the difficult decision to split up, and Joanna's mother Naomi—a Navajo herself—had taken her live on the Navajo reservation up near Kayenta, far away from the Wilcoxes…and their clan's scheming leader.

The stratagem had been necessary, Joanna supposed, but at the same time, she knew being raised for a good chunk of her life among her mother's people rather than the Wilcox clan had made her feel forever apart from them.

Just like the man standing before her now, she didn't quite know where to fit in.

"Well, you're helping me make great progress," she told Randall Lenz. "Another day like this, and I think I'll have it all handled—as long as Addie doesn't send any more massive snowstorms our way."

Something flickered in his cool blue eyes. Belatedly, Joanna remembered that Randall had been responsible for the death of Addie's mother, even though the whole thing had been a terrible accident. Even so, she knew the two of them had done their best to avoid one another ever since he'd come to live in Flagstaff. Probably, it hadn't been very tactful to bring up the subject of Addie Grant.

However, Randall's voice was calm and unruffled as he said, "I think we're in the clear. At least, the forecast says we're coming into a warming trend, and I doubt she'd tamper with that."

Most likely not. Addie, just like Joanna herself, didn't tinker with the weather any more than was strictly necessary. All the storms that had descended on Flagstaff this past season really weren't any of her doing. She might have removed the stopper from the bottle, so to speak, but it wasn't as if she'd spent all winter calling snowstorms into the area. From what Joanna had been able to tell, her clan's other weather-worker was as sick of continually having to dig herself out of the snow as anyone else.

"No, probably not," she agreed. Even as she spoke, though, an odd little thought flickered through her mind.

She liked standing there and talking to him. And it wasn't just being able to take a break after a few hours of some pretty hard labor. No, she liked the clarity of his eyes, so different from the dark eyes of the Wilcox men. She liked the sound of his voice, smooth and deliberate…the way she could see the muscles in his throat move as he took another swallow of water from the bottle she'd provided.

Why hadn't anyone told her that Randall Lenz was a very attractive man?

Well, it probably wasn't the sort of thing that Addie would have even noticed, for a variety of perfectly understandable reasons. And no one else in the clan had had much contact with him, after all. If Joanna had been the type to meet up for coffee and gossip, maybe she would have heard something from her cousin Lorelei, who'd rented Randall the house where he now lived. She didn't know Lorelei well, but she knew the other woman was the chatty type.

Joanna, on the other hand….

Maybe because she'd spent a large chunk of her formative years being sheltered from the Wilcox *primus,* she'd never been the type for confidences. Her mother had raised her to take care of herself…along with being circumspect to the extreme…so she'd never been as much into the whole clan-togetherness thing as most of her cousins. She went to the holiday parties that Connor hosted, because avoiding those would have been horribly antisocial, but mostly, she kept to herself.

Anyway, if she'd kept her toe in the waters, so to speak, possibly she would have heard that Randall Lenz was something of a looker. Older than she was, true, maybe by as much as ten years. Not that it really mattered.

It shouldn't matter at all, she told herself. *He's here helping you out, not looking for a hook-up.*

And neither was she. Her dating life was as fractured as her fence. She'd had only two romantic relationships in her life, one with a distant Wilcox cousin, the other with a civilian. That one had lasted a little longer, but when he'd started pressuring her to make things more serious, she backed out. At the time, she'd told herself it was only because she hadn't felt enough for him to tell him who and what she really was—what being a Wilcox *really* meant—but even then, she'd known there was a lot more going on than that.

She just hadn't wanted to make herself vulnerable. Ever since then, she'd kept to herself. It was easier that way, even if it sometimes got lonely in the big ranch house all by herself, with only her cat and the alpacas for company.

If Randall noticed the odd pause in their conversation, he didn't show any sign of it. He drained the rest of the water in his bottle, then set it on the ground a little ways away from where they'd been working. Before they'd taken their break, he'd shoved his work gloves into the pocket of his jeans, but now he pulled them out and put them back on again.

"Ready to get to work?" he asked.

She nodded. Randall Lenz was definitely all business, and she liked that.

With any luck, it would make things a lot less complicated.

The setting sun glared into Randall Lenz's eyes as he pointed his truck toward the house south of Route 66 he'd been renting for the past nine months. His muscles ached, but in a good kind of way, telling him that he'd put in an honest day's labor. Two large sections of fence had basically been rebuilt, and the repairs that remained weren't quite as extensive. He and Joanna should be able to get those taken care of by mid-afternoon tomorrow at the very latest.

Joanna.

He didn't know what he'd been expecting to meet him as he drove out to her property, but he knew that Joanna Wilcox was not it. When she'd gotten out of that Polaris and walked toward him, he'd had to keep himself from staring at her in shock. No, Jasper hadn't said much about his cousin, had only said she owned an alpaca ranch out on the northeast edge of town, but still, Randall supposed he'd imagined her in his mind's eye as a rough, outdoorsy sort of person, maybe around his own age.

What he hadn't expected was a goddess.

Her silky black hair had been pulled back in a ponytail, but the day's fresh breeze had still caught it, playing with the ends, showing that it fell nearly to her waist. The eyes that met his had been as dark as her hair, slightly almond shaped in a perfect oval of a face. Although he didn't know anything about her, the analytical side of his mind had catalogued her features and surmised she was probably part Native American. Not a huge surprise, since he knew that the Wilcoxes had a fairly large Navajo strain running through their clan.

His training had kicked in, and he'd managed to keep himself from gaping at her. Honestly, he didn't even know why he'd experienced such a strong reaction to that first glimpse. While he'd abandoned any attempt at having a personal life years earlier, he still had met plenty of beautiful women over the course of his life. It wasn't as though he was some sort of inexperienced kid who'd never seen someone so physically perfect.

Now, as he pulled into driveway of his house —the one-car garage housed his beloved Audi, which he couldn't quite bring himself to sell—he could only shake his head at himself. While he hadn't exactly taken a vow of celibacy or anything, he also hadn't done much to disrupt his current extremely solitary life. Some might have called it penance for what he'd done to the witches and warlocks who'd been held for so many months at the facility in Virginia he once commanded...or maybe it was his way of trying to atone for the death of Addie Grant's mother.

Either way, he'd kept to himself since arriving in Flagstaff. Trying to explain his situation to a civilian would have been nearly impossible, and he wouldn't have felt right about forming a relationship with a Wilcox witch. Not that many of them were available; those who hadn't yet married were far too young, in their early twenties for the most part, and the few who were closer to his age and who'd ended up divorced—although divorce appeared to be very rare in witch clans—hadn't evoked much interest. Maybe it was only that he didn't think he was emotionally able to take on someone with the baggage of children and a failed marriage, not when he had so much baggage of his own. He still felt like a fish out of water in Flagstaff; he'd never been the type to care much about fitting in, and yet he couldn't deny that there was something almost alluring about the idea of a clan, of being so intimately connected to one's family. His parents had given him every advantage, and yet underneath his overall contentment with his life had always been the wish that he could have known where he'd come from.

And now...Joanna.

She's way too young for you, he told himself as he got out of his truck and let himself into the house through the back door. Although he could have used his witchy inborn gift of being able to unlock doors with a thought, he always used a key.

Some habits were hard to break.

At least, he thought Joanna was too young, even though she possessed a self-assurance that was often rare in those under thirty. He couldn't detect any true signs of age in her face, however. Maybe the faintest hint of laugh lines around her eyes, although he wasn't entirely sure of that.

But even if she was thirty, that still made him ten years older than she.

And she hadn't shown the slightest sign of interest in him. He'd taken his cues from her and had been matter-of-fact and brisk, and she'd seemed just fine with that. As he should be. He shouldn't even be thinking about getting involved with a Wilcox witch.

Just the mere fact that his mind had decided to take him in that direction told him how much of an impact she'd already had. He was used to looking at women as coworkers, sometimes allies, sometimes adversaries, and not much more. Physical attraction had never overwhelmed him like this before.

Which meant exactly what?

"That you're losing your grip," he said aloud. He went to the refrigerator and steadfastly ignored the six-pack of Kiltlifter Ale that sat there, and instead lifted out the pitcher of water inside and poured himself a glass.

The cool liquid on his throat felt good. Joanna had given him plenty of water to drink, and it hadn't been a warm day—although he'd definitely gotten heated up as he worked—but repairing fences was thirsty work, no matter how you looked at it.

And they still had more to do.

Which meant he'd be back the next day. Even if nothing happened—and he had no reason to believe it would—the prospect of spending a few more hours in Joanna Wilcox's company made him much more cheerful than he'd been lately.

If nothing else, he'd get to see her, hear her throaty laugh. Small things, he supposed, but these days, he had to take what he could get.

Or at least, take what the universe offered him.

2

ANOTHER STROKE WITH THE HAIRBRUSH, AND then Joanna forced herself to pick up the elastic band that lay on the vanity and pull her hair back into it. Part of her had wanted to leave it down, to let it fall to her waist so Randall could see what it looked like when it wasn't confined to a hair band, but the rational part of her mind told her that was a stupid idea. How the hell could she get any work done if she had hair flying every which way?

Honestly, she didn't know what was going on with her brain. Their parting the day before had been prosaic enough, with her thanking him for coming out and him confirming that she wanted him back at ten the next morning. With that arrangement agreed upon, he'd gotten into his dusty Nissan pickup truck and driven down the lane that connected her property with the highway.

But she'd stood there for a long time after he was gone, staring after the disappearing truck. It was far too muddy for the little Frontier to have left a trail of dust behind it, but she still fancied something of him lingered in the air, a hint of his presence that couldn't be erased.

Eventually, though, she'd gone into the house, fed the cat, and fixed herself a bowl of soup. She tended to make big batches of soup or stew or chili at the beginning of the week so she could feed herself off that for days, but that night, the minestrone had lost most of its charm. Even as she ate, she found herself wondering what Randall Lenz was up to, what he was having for dinner. Did he cook for himself, or subsist on takeout? And if he did live on restaurant or fast food, would he appreciate a home-cooked meal?

Maybe she should invite him over for dinner.

No, that was a bad idea. She didn't know why she found herself so attracted to him. All right, he was objectively good-looking, with those piercing eyes and those regular, chiseled features. The little hint of gray at his temples just made him that much more handsome, in her opinion. She could tell he would probably age well.

Planning on growing old with him? Joanna mocked herself, although that inner voice didn't have quite as much bite as she'd hoped, as if it, too, was sort of curious as to where things with Randall Lenz might end up.

They weren't going to end up anywhere. He was going to come back and help her fix that remaining stretch of fence, and then he'd be done and would leave her life as quickly as he'd entered it. End of story.

And she needed to make sure she paid him. The day before, she hadn't been able to think of a way to bring up the subject without sounding horribly awkward, but she knew that today she needed to hand him a check as she thanked him for all the work he'd done. She'd heard through the family grapevine that Connor had given him a stipend, just as though he was another member of the Wilcox clan, and so Randall couldn't be hurting for money too much. All the same, she was not the sort of person to expect someone to work for free.

Joanna got her checkbook out of her desk drawer and wrote out the check. If Jasper had come and done the same work, she would have paid him five hundred dollars, and so she guessed it would only be fair to pay Randall the same amount.

When she was done with that task, she folded the check in half and stuck it in the pocket of her jeans. Resolutely, she forced herself away from the mirror instead of taking one last look at her hair and her lip gloss, and headed downstairs.

Five minutes until ten.

Stupid to feel this anxious about him coming over. Even if she had to admit to herself that she found Randall attractive, she also needed to recognize that he wasn't the world's nicest person. He'd shot Addie's mother. He'd rounded up all those orphan—that is, clan-less—witches and warlocks and kept them imprisoned at the SED facility in Virginia. True, he'd apparently seen the error of his ways and freed them all, sacrificing his position with Homeland Security in the process, but the man was no angel. And—

Someone knocked on the front door.

Joanna hurried to answer it. Standing outside on the porch was Randall Lenz, dressed much the same way as he'd been the day before, only now he wore a pair of mirrored aviator sunglasses that shielded his eyes from the morning glare.

He looked almost unspeakably hot in those sunglasses.

"Come in," she said, finding her voice. "There's still some coffee. Do you want any?"

"No, I'm fine," he replied as he stepped inside.

That's for sure, she thought.

It was impossible to miss the way his gaze quickly roved the living room, assessing his surroundings. That was the look of someone taking note of exits and windows, she realized, not necessarily appraising the interior design.

Which was probably just as well. Joanna loved her house, loved the warm wood walls and the heavy beamed ceiling overhead, the substantial river rock fireplace, but she knew it probably wasn't going to win any design awards.

"I went ahead and brought the poles around to the work site," she said quickly, not wanting an awkward silence to develop. "I figured that would save us some time."

He nodded. "Then we might as well get to work."

His comment closed the door on the possibility of any small talk. Joanna told herself that was probably for the best, since she'd never been much good at chitchat anyway.

"We can go through the kitchen," she told him. "It's faster, since it faces out toward the pastures."

Without waiting for a reply—and good thing, because she didn't get one beyond a faint head tilt —she led him from the living room, past the dining area, and on into the kitchen. The back door opened onto the porch that wrapped around the entire house, and she descended the stairs so she could follow the path as it wound its way back toward the pastures.

The day promised to be bright and sunny, and

because there hadn't been any rain or snow for more than forty-eight hours, some of the mud was finally starting to dry out. And thank God for that, because even as a weather-worker who could appreciate all four seasons and their infinite variations, she'd never been a huge fan of the gluey mud that inevitably resulted from springtime snow melt.

They got to work at once. Because they'd already gone through pretty much the same process the day before, they didn't have to waste much time on strategies or planning, only setting the rails in place and making sure the footings on all the posts were secure.

From the next pasture over, the alpacas looked on with interest. Since they tended to be placid creatures, Joanna knew she didn't have to worry about them getting too cranky about being all clumped together like that, although they'd obviously be happier when they had more room to spread out. Luckily, at the moment they seemed inclined to watch the goings-on from where they stood, rather than try to roam a little closer.

When she and Randall paused to take a water break a little before noon, however, his gaze strayed to the cluster of animals watching them from a few yards away. "Why alpacas?" he asked.

Well, at least that was an easy enough question to answer. "They came with the ranch," she said, then sipped some water from her bottle. "I wanted to buy a place with some land, and the couple who owned the property were retiring and moving to Tucson. So, instead of trying to find new homes for the animals, I took them along with the house. I actually got a really good price because I was buying the whole thing as a package deal."

Randall appeared to consider her reply for a moment, still with that slightly narrow-eyed, speculative expression on his chiseled features. "Some might say that was a lot for one person to take on."

Joanna shrugged. "I needed to have something to do with my time. I really didn't want to get a normal job the way most Wilcoxes do. But having the alpacas gives me a decent income stream, and keeps my civilian neighbors from wondering how I earn a living."

"There's a lot of money in alpacas?"

She could tell he was asking from a place of genuine curiosity, and not because he was trying to dig into her finances, so she didn't take offense at the question. "More than you might think. Demand for alpaca wool always outstrips supply, and because my alpacas are from very good stock, the weanlings are also worth a lot."

Randall absorbed this information before asking, "And it's not a problem keeping them outside all the time? This past winter seemed fairly harsh."

To someone who'd spent the past ten years or so living in Virginia, Joanna supposed it probably had. Even compared to New York City, Flagstaff could be damn cold. "Alpacas evolved in a place that has twice the altitude of Flagstaff. This is nothing to them—they actually have a harder time with hot weather than they do with cold. They have a shed where they can hang out on the really sunny days, but they like the shade from the trees better."

The property's former owners had planted a variety of trees around the pastures—oaks and maples and sycamores. Aspen trees ringed the house itself and provided an extra measure of privacy. Actually, it was partly the trees that had made Joanna decide this place needed to be her forever home. Growing up in Navajo territory, she hadn't had many trees around except some scrubby juniper. She loved the shade the trees on her property provided, loved watching them through all the seasons of the year, even in the winter when they lifted bare, graceful branches to the sky.

Not that she would tell Randall Lenz anything like that. It would be far too personal a confession.

He smiled then, the shift in expression

lighting up his icy blue eyes and showing a flash of white teeth. She got the impression he didn't smile like that very often, which was too bad. It made him seem much easier to know.

"I suppose I wasn't expecting to find a witch who raised alpacas when I came to Flagstaff," he said, then drank some more of his bottled water. "But I'm finding that you Wilcoxes are a diverse lot."

On the surface, Joanna wouldn't have thought so, since the Wilcox clan tended to present a fairly uniform appearance—tall, dark-haired, dark-eyed, good-looking people. There were variations, of course, but they still tended to share a certain look.

On the other hand, they were just as individual as any other group of a similar size, each with their own talents and strengths, foibles and failings. Because she'd been raised away from the clan for a good chunk of her life, Joanna thought she could be a bit more objective when it came to appraising the Wilcox family. All the same, she was proud to be one of them. In the past, there might not have been quite as much to be proud of, but a lot had changed since Connor took over from his late brother.

She kind of doubted Damon Wilcox would have allowed someone like Randall Lenz to settle in his territory.

"We try to be," she said lightly.

So many questions crowded her mind, but Joanna didn't think it would be appropriate to ask any of them. She and Randall barely knew each other, after all, and so she doubted he'd appreciate her inquiring whether he'd made any effort to locate his own clan, or if he'd done any experimenting to explore the limits of his own gift. According to Addie and Jake, Randall's talent was luck. Joanna's cousin Lucas had a similar gift, although he didn't do much with it beyond letting it enhance his life in a myriad of subtle ways.

Did Randall think he was lucky? On the surface, it might not look that way, considering he'd lost his job with Homeland Security and been forced to resign in disgrace. He'd been successful in his former life, had a big house in Virginia and an important job, and now it seemed as if he didn't have much of anything.

Then again, maybe he considered that a fair trade-off for discovering he was actually a warlock, and not just an ordinary man.

He didn't say anything, only swallowed some more water and then set the bottle down on the passenger seat of her Polaris, which she'd parked a few feet away from the section of fence they were currently working on. Since she could tell he wanted to get back to work, she also set down her bottle and picked up one of the rails that were lying on the ground nearby.

"Let's get to it," she said.

A few hours later, they were done. The job had taken a little longer than Joanna had expected, but still, it was barely two in the afternoon, leaving Randall plenty of time to do something else with his day if he was so inclined. He stood and surveyed their handiwork, then gave a satisfied nod.

"It looks good," he said. "But I think the fences in the next pasture down probably need some attention, too."

"They do," she admitted. "Or at least, they probably will sometime in the next six months. They'll hold for now, though—these were the ones that needed the most work right away."

Joanna stopped there, since part of her wished she'd asked him if he wanted to go ahead and fix the fences in the third pasture. If nothing else, that would have kept him around her property for a few more days.

But she had a feeling he would have seen right through such a ploy. Better to let it go. She couldn't deny that she'd liked having him around the past couple of days, and yet she knew that pushing for anything else would be a mistake.

Randall didn't seem inclined to argue with her. He pulled off his work gloves and shoved them into his pocket, then nodded. "Well, if there isn't anything else you need help with, I guess I'll be going."

Damn. She didn't want him to leave, but any excuses she could come up with as reasons to stay would sound pretty feeble. "Thanks so much for all the help, Randall," she said. "I really appreciate it."

"It's no problem," he replied. "I liked being able to work out in the fresh air for a bit."

That probably would be a nice change after spending all those years working behind a desk. Then she realized she'd almost forgotten something. She scrabbled in the front pocket of her jeans and pulled out the check she'd written earlier that morning. "Here you go," she said, extending the piece of paper toward him.

He stared down at the check as though he'd never seen one before in his life. "What's this?"

"A check," she said, even as she wondered whether she'd made a serious misstep. "You didn't think I was going to make you do all this work without paying you for it, did you?"

A long moment passed as he gazed back at her, expression impassive. For the first time, she could see why Addie had found Randall Lenz so intimidating...and scary. Those blue eyes of his might as well have been chips of ice.

When he spoke, though, he didn't sound angry. No, his tone was almost amused.

"I didn't come here to help you out because I expected to get paid," he said. "I owe the Wilcox clan a debt of gratitude for giving me someplace to land. This was just part of repaying that debt."

Oh. She supposed she should have guessed he'd look at the situation that way. While she could appreciate such a stance, she still hated the idea of making him spend two days performing back-breaking work with not much to show for it.

Well, she'd just have to come up with some other way of saying thank-you. An idea occurred to her almost immediately, but she wasn't sure if she dared...especially since she knew deep down that her motivation sprang from something more than merely wanting to show her gratitude for all the work he'd done on the property.

Still, she also knew that if she didn't blurt it out now, she might not have the opportunity—or the courage—to do so again.

"If you won't let me pay you, then will you at least let me make you dinner tomorrow night?" she asked. "This isn't a Wilcox clan thing...just a me trying to say thank-you thing."

He was silent for a moment, expression still

unreadable. Had he developed that poker face while interviewing all the "orphan" witches and warlocks he'd collected?

Then he inclined his head ever so slightly and said, "I'd appreciate that, Joanna. I'm not much of a cook, so it's frozen food when I'm not getting take-out or things from the deli at Sprouts."

"Well, then," she replied, relieved that he hadn't shot her down...but also wondering just what the heck she'd gotten herself into. "It's time you had a home-cooked meal. Any dietary restrictions I need to know about?"

"No." A small glint had entered his eyes, as if he'd wondered whether to make something up, just to make things more difficult for her. "No food allergies, nothing I need to avoid. You just make what's easiest for you."

Oh, she'd do a lot more than that. Since he hadn't given her any restrictions, she'd make sure she'd prepare something that would knock his socks off. Maybe not a standing rib roast or anything quite that fancy, but the nights were still cool enough that she could put together something hearty and fun. Coq au vin...lamb stew... possibly elk tenderloins if she could lay her hands on some.

"I'll figure it out," she replied, glad that she sounded casual and not at all as though her brain had suddenly switched into overdrive as she tried to decide the best thing to make for their dinner. "Tomorrow at seven?"

A corner of his mouth lifted. "Tomorrow at seven," he echoed. "See you then."

He tilted his head toward her, then turned and headed toward his truck, which he'd parked over by the detached garage. It was hard not to stare at his rear end in those faded jeans, because they definitely were filled out nicely.

Then he was safely inside the vehicle and beginning to move down the lane that led to the highway. A moment later, and he was gone.

Joanna let out a breath...and hoped she hadn't made a huge mistake by asking him to dinner.

3

RANDALL FIDDLED WITH THE COLLAR OF HIS shirt and wondered if he'd overdone things. No, it wasn't as if he'd put on a tie or anything—ties were one part of his former life that he'd been all too happy to leave behind—but Joanna had only seen him in flannel work shirts and his most worn-out pairs of jeans. For their dinner, he'd put on a gray button-up and a newer pair of jeans, thinking he didn't want to look as if he'd showed up to help her clean out the tool shed or something, but now he found himself worrying that he might come off as trying too hard.

Because this wasn't a date or anything. It was just Joanna feeding him dinner because he wouldn't take her money.

In the moment when she'd extended the check to him, he'd experienced a flash of resentment before he realized she wasn't trying to condescend to him. No, she'd only been attempting to show her gratitude for the work he'd done. Sooner or later, he hoped he'd figure out that the world he moved in now was very different from the one he'd lived in for most of his adult life, but he still hadn't quite shaken some of the reactions that had been ingrained in him over the past decade or so.

At least, he hoped it wasn't a date.

No, scratch that. Part of him very much wanted this dinner to be a date...even as at the same time he knew that getting involved with a Wilcox witch wasn't in the program. He was supposed to be living a quiet life here in Flagstaff, not attracting any attention, not making waves.

True, that restriction was one he'd put on himself, because neither Connor nor Angela—nor anyone else in the clan—had told him he couldn't have a personal life. But Randall knew he didn't want that sort of complication. He'd been granted a second chance...something that very few people ever truly got...and he didn't want to make a hash of things.

As usual, he was probably creating complications where there truly were none. Joanna wanted to cook for him because doing so would be an easy way of repaying her debt. And obviously, she'd guessed that he probably hadn't been getting many home-cooked meals lately. The last one had been Christmas dinner at his mother's home in Manhattan, although the rest of the time he'd been in New York, they'd gone out to eat. Barbara Lenz was a good cook, but she'd wanted to give her son a chance to get some of the food she assumed he must have been missing during his exile away from what she regarded as the "civilized" world.

Not that she knew too much about what was going on in his life. He'd told her he was in Arizona, but he hadn't said precisely where. "I move around a lot," he'd said vaguely, implying that he was living a vagabond existence, hopping from Airbnb to Airbnb while he tried to get his life figured out. She hadn't been happy about that, but she also hadn't pressed him. His mother possessed a lot of wonderful qualities, and discretion was only one of them.

When he'd first come to Flagstaff, he'd made a day trip to Phoenix to set up a mailbox at a UPS store there, and also to establish an account at a bank far enough away from his actual home base that it should be safe. He needed a place where his official mail could be delivered, and also an address where his mother could mail him Christmas cards and other correspondence if she was so inclined, and to his relief, she hadn't asked too many questions. Maybe he was taking too many precautions, but he felt that keeping his actual location something of a secret was best for everyone involved.

Whether such caution was truly necessary, Randall had no idea. He'd taken those steps to distance himself from the Wilcoxes just in case some part of his past reared its ugly head. After everything they'd done for him, the last thing he wanted was to bring any trouble to their part of the world. True, thanks to Jake Wilcox's hacker brother, any connection between Randall Lenz and Flagstaff, Arizona, had been effectively erased, but it still seemed better to play it safe.

At any rate, he figured he'd go to dinner, thank Joanna for the meal, and cut things off cleanly there. She would have no reason to see him after tonight—well, at least not until she decided to make the repairs on the remaining pasture fences on the property.

That would be some time in the future, though, and there was every likelihood that she'd call her cousin Jasper to assist her rather than reach out to him again. Randall didn't know whether he really enjoyed that prospect, but there also wasn't much he could do about it. In general, Jasper handled that sort of thing, and it was only because he'd been busy with another job that he'd called Randall in to lend a hand.

Since there wasn't much he could do about his outfit except take everything off and change it out for something that might look a little less formal —and because doing so would make him late for dinner—he shrugged at the mirror and got his jacket from the hall tree that stood in a corner of the small living room of his rented house. The place was so tiny, it didn't have a coat closet. Not that it really mattered, since he was the only one living there anyway.

The drive to Joanna's house took about fifteen minutes. He hadn't been there after dark before, and he almost missed the turn-off to the small private lane where her property was located. Luckily, he caught himself in time and turned onto the road with only a small scatter of gravel.

Lights shone from almost every window as he pulled up and parked in his usual spot by the garage. The place looked homey and welcoming, a refuge from the harshness of the world.

And that, he told himself as he got out of his truck and walked toward the porch, was laying it on a little thick. Joanna's place was a house and nothing more.

But he had to admit that it was sturdy and well-built, obviously constructed to withstand the worst that Flagstaff's winters could throw at it. He'd taken note of the stacked logs in the bin on the back of the porch when they'd walked out to the pasture the day before. Clearly, Joanna was prepared in case a spring storm came along and buried everything in a few feet of snow. Randall knew that was always a possibility, since he'd been warned Flagstaff could get snow as late as Memorial Day...although he had to hope that wouldn't be a problem this year.

The door opened within a moment of his knock. Joanna gazed out at him, looking truly spectacular in a simple black dress and shiny black cowboy boots, with turquoise gleaming at her neck and ears and wrists.

So much for worrying about being overdressed.

"Hi, Randall," she said. Her tone was almost a little too casual, but maybe she also felt awkward about dressing up for dinner after the work clothes she'd worn to repair the fences. "Come on in. I just have a few last-minute things to do in the kitchen, and then we'll be ready to sit down."

He nodded and entered the house. Whatever she was making, it smelled incredible—warm and somehow spicy at the same time, redolent with garlic and basil and something else he couldn't quite identify.

"Here," he said, and handed over the bottle of wine he'd purchased earlier that day at Vino Loco, a wine bar and shop in downtown Flagstaff. "It's a cab. I hope that works."

"It's perfect," she replied, looking both startled

and pleased at the same time. "I made beef ragout, so that'll go great."

Since he'd had an inkling she would make some kind of beef dish, he'd gone for the cabernet. Good to know that his instincts still seemed to be intact...or maybe it was just his gift of luck kicking in at exactly the right moment.

"Do you need help with anything?" Randall asked. It might have been a while since a woman had invited him over to her house for dinner, but the manners his parents had ingrained in him hadn't deserted him completely.

Joanna smiled. Was that a hint of amusement in her tip-tilted dark eyes? "No, I'm good," she said. "But you can open the wine. There's a corkscrew on the table."

That he could manage. He nodded at her and went into the dining room while she headed back to the kitchen. The corkscrew was fancier than he'd expected, a waiter-style piece with a polished wood handle inlaid with turquoise. He wondered if she'd gotten it in Navajo country somewhere.

Opening the wine only took a moment. Randall set the bottle back down on the table, noting the heavy earthenware dishes with their warm red glaze, the equally rustic place mats done in shades of red and brown and cream. In the center of the table, a trio of pillar candles sat on black iron holders.

In all, the table looked just as welcoming as the house itself had appeared to him as he drove down the lane a few minutes earlier. The knot of tension that seemed to have taken up permanent residence at the base of his neck loosened slightly, even though he thought he should be even more ill at ease, considering that he didn't quite know how he should behave around Joanna Wilcox.

How about you relax and go with the flow for once? he asked himself, although the question was mostly rhetorical. He'd never been the type to go with the flow about anything.

But he didn't have time to worry, because Joanna returned carrying a large bowl of salad, followed by a basket of rolls, and then another big bowl, this one filled with the ragout. The aroma that drifted from it was so savory, Randall's mouth actually began to water.

"I think that should do it," she said as she put the bowl down on a potholder she'd set out to protect the tabletop from the hot ceramic.

"It looks wonderful," he responded.

"I hope so."

She went ahead and sat down, and Randall, who'd been hovering next to the table the entire time, followed suit. This show of gentlemanly behavior earned him the faintest lift of an eyebrow, as if Joanna wasn't convinced that he needed to be quite so polite.

Again, that was how he'd been raised, and he didn't see any reason to change his behavior now. He picked up the cloth napkin at his place setting and put it in his lap, and Joanna spread her napkin over the skirt of her dress.

"To getting it done," she said as she lifted her glass.

There was a nice, neutral toast. Or at least, he assumed she was referring to the work they'd performed while repairing the fences, and nothing more than that.

"To getting it done," he repeated, and dutifully clinked his wine glass against hers.

For a few moments, they were silent as they dished up their food. The salad looked beautiful as well, with grape tomatoes and freshly grated parmesan cheese and croutons that turned out to be homemade.

"Oh, they're easy enough to make," Joanna told him in response to his question. "I don't like store-bought ones very much. So I made those, and the rolls. The salad dressing, too."

This revelation made Randall look at her in surprise. "It sounds like you should be running a restaurant, not raising alpacas."

She chuckled. "Oh, I like to cook, but I don't have the right disposition to be in the restaurant business. One obnoxious customer, and I'd be telling them to their face what I thought of their one-star Yelp review."

He couldn't help smiling in response to that statement. True, Joanna Wilcox didn't seem like the sort of person who would suffer fools very well. And nor should she. Since he had very little use for idiots himself, Randall thought that was just one more thing he liked about her.

Not that there had been a shortage to begin with.

The food tasted even better than it smelled. Although he'd been subsisting mainly on takeout, he couldn't really claim that he'd been deprived of great cuisine, since Flagstaff had a surprising number of very good restaurants for a smallish city. However, the ragout and the rolls and the salad were still better than anything he'd gotten from any of the places in his usual rotation.

"This is all wonderful," he told her, and she gave a small lift of her shoulders, as though the only response she could think of was to be at least partly self-deprecating.

"It's nothing fancy," Joanna protested, and Randall shook his head.

"Take the compliment and enjoy it," he said, and this time she actually laughed.

"Still giving orders, Agent Lenz?" she shot back.

If someone else had addressed him in such a

way, he probably would have taken offense. He'd done his best to leave that identity behind on the East Coast. But because it was Joanna Wilcox teasing him, he only shook his head. "Bad habit," he replied, his tone casual. "I'll try to do better."

She watched him for a minute, glass of wine in one hand. Her gaze was speculative, and he wondered if she would have even uttered her next words if she hadn't already drunk almost half the glass.

"You're different from what I expected."

Considering what Addie Grant had probably told Joanna about him, that had to be a good thing. Still, he was willing to play along. "Different how?"

"Just...different." She took another sip of wine and then put down the glass, but although she reached for her fork next, she didn't seem inclined to get herself another bite of ragout. "You know, I was kind of shocked when you showed up on my doorstep Wednesday."

"Jasper didn't tell you I was coming?"

She shook her head. "No. He just told me that he couldn't make it but he had someone else he could send over."

Well, that seemed kind of par for the course where Jasper Wilcox was concerned. Randall thought he was a fairly good judge of character, but he'd be the first to admit that he hadn't quite figured out Jasper. On the surface, he seemed like your typical counter-culture sort, right down to the longish hair and multiple tattoos. However, he appeared polite and well-spoken enough...when you could get him to talk at all. The voluble type he was not.

But because it had been a combination of Jasper's talent at making counterfeit I.D.s—his magical ability was to make small, permanent illusions—and Jeremy's gift for hacking computers that gave Randall a new identity as Randall Garnett, resident of Flagstaff, Arizona, he couldn't complain too much. Since he'd already had first-hand experience of how good the work of those two men actually was, he knew he didn't have to worry about anyone tracking him down.

If anyone was even looking. He'd gotten the distinct impression that everyone in DHS, from Under-Secretary Bryant on down, was glad to see the back end of Randall Lenz. For all he knew, his precautions mattered very little.

"Guess he wanted to surprise you," Randall said with a smile. Then, because both he and Joanna needed a refill, he reached for the bottle of wine and poured a bit more into each of their glasses.

"That sounds like something Jasper would do," she responded after murmuring a thank-you for the additional wine. "Not that I'll admit to being an expert. He may be my cousin, but I don't really get him."

"I doubt anyone does," Randall said. "I'm sure that's how he wants it."

"Probably."

They both fell silent then as they returned to their food. That little break they'd taken as they spoke had given him his second wind, and he reached for more ragout once he finished what was on his plate. Joanna didn't say anything, but he thought he noted a satisfied glint in her eyes as she watched him eat. Like a lot of cooks he'd known, she seemed to derive more pleasure from seeing people enjoy the food she made than eating it herself.

Not that she deprived herself. No, she ate with a healthy appetite and clearly didn't seem to have any hang-ups about overeating. And although she was very slender, it didn't seem to matter how much food she put on her plate. He guessed she kept active enough with the alpacas and the other chores around the ranch that she pretty much burned off anything she took in.

"About the fence on the third pasture," he began, surprising himself a little. He'd been thinking about it as he ran errands and did some work around the house, but he hadn't thought he'd broach the subject with Joanna. It was her property and her decision, after all.

"What about it?" Her expression hadn't changed, so if she thought it odd for him to bring up the topic when they hadn't mentioned the fence all night, she showed no sign of it.

"I really don't mind helping you get all of it repaired," he replied. Since he'd already opened his mouth, he figured he might as well go for the gold. "That is, I don't see the point in not fixing all the fences at once."

Now her mouth curled slightly in amusement. "You don't like leaving a job half done?"

When she put it that way....

"I guess not," Randall admitted. He always had been a stickler for order, for finishing what he'd started. When he was a kid, his mother never had to bug him about cleaning his room or doing any regular chores, like rinsing the dinner dishes or watering the plants on the patio. "But if you have other plans, then obviously, you can leave it for whenever doing the repairs will fit better in your schedule."

"'My schedule,'" she repeated, then chuckled. "I don't have a schedule, Randall. Or at least, I don't have much of one beyond whatever the alpacas have in mind. Since two of my girls are about to have their babies, I need to be around for that, but because they've already been moved to the other pasture, it shouldn't matter too much."

She hadn't shot him down or told him that

Jasper would take care of the fence. That had to be a good thing, didn't it?

"The noise won't bother them?" Randall asked, thinking that Joanna seemed fairly *laissez-faire* about the impending birth of the alpaca calves...or whatever they were called.

"Probably not." She sipped some wine and broke a piece off the half roll that lay on her plate. "Alpacas are pretty mellow creatures. Every once in a great while, there might be a complication, but overall, they're a lot easier to deal with than horses or cows or even goats." A pause there, and then she added, expression brightening, "Actually, they get along really well with goats. I've been thinking of buying a few, but I hadn't gotten around to it yet."

Having spent his entire life in the city, he knew very little about goats, except that they were eating machines and liked to jump on things. Keeping goats sounded like a lot of work to him, but he had no doubt that Joanna could handle adding a few goats to her herd of alpacas.

The important thing was that she seemed open to having him continue to work on repairing the fence. He didn't have any major claims on his time, either; he drove for Door Dash and Instacart on an off-hand basis, but it wasn't as if he had regular hours for those gigs. The days he'd been working here at Joanna's ranch, he'd simply marked himself as not available.

"That's good to know about the alpacas," Randall said, hoping he sounded casual. "Do you want to work on the fence over the weekend, or should I come by on Monday?"

Her brows drew together as she appeared to consider her options. "Let's start on Monday. There's a good chance that Polly and Snow will have their babies during the weekend, and then that'll be over with before we start hammering again."

Probably not the most fortunate choice of words. Joanna seemed to realize that as well, because a faint flush appeared on her high cheekbones, and she reached for her glass of wine and took a quick sip.

Randall knew better than to say anything. He remained silent as well, using the last few bites on his plate as cover for his lack of response.

That wasn't the end of dinner, though—Joanna picked up their plates and went into the kitchen, then came back with a couple of slices of chocolate cake.

"I suppose I should've asked whether you liked cake," she said as she set a plate in front of him. "But you said you didn't have any dietary restrictions...."

The words trailed off as she gave him a quick sideways glance.

"I don't," he said. The cake looked as amazing as the rest of the dinner—lush and dark, with a generous coating of fudge frosting. "And I like chocolate cake very much. Thank you."

Relief clear in her expression, she sat down and picked up her fork. Randall did the same, and took a bite of cake. It tasted just as luscious as it looked, and was even better than the cakes his mother used to get him for his birthday when he was a kid. He rarely ate sweets anymore, but he couldn't regret having this slice of cake. It was a little piece of heaven…just like Joanna's ranch.

Or maybe the woman herself.

He probably shouldn't be thinking those sorts of things. Not when he'd had half a bottle of wine, and his inhibitions might not be entirely intact. Still, he had to wonder how a woman like her could possibly be unattached. It wasn't that he thought a woman's worth depended on her skill in the kitchen—far from it—but she was smart and capable and beautiful, and the Wilcox warlocks must have been singularly undiscerning to allow such a paragon to escape their notice.

As they ate, she made a few comments about how her mother had taught her to cook, and how she'd kept up the practice once she was living on her own. "It's something to do," she said. "And

I'm always having cousins ask me to bake cookies for their book club get-togethers or cakes for birthday parties. It's fun, and I kind of like the thought of Wilcox kids getting to have goodies baked by another Wilcox. Just keeps it all in the family, you know?"

He nodded. Family seemed to be all-important to witch clans, and Randall thought he understood. They had to present a united front to keep their magic secret from the civilian population, and so that inter-connectedness was key to their preservation.

At the same time, though, he guessed that he'd never be able to completely immerse himself in the Wilcox clan, despite being a permanent guest. He wasn't one of them, and so would forever be kept at arm's length. The situation bothered him somewhat, since he'd begun to feel weary about being perpetually on the outside. On the other hand, he hadn't come from a big family—both his mother and father were only children—and so it was a bit difficult to miss what he'd never had.

"It's nice of you to do that," he responded, although he hoped privately that all those Wilcox cousins who were asking Joanna to make their cookies and cupcakes were at least providing some funds for materials so she wouldn't be doing all of that out of her own pocket.

Probably not his business, but....

"They're not imposing on me," she said, dark eyes twinkling.

"Did I say they were?"

"You didn't have to," Joanna replied. Her mouth twitched in amusement. "I could see it in your face."

Well, then, he'd have to work on that. He'd always prided himself on keeping his cards close to the vest, so to speak. Then again, when he'd been interrogating subjects back in the day, he wasn't doing so after drinking half a bottle of wine.

He shrugged and reached for the glass of water at his place setting. It was still more than half full, and he knew he should have been drinking more of that during dinner than so much wine.

"I wouldn't presume," he said, and she chuckled.

"No, you wouldn't," she said. "But you'd think it real loudly."

About all he could do was shake his head as he replied, "I suppose I'm still figuring out the Wilcox clan."

"You'll get used to us. It hasn't even been a year yet." She paused there, expression turning thoughtful. "Do you miss it? Your work, that is."

Joanna Wilcox was the first person who'd ever asked him that question. Randall knew most of the Wilcoxes believed he must be glad to be away from Homeland Security and with his own kind, even if they weren't his clan. Most days, he was. Once he'd realized that the work he cared about so much had been hurting people rather than keeping them safe, the choice was clear.

But even though he knew in his heart that he'd set his feet on the right path, he did miss the work sometimes.

The sense of purpose it had given him.

These days, he often felt like an unmoored boat, drifting lazily down a river with no paddle and no way to steer. He didn't like that sensation; he'd always been the sort of person who'd woken up each morning knowing what he needed to accomplish that day.

"Sometimes," he admitted, although he didn't say anything else. That one word was more than he'd revealed to anyone else over the past nine months.

Joanna nodded. "You'll get it figured out."

Randall wasn't sure if he shared her sanguine view of the situation. No one in the Wilcox clan had been anything other than pleasant to him, but all the same, he wasn't one of them and never would be.

To be fair, though, he could have made more of an effort. Tom Wilcox, a detective with the Flagstaff P.D., had even reached out to him and said they could probably make room for him on the force if he was interested. At the time, he'd only been in town for a few months, and so he hadn't been ready to make that sort of a commitment. He'd given Tom a neutral reply, saying he'd consider it but hadn't quite decided what he wanted to do yet. The other man had accepted the answer with good grace...but he also hadn't repeated the offer.

Honestly, Randall couldn't quite picture himself writing parking tickets or pulling over drunk drivers. Being a cop was a necessary occupation, and yet....

He realized Joanna was watching him with what looked like sympathy in her expression. And he didn't want that. He might not have figured out where he was going, but that didn't mean he wanted her—or anyone else—to feel sorry for him.

"I'm sure I will," he said. Because he didn't want the conversation to steer into more personal territory, he thought it was a good time to put an end to the evening. "And thank you for dinner. Everything was wonderful."

Something in her face seemed to go still, as if she'd recognized his words for what they were. "No, thank you. I'd still be fighting with that fence if it weren't for your help."

Thank God she wasn't going to try to prolong things. "It's not a problem," Randall replied as he lifted the napkin from his lap and set it on the tabletop. He rose, adding, "I'll be here at ten on Monday."

Joanna smiled, but the expression looked a little stiff. "I'll see you then."

She got up from her seat as well, going to the coat closet so she could retrieve his jacket for him. He put it on, even as he wondered if there was something else he should have said.

No. He needed to keep this all business with Joanna Wilcox, no matter how much he might be attracted to her...no matter how much he might enjoy her company.

"Have a good weekend," he told her, and made himself walk out the front door.

He didn't look back.

He didn't dare to.

4

Because it had been a one-pot meal, there wasn't a lot of clean-up. Even so, Joanna stayed in the kitchen longer than she needed to, wiping down the counters and the stovetop to make sure everything sparkled.

For some reason, she really didn't want to go upstairs and straight to bed.

Her lonely bed.

Oh, get over it, she scolded herself. *What did you think was going to happen? That Randall Lenz was going to sweep you off your feet and carry you up the stairs in some kind of silly* Gone with the Wind *moment?*

Probably not. If nothing else, she couldn't think of many people who were less like Rhett Butler than Randall Lenz.

There had been a moment here and there

when she'd caught Randall's gaze lingering on her, had wondered if she'd seen a spark of something beyond polite interest in those fascinating, icy eyes. She was probably flattering herself, though.

Then again, if he wasn't interested, why had he pushed to come back on Monday and help her fix the remaining fence? It wasn't as though rebuilding split-rail fences was anyone's idea of a good time.

He could just be the old-fashioned type. Not that Joanna had ever been one to rush into bed with someone...but he could have at least tried for a goodnight kiss.

She definitely wouldn't have stopped him.

Holding back a sigh, she surveyed the kitchen and determined that it was about as clean as it was going to get, unless she got out a toothbrush and started scrubbing in the corners. Since she was way too tired for that, she figured she might as well call it a night.

The stairs felt especially tall that evening, for some reason. When she got to the upstairs hallway, Sassafras, her big calico cat, gave her an annoyed look through slitted green eyes, but she didn't move, forcing Joanna to step over her as she headed into her bedroom. Sass didn't like strangers and had bolted for the shelter of the second story as soon as she heard Randall's voice.

But if he came over enough, she'd get used to him eventually.

That makes two of us, Joanna thought with an inner grin.

And really, despite the lack of a kiss, she thought the evening had gone very well. The conversation had never lagged, and Randall seemed genuinely interested in what she was doing here on her little ranch. He'd even offered a few personal tidbits—not many, but sufficient to show he trusted her enough to share some information about himself.

There was still so much she didn't know, however. Obviously, he hadn't been married when he'd made a break with Homeland Security, but maybe he'd been divorced for a while. Or possibly he was the type to make his work his entire life. That was more the impression she'd gotten, although she didn't dare ask.

Well, he was coming back on Monday. Maybe he'd let drop a few more morsels of personal information, and maybe he wouldn't. Joanna had to admit that repairing fences didn't necessarily offer the best conditions for offering revelations about your personal life, but she tried to stay hopeful. And honestly, just knowing he planned to return was good enough for now.

She went through her usual rituals of washing her face and applying moisturizer, brushing and flossing and following it all up with a swig of mouthwash. When she settled into bed, though, she couldn't help noticing how quiet the house was…how big the king-size bed felt with just her in it.

Funny how all that space had never bothered her before. If asked, she would have said she liked her solitude, that she had enough to keep her busy and never regretted her single state.

Well, she was regretting it now. Or at least, hoping it might change in the near future.

Unlike Randall, she'd grown up knowing all about her witch heritage. Yes, she'd spent more than a decade hidden away on the Navajo reservation, but her mother had told her the truth about her situation, and had always impressed on her that—with any luck—the current state of affairs would be a temporary one. As one of the Diné, Naomi hadn't been a Wilcox, but she'd had her own powers. Not exactly a seer, she still had very good instincts about the world. Although she'd never come out and said anything directly, her attitude had always suggested that she knew more about what was to come than an ordinary woman possibly could.

At any rate, when Damon Wilcox died unexpectedly and Connor took over, Joanna's mother had said it was time for her to reacquaint herself with that side of the family, and that everything would be different from now on. It definitely was…more different than maybe any of them could have imagined.

But one of the things Joanna had heard from a very young age was that witches and warlocks generally recognized their soul mates early on, and that was why divorce tended to be rare in witch clans. She wasn't sure how much of that she believed—after all, her parents had gotten divorced, although their situation wasn't exactly normal—but she'd absorbed the information and tucked it away. As the years went on and she hadn't met anyone who kindled that little spark within her, she started to wonder if being half Navajo had somehow prevented her from making a soul mate connection with any of the warlocks she met. It wasn't even a somewhat natural aversion to hooking up with a cousin, albeit a distant one; none of the McAllister warlocks she'd met had done it for her, either. After her thirtieth birthday had rolled around a few months back, she'd decided she wasn't going to worry about it anymore, that obviously something had gone wrong with her internal wiring and she'd better brace herself for a lifetime spent alone.

And then Randall Lenz had—quite literally—shown up on her doorstep.

This felt different from any attraction she'd experienced before. The two times she'd found someone attractive and interesting enough to become intimate with them, it had been almost an afterthought. She'd slept with those men because she'd thought that was what you were supposed to do. There hadn't been any kind of real connection, and she'd broken off those relationships—one with a civilian and one with a Wilcox warlock from Williams—almost before they had a chance to really get started. They'd just felt...wrong.

Whereas Randall Lenz felt oddly right to her.

Joanna stared up at the ceiling, trying to tell herself that she was overreacting. Yes, the man was attractive...and unlike anyone else she'd ever met. He could put in a hard day's work without a single word of complaint. During dinner, there hadn't been a single moment of awkwardness, not even when she'd teased him about giving orders.

As soon as those words had left her mouth, she feared she'd gone too far. But he'd taken the whole thing in stride, even smiling slightly. For all she knew, he'd enjoyed the teasing. She had a feeling there hadn't been too many people in his former life with the guts to do that sort of thing.

So...yes, there was a lot to recommend Randall Lenz.

And just as much to make him squarely off-limits. Joanna counted Addie Grant as a friend, and she didn't even want to think what the other woman would say if she casually mentioned she was considering Randall Lenz as a romantic partner. Addie would certainly view her interest as a betrayal.

Or maybe not. Addie would probably never want to go on a double date with her and Randall, but she'd also been pretty composed the few times she'd spoken about him, as if she'd done her best to put everything that had happened in the past. She and Randall couldn't be friends, but she was prepared to be civil.

And all this speculation was jumping the gun. Absolutely nothing had happened tonight, and Joanna had no reason to believe anything would happen when he showed up at her house on Monday morning.

Well, except that her fence would get fixed.

Joanna rolled over on her side and told her mind to shut up. Endlessly speculating wasn't going to change anything. Monday would come, and she'd see what the day brought.

Now, though, it was time to go to sleep.

Randall was at the house exactly at ten o'clock. Exactly how he'd managed to be so precise, Joanna didn't know. Flagstaff wasn't a huge town, but the traffic there could still get nasty, especially in the downtown area where he lived.

Because they were going to be working, she hadn't made any special effort with her appearance, although it had taken an effort of will to prevent herself from putting on a second coat of mascara or exchanging her usual tinted lip balm for something a little deeper. No, she'd braided her hair out of the way and put on a faded chambray shirt and jeans with ripped-out knees, and told herself any primping would be silly.

And since he showed up in old jeans and a flannel shirt with some frayed spots along the cuffs, she was glad she'd followed her instincts.

"Coffee?" she asked him as he followed her into the house. "I made some extra, just in case."

"Thanks, that would be great."

Relieved, she went into the kitchen and poured him a cup. "Milk or sugar?"

"None, thank you."

Joanna supposed she should have guessed that he would drink it black. Since she took it the same way, she didn't have to do anything after she'd poured herself a cup except blow on it to cool it down a bit.

A moment passed as they drank their coffee in silence. Not an uncomfortable silence, though; more like they both knew they'd be exerting themselves soon and so were conserving their energy.

Then he asked, "Did the babies arrive?"

She blinked at the *non sequitur,* but then

smiled. "The *crias?* Yes, one on Saturday and one on Sunday. Both females. I haven't decided what to name them yet, though."

"'*Crias*'?" Randall repeated. "Is that what the babies are called?"

"Yes. They're adorable, too—all wobbly little legs and big eyes. But they're doing great. You can take a peek at them when we go out to the pasture —I need to check on them anyway."

He nodded, apparently amenable to that plan. Something about the little exchange had broken the ice between them, and Joanna realized she didn't feel as awkward around him as she'd feared, even if she'd been forced to admit to herself that she found him far more interesting than she should.

Eventually, they both finished their coffee and headed outside. As promised, the *crias* were out in the pasture with their mommas, standing in patches of sunlight and looking happy and healthy. There hadn't been any problems with either birth, and both babies were up and about on their wobbly, gangly legs within an hour of being born. Joanna had put jackets on them for the overnight hours, since mid-April in Flagstaff could still be downright cold, but she had taken them off as soon as the sun was up and shining brightly.

Randall paused at the fence that surrounded

their pasture and watched them for a moment. One of the *crias*—the white one—was getting a late morning snack from her mother, while the slightly larger of the two, a little brown wisp of energy, wandered around the sunny side of the paddock, apparently fascinated by the movement of the wind in the new grass.

"I didn't expect to see them up and about like this," he commented as she came to stand a foot or so away from him.

"Oh, yes," Joanna replied. "They're like horses that way—they get moving really quickly. If they hadn't, I would've had to call the vet to have them checked out. So far, though, I haven't had any complications with any of my alpacas. They're a hardy lot."

"Apparently." He was quiet for another moment, studying the animals, and then he turned away, his manner now brisk. "Well, I suppose we'd better get started."

As much as she would have liked to stand there and spend another minute or two watching the adorable little *crias*, she knew it was probably time to get to work. Without comment, she headed over to the empty pasture where the remainder of their task waited for them. As before, she'd hauled out the rails in advance so they wouldn't have to waste any time getting set up.

By that point, they pretty much had the procedure down to a science. Without speaking, they started taking down the damaged rails and replacing them with new pieces, working together, each of them seeming to instinctively know the other person's rhythm.

Joanna had never been one to shy away from physical labor, but she knew there was something different about this, about having a partner who could somehow tell when something was too heavy for her and who would reach out to lend a hand without her even having to ask. It made the work go quickly and easily, although she realized there was no way they'd be able to get this pasture finished before lunch.

Luckily, she'd planned for that contingency.

"Take a break?" she asked after glancing up at the sky and guessing that it had to be almost one o'clock. "I'm ready for lunch."

One dark brow lifted. "Did you cook again?"

"I did," she admitted, then added with a grin, "But over the weekend. Just some leftover ham and corn chowder. I swear I didn't go to any huge effort."

He let out an unwilling chuckle. "Okay. If you say so."

Still smiling, she led him back to the house. While he was washing up—and after she washed her hands as well—she got the storage container of leftover soup out of the fridge and poured most of it into a saucepan to heat up. Some people probably would have used a microwave for such a task, but she'd found that something like chowder did better on the stovetop.

When Randall came out of the bathroom, he sniffed the air appreciatively. "That smells great."

"It is great," she said, figuring she might as well not bother with false modesty when it came to her cooking. "An old recipe of my mother's. Sticks to your ribs, as she likes to say."

"Does she live in Flagstaff?" he asked.

"No, she's still up by Kayenta—that's in Navajo territory," Joanna added, realizing he was still fairly new to the area and probably hadn't even heard of the tiny town that was her mother's home. "I think she decided a while back that she really didn't want to get involved in Wilcox drama."

That remark made him raise an eyebrow again. Most likely, he was wondering why her mother had married a Wilcox in the first place if that was how she viewed the clan. In fact, Joanna had asked her mother much the same thing a while back, and Naomi had only shrugged and said, "Sometimes the heart and the mind aren't on speaking terms."

At the time, she'd only wanted to shake her head at her mother's comment. Now, though,

Joanna thought she was beginning to understand what Naomi had meant.

"Anyway," she went on, mostly so Randall wouldn't have a chance to interject, "this is just about ready. Can you get me a couple of bowls from that cupboard over there?"

She pointed to the cabinet in question, and he went over to it and retrieved a pair of bowls. "Here you go."

Joanna took them from him and set them down on the counter next to the stove, then got a ladle out of the stoneware urn that held her most used utensils. After filling up each of the bowls, she handed one to Randall. "That should be enough to get you started. I'll meet you in the dining room."

A nod, and he walked over to the dining table and sat down. She took her own bowl and a pair of spoons and some napkins over to the table, then set them all down. Since she'd already put out place mats and water glasses, all she had to do next was fetch a pitcher of filtered water from the fridge and set it down on the table as well.

"See?" she said after she settled herself in her own chair. "Nothing fancy."

"But still excellent," he said. "This is just what I needed, so thanks."

A happy little flush touched her cheeks, one she hoped he wouldn't notice. Between her own natural skin tone and the tan she'd already picked up from working out in the sun, a blush probably wouldn't be too obvious.

Hopefully.

They ate quietly for a few minutes. The corn chowder was one of her favorite soups, but she generally didn't make it during the warmer months, so this might be one of her last chances to have it before autumn rolled around again. That was another thing she enjoyed about cooking —choosing the right recipes for the right occasions and times of year, always trying her best to utilize what was fresh and in season whenever possible. Temperatures were too cold overnight for her to have started work on her vegetable garden, although she had trays of seedlings germinating in the section of the shed that she'd converted to a greenhouse.

"I noticed your alpacas are pretty woolly," Randall remarked after he'd eaten about half his bowl of soup. "When do you shear them?"

"In a couple of weeks," Joanna said, pleased that he'd been observant enough to notice that detail. But why should she be surprised? The guy used to work for Homeland Security; he'd probably been trained to detect all sorts of details that a regular observer would never pick up. "That's late, but we don't really start to heat up until the end of May, and we can still get some pretty low overnight temperatures before then. I try to play it safe."

"Well, they look happy and healthy, so I'd say you're doing a good job."

His praise made her absurdly pleased. She didn't know why she should care so much what he thought of how she managed the ranch and the animals on it—she'd never been the type to worry what other people thought as long as she knew she was doing the right thing—but she supposed she could chalk up her reaction to her overall infatuation with Randall Lenz.

No, wait…"infatuation" was way too strong a word to use. Attraction, sure. It was easier to admit she found him physically appealing than to acknowledge to herself that more than just her body might be involved in the way she reacted to him.

Even if deep down, she already knew the truth.

"I try," she said lightly. "There was a learning curve at the beginning, but I've owned this place for almost seven years now, so I think I've got it mostly figured out."

"'Seven years'?" he repeated, now looking surprised. "What, did you buy it when you were in high school?"

Once again, a disconcerting little burst of happiness went through her. The words had been partly teasing, but she got the feeling he really did think she was quite a bit younger than she actually was. "I turned thirty in January," she pointed out.

Maybe her ears were deceiving her, but she could have sworn he murmured "good" before he lifted another spoonful of corn chowder to his mouth. Was he happy there wasn't quite as big a gap in their ages as he'd first thought?

Randall swallowed, then said in a much more distinct tone, "That's still a lot of responsibility for someone in their early twenties."

She shrugged. "Like I told you before, I wanted a place where I could be doing something. I didn't want a desk job. Two years of college told me I just wasn't into it."

"It's not for everyone," he agreed.

Joanna had been studying his face, looking for a sign he was disappointed that she wasn't a college graduate, but she couldn't find one. That had to be a good thing, right?

"Where did you go to college?" she asked.

The question evoked a flicker in his cool-hued eyes, but she didn't know him well enough to guess what it could have meant. "Columbia," he said easily, without hesitation. "I majored in political science."

"So, you always wanted to work for the government?"

"Not at first," he replied, and now she could

clearly see the strain in his lean, cleanly chiseled features. "My father died on 9-11. That's the main reason why I decided to go to work for Homeland Security after I was out of college."

Shock flared through her. Growing up in Arizona, she'd been fairly far removed from the tragedy, especially since people in witch clans didn't tend to travel much, and so it wasn't as if anyone in the Wilcox family had been involved... beyond their greater connection as citizens of the United States.

"I'm so sorry," she murmured.

His shoulders lifted, but she could tell the response was an automatic one and didn't necessarily reflect his actual feelings on the matter. Even though his loss had been decades in the past, he clearly was still affected by it. "It was rough," he said, although his tone was even, betraying nothing of the havoc such a loss must have wreaked on his life. "Luckily, we had a good support system. My mother finally remarried about eight years ago."

Joanna thought that must be a sign that she'd allowed herself to move on, even though she'd had to let more than a decade pass before she felt comfortable allowing someone else to take up a permanent place in her life. Because she got the impression that Randall didn't want to dwell on the loss of his father, she asked, "What does your mother do?"

Was that the faintest hint of a smile on his thin lips? Probably; not much got past Randall Lenz, so he would have noted the change of subject as exactly what it was. "She owns an art gallery in Soho. Howard, her husband, is an investment banker. He actually knew my father back in the day—that circle isn't very large."

"'Circle'?" Joanna repeated. She knew he'd been raised by civilians, hadn't even known he was a warlock until a zap from one of Addie's lightning bolts had awakened his hidden powers, so she wasn't sure what he meant.

Now the smile was obvious. He lifted another spoonful of corn chowder to his mouth and swallowed before replying, "I guess what you'd call upper-crust New York society. The people who go to charity galas and live in multimillion-dollar brownstones and penthouses."

He said the words in such a deprecating tone that she guessed he wasn't too impressed by those trappings of wealth, having grown up around them. Obviously, he didn't have any problem with slumming in his small rented cottage and driving for Door Dash…or if he did, he was very good at hiding it.

Then again, he'd worked as a government agent for years. He was probably very good at concealing his opinions, if the situation called for it.

Still, she didn't get a snobbish vibe from him at all. Good thing, because otherwise, she didn't think she had a lot to offer someone who was used to five-star restaurants and having the very best of everything.

"Flagstaff must be a real change of pace, then," she said, doing her best to keep her tone noncommittal.

The laugh lines around his eyes crinkled a bit. "I guess so. But I like it. And really, I sort of stopped doing the high society thing as soon as I started college. Then 9-11 happened, and...." The words trailed off, and he shrugged again. "Anyway, there isn't much time for society galas when you're working as an agent for DHS. I left all that behind long before I ever came to Arizona."

That statement sent a wave of relief through Joanna. At least she didn't have to worry about him pining for a life he could never have again.

"Well, I'm glad that fancy upbringing didn't keep you from doing a damn good job repairing split-rail fences," she remarked, and she could almost see how the tense set of his shoulders relaxed slightly.

That ghost of a smile was back on his finely sculpted lips. "It's actually a lot more rewarding, too."

She chuckled, and they went on to finish the rest of their soup. Afterward, it was back out to the aforementioned fences, the two of them slipping into an easy rhythm once again. And when late afternoon rolled around and it was obvious they'd need another day to finish the project, he didn't seem too put out by the prospect.

"I'll see you at ten tomorrow," he told her, and she nodded.

"See you then."

That was all—he got in his truck and drove off after their exchange—but Joanna knew there was an undercurrent to their comments that couldn't be ignored.

They were both looking forward to that meeting far too much.

5

As he drove out to Joanna's house, the bright morning sun shining right in his face, Randall wondered if he'd lost his damn mind. Right then, that seemed like the most likely explanation for his behavior.

Because any sane man would have recognized his attraction to Joanna Wilcox for what it was, and found a convenient excuse to back out and let Jasper help her finish the rest of the fence-repair project. He couldn't allow himself to get involved with her. It was way too risky.

Or at least, Randall wanted to believe there was some level of risk involved, because that way, he could back out without feeling as if he'd done something wrong. Better that than acknowledge she'd somehow managed to slip into his heart and occupy a space there he hadn't even known existed.

And that just wasn't right. He hadn't exactly defined a set amount of time for the penance he needed to perform to somehow atone for the death of Lissa Grant and the way he'd held all those witches and warlocks in the SED's testing facility in Virginia, but he doubted a mere nine months was enough time to have the universe forgive him for those sins.

But here he was, heading east to Joanna's secluded little ranch tucked up against the skirts of Mount Elden, his mind already thrumming with anticipation at seeing her again, at hearing her warm yet somehow ironic voice, of seeing the bright flash of her smile and the gorgeous fall of her raven-dark hair. Obviously, his willpower had gotten shot to hell over the past few months.

Not enough discipline in his life, probably.

However, since he'd already promised Joanna that he would come out and help her finish the fence repairs, there wasn't much he could do. Backing out would have been even more obvious than showing up and acting like a lovestruck schoolboy around her.

All right, it probably wasn't that bad. They'd exchanged a few heavily charged glances, but things hadn't advanced past that point. After dinner the other night, he'd thought there had been a moment when they both could have leaned in for a kiss. Thankfully, though, the moment had passed. And yesterday had been utterly ordinary, just the two of them working hard all day, with only a brief break in between for lunch. They'd exchanged a few confidences about their pasts, but nothing that couldn't have been shared between friends. It didn't have to go any farther than that.

He pulled into the long lane that led to her house after the solar-powered gate opened to let him in. Dust plumed up from his tires as his truck rattled along the gravel road—a good sign, telling him the ground had dried out enough that today's work wouldn't be quite the muddy mess it had been the first day he'd come out here.

Because they already had a routine going, he knew to park in front of the detached garage and walk over to the pasture. A load of rails already waited in the trailer Joanna used to haul things around the property. However, she wasn't standing by the fence they'd been working on, but was over by the pasture where the alpacas grazed on the hay she'd scattered on the ground. The nights were still too cold for grass to have started growing, which was why she had to keep feeding them hay for the time being.

Her gaze was fixed on the two baby alpacas —*crias,* he reminded himself. But she looked over at once at the sound of his footsteps on the gravel path, and a flash of a smile passed over her face.

God, she's beautiful, Randall thought, and a wave of need passed over him, just seeing her as she stood there in her faded jeans and a truly horrible orange and green plaid shirt.

That need wasn't even exactly physical desire, although he knew that was part of his reaction as well. No, it was more a hunger to be part of her life, to be able to spend his days with her, whether that was fixing fences or weeding her vegetable garden—he'd seen the raised beds off to one side of the house near the kitchen door, although the earth lay fallow for now, waiting for warmer days —or simply walking amongst the trees that ringed the property and made it feel so secluded, so private.

A little slice of heaven, really.

"Morning," he said, doing his best to sound casual. Once upon a time, he'd been damn good at making sure the people around him could have had no idea what he was thinking. Now, though, he had to wonder if Joanna Wilcox could see right through him, could see how badly he wanted to pull her into his arms and kiss her, even if he knew that would be a spectacularly bad idea.

"Morning," she responded. There was just the faintest flush to her olive skin, although that could have had something to do with the chilly morning air. He didn't want to flatter himself that it could have been a reaction to him. "Want to help me name the *crias?*"

For a second or two, Randall could only stare at her. That she'd entrust such a special task to him was surprising, to say the least. He found his voice. "I don't know much about naming alpacas."

Her dark eyes warmed with amusement. "You've never had any pets?"

He thought of Charlie, the golden retriever who'd been a faithful companion through a big chunk of his youth. "When I was a kid," Randall replied. "It's been a while."

"Then you'll do fine," Joanna said. "It's not like I'm asking you to christen a boat or something."

With a twinge of inner amusement, he recalled the "Boaty McBoatface" scandal in the U.K., where the government had made the unwise decision of asking the public to weigh in on the naming of a new warship. "True," he agreed, fighting back a smile. He looked over at the two *crias*. They seemed visibly bigger today, but maybe that was only because they looked a lot steadier on their feet. One was white, the other a soft, warm brown that made him think of hot chocolate. "How about 'Coco' for that one?" he suggested as he inclined his head toward the *cria* in question.

"That's perfect," Joanna replied, face lighting up with pleasure. "What about the white one?"

He studied the little alpaca. It wasn't pure white, more a soft ivory color—a little splashed with mud on its fragile-looking legs. "'Snow'?" he said.

"That's her momma's name," Joanna replied, although she was still smiling.

Well, he supposed he couldn't bat a thousand all the time. "'Sugar'?"

To his relief, she nodded. "That works. Coco and Sugar. I like it. And they'll be easy names for their new owners to work with."

Randall wasn't sure he liked the sound of that. "New owners?"

"Oh, I can't keep all of them," she said. Although her tone was casual, something in the way she studied his face seemed to tell him that she understood why he wouldn't be happy to hear about selling off the baby alpacas. "They stay with their mothers until they're weaned and steady enough to be on their own. But I actually make a lot more money selling off the ones I can't keep than selling their wool—although that's a big part of my business, too."

He probably should have thought of that. While he didn't know much about alpacas, he'd been friends with people whose families had farms out in the country and raised horses, and he assumed the situation couldn't be all that different —you kept the ones you wanted to use for breeding stock, but the rest got sold off as necessary. And although Joanna's ranch seemed large for Flagstaff, where most lots were the normal third of an acre or less, he realized it still couldn't hold unlimited numbers of alpacas. Sooner or later, she'd have to get rid of some of them.

"Of course," he said. A pang went through him at the thought of the *crias* he'd just named being taken away from this beautiful place, although he knew that Joanna would be careful about finding them new homes and wouldn't sell them to just anyone.

She gave him an encouraging smile. "And that won't be for months and months. They'll have all summer here—which is why we should get this fence fixed, so they'll have more room to spread out."

Right. He nodded and said, "Then let's get to work."

~

Joanna honestly hadn't thought Randall Lenz would have such a soft spot for the *crias*. But she'd seen it in his face. He didn't want her to sell Coco and Sugar.

Maybe she wouldn't have to. She'd sold several

alpacas last year, and there was enough room for everyone at the moment. It would be nice to watch them all grow up together.

Well, she didn't have to make any decisions right away. As she'd told him, it would be months and months before the *crias* were old enough to be sent off on their own.

This stretch of fence was longer than the one they'd worked on the day before, but the individual sections were in better repair, and so she thought it probably would take about the same amount of time, maybe a bit more. They wrapped up the first part around one, and she suggested lunch. This time, Randall didn't try to argue, but only went inside with her, where they sat down and ate the sandwiches she'd made that morning after she was done with breakfast.

And they kept the conversation light, only talking about her plans for the vegetable garden, places they liked to shop in town, what she thought the weather would be like that summer. They left the past alone, and didn't bring up anything too personal.

Because of that, Joanna thought it might be safe to ask him to stay to dinner. Nothing as fancy as last time, but he'd put in two more days of hard work, and she wanted to thank him with something more than a sandwich and a few bottles of water.

Even so, when the time came—when they laid the last rail just as the pasture fell into deeper shadow, the sun having disappeared behind the mountain more than a half hour earlier—she found it difficult to say the words. She might have told herself this was just another way of saying thank-you, but she knew differently.

She didn't want to say goodbye today and wonder if he would just walk right out of her life.

"Stay for dinner," she blurted as Randall began to pull off his work gloves.

A flicker of surprise passed over his lean features before his face went blank again. "You don't have to keep feeding me, Joanna," he said.

"I know I don't have to," she replied. "I want to."

He stuck the gloves in his pocket, and then sent a rueful glance down at himself. His jeans were smudged with dirt and dust, and his shirt wasn't in much better shape. "I'm kind of a mess."

No, you're hotter than hell, she thought. She liked the smears of dirt on his muscled forearms where he'd rolled up his sleeves, liked the warm tan the past few days of working in the sun had awakened in his skin.

"So am I," she said, gesturing down at her own dusty clothing. "It's not like I'm going to feed you filet mignon or chicken cordon blue. I just thought I'd grill a few burgers and throw a bag of fries in the air fryer."

"You're not making them from scratch?"

Joanna guessed from the way an eyebrow lifted that he was teasing her. And yes, normally she wouldn't deign to feed a guest store-bought fries, but making them was time-consuming, so she always had a bag in the freezer just in case.

She had made the buns herself and then frozen them, but she wouldn't bother to point that out.

"Nope," she said cheerfully. "No fuss, no muss. Just a couple of ranch hands having a burger at the end of the day."

To her relief, he smiled. "Well, when you put it that way—"

"Good," Joanna said. "Let's go inside and get washed up."

They headed into the house. She let him use the powder room on the first floor, while she went upstairs to her bathroom to wash her hands.

And brush her hair, and put on some tinted lip balm. Anything more than that, and she knew she'd look as though she was trying too hard, even though it had been difficult to resist the impulse to wash her face and start over from scratch.

When she descended the stairs, she found him studying the picture of her and her parents that stood on the juniper mantel. The photo had been taken when she was nine years old, back in what she liked to think of as the good times. It wasn't that she regretted spending a decade with her mother's family and learning about that side of her heritage, but that things had been so much simpler when her parents were together and she'd thought the world would never change.

Well, the world had sent her a hell of a wake-up call when she turned ten.

As soon as he heard her footsteps on the wooden floor, Randall looked away from the photo and over at her. "Sorry," he said. "I didn't mean to snoop."

"You're not snooping," Joanna told him. "It's not like I had that picture hidden in a drawer or something."

His shoulders lifted. "Maybe."

"It's not a big deal. I talk to my father. I'm friendly with his family."

Surprise flickered over Randall's features. "He remarried?"

"Yes." Now, more than fifteen years after that particular event, Joanna could allow herself some detachment. At the time, though, when she'd learned of her father's new wife, she'd been outraged. How dare he move on with his life when her mother had stayed buried up by Kayenta to protect her daughter from Damon Wilcox? Naomi had been resigned, saying she'd never expected her former husband to spend the rest of his life alone. "He married a civilian. They have a son and a daughter. They're both a lot younger than I am, so they're still in high school."

"Hmm."

That was all Randall said, but she could still detect the disapproval in his tone. Was he thinking that her father's second marriage had been some sort of betrayal, and was feeling defensive on her behalf?

Something warmed inside her, even though Joanna had thought she was long past feeling betrayed by her father's actions. It had happened, and she'd dealt with it and moved on. Even so, every time she saw him with his new family, she found herself wondering what her life might have been like if he'd been there all along, instead of all but disappearing from her world when she was only ten years old.

"Anyway," she said as she moved into the kitchen, "what kind of cheese do you want on your burger? I've got cheddar and swiss."

"Swiss," Randall replied promptly.

Why did that not surprise her? Since she was partial to swiss, too, she got out the package of cheese from the fridge, along with the ground beef. Over one shoulder, she said, "You can set the table. The place mats and napkins and silverware are in the sideboard in the dining room."

If he was surprised to be ordered around so peremptorily, he didn't show it. He gave her a nod and went off into the other room, then got to work. Probably, he was glad to have something to do while she got the food together.

Not that there was much work involved in preparing this particular dinner. She hauled out the air fryer and started it preheating, and retrieved the package of truffle fries from the freezer. Her stove was the kind with a grill built in between the burners, and so she didn't have to worry about taking the burgers outside to barbecue them. Within a few minutes, she had everything going—the fries crisping in the air fryer, burgers starting to sizzle on the grill.

Randall came back into the kitchen and asked, "Need help with anything else?"

"You can get some glasses down from that cupboard." Joanna inclined her head toward the cabinet.

He opened it and pulled out a pair of tumblers. Before she made the request, she'd wrestled with whether they should have some wine again, then decided that probably wasn't a good idea. She was trying to avoid sending any kind of message, and that was why she'd directed him to the cupboard with the regular glasses and mugs, and not the wine glasses.

"Water from the dispenser?" he asked, gaze

moving toward the water bottle that sat on a ceramic crock on its metal stand in a corner of the kitchen.

"Yes, please."

She flipped the burgers while he filled the glasses. The food was almost ready, so she quickly made up a plate with cheese, sliced tomatoes, and lettuce, and took it out to the dining room. Everything was ready—and she was happy to see that Randall had gotten the silverware in the correct positions. Maybe it was silly to worry about something like that, but she had to wonder what was going on with a grown-ass man who didn't know the knives were supposed to be on the right-hand side.

The buns had been toasting in her countertop convection oven, so she got them out and put the burgers on them, then dumped the fries into a waiting bowl. She brought everything to the dining room, where Randall was waiting.

"I could've helped you with that," he said as she set down the burgers and the fries.

"You got the water," she replied. Then she realized she should have asked him if he wanted something else to drink. She didn't have any soda in the house because she couldn't stand the stuff, but there was a pitcher of sun tea in the fridge. "Unless you'd like some iced tea," she added hastily.

"Water's fine. I try to avoid caffeine at night."

"Me too."

They both sat down, and were quiet for a few minutes as they assembled their burgers and dished some fries onto their plates. Randall took a bite of his cheeseburger and shook his head. "You said dinner was no big deal," he remarked, "but this burger is better than anything I've had in any of the restaurants here."

"Thanks," Joanna replied. "But it honestly wasn't any real work. I'm glad you like it, though."

He shook his head at her self-deprecation, but he also didn't try to argue. No, he showed his appreciation by taking several more large bites of his burger before he appeared to realize there were French fries as well. A pause to drink some water, and then he finally reached for a fry.

"So," he said, his tone casual, "are you going to move some of the alpacas into the third pasture tomorrow?"

"Probably," she replied, relieved by the change of subject. While she was glad to know he liked her cooking, she also didn't want to keep fending off compliments. "It'll give everyone a chance to move around a bit. I'll keep Sugar and Coco and their moms together, though, because it seems like they're all getting along really well."

Randall nodded, looking pleased that the *crias*

wouldn't be separated. Tone too casual, he said, "Any more projects you need help with?"

Joanna smothered a smile. *Bit too transparent with that one, Randall,* she thought, even while she glowed with inner happiness that he apparently wanted to keep hanging around just as much as she wanted him to.

Problem was, she didn't have much she needed assistance with. Moving the seedlings from their flat in the greenhouse space would be a lot of work, but it would be probably a month before it was safe to do so. She needed to wait until there was at least a week of above-freezing overnight temperatures, and that meant sometime in the middle of May.

But....

"You know anything about security systems?"

His clear blue eyes lighted with interest. "Some. You think you need one out here?"

"Oh, it's not for the house," she explained. "I think I want to install a keypad on the gate. The motion-activated system that's there now came with the place, but I've had enough people come wandering up the lane to make me think I need more of a deterrent than just those 'private property' signs."

"Then you should definitely switch it out," he said. Now his expression was almost hard, as if he was annoyed on her behalf by all those trespassers and all too willing to do whatever it took to get rid of them.

Maybe she should have been annoyed by that protective urge—she was used to taking care of herself—but she also had to admit that his desire to look out for her was oddly appealing.

And to be fair, at least half of the interlopers were merely people who'd gotten lost while trying to find her neighbors, but she'd also gotten enough solicitors and looky-loos that she thought it would better to make it much harder to get on her property. While she liked living alone, she didn't like strange men appearing on her doorstep.

Well, unless the man in question was Randall Lenz....

"Then maybe you could come over and look at some websites with me, help me figure out what would work best?"

Even as she asked the question, Joanna wondered if she was being way too obvious. Then again, she really did want to upgrade the gate, and since he used to work for Homeland Security....

He'd been taking a bite of burger, and so he had to pause and finish chewing before he could reply. "Sure," he said. "And I'll look at what you have installed now so we can make sure the specs line up."

"Great. Same time?"

"Sounds good."

Well, that was settled. And without any fuss, either. Would he object to her making a big lunch? It had been a while since she made chili and cornbread. But she supposed she could just tell him she'd been planning to cook up a big batch anyway. He shouldn't find anything too strange about that.

He asked about her neighbors, whether they had small ranches like hers or just preferred to live in a part of town where the lot sizes were bigger and people had a little more room to spread out. Joanna told him about the McHenrys down the road, who'd sold their big ranch over in Chino Valley but still kept horses, and Oscar Salazar, who grew the most amazing organic tomatoes.

"And Jack Meyer," she finished, smiling a little. "I don't know exactly what he does, but I'm pretty sure he's one of Flagstaff's biggest pot suppliers."

Randall's eyebrows lifted. "And he hasn't been arrested?"

Trust Mr. Law and Order to ask a question like that. Still wearing a smile, Joanna said, "We legalized recreational marijuana here in Arizona, you know."

Her companion didn't seem too impressed by that statement. "Maybe so, but you still need a lot of permits to be a grower."

Joanna supposed that was true; she hadn't

really investigated the situation in depth, since she didn't have any plans to take up smoking pot. With a shrug, she said, "Jack keeps a pretty low profile. It's just a guess, anyway—he doesn't have a job, as far as I can tell, and he doesn't leave the house much, but he always has people coming and going at weird hours. Maybe he's a cult leader."

This suggestion earned her a pained glance. "More like he's living in a grow house."

That was pretty much what Joanna had secretly imagined as well—a place filled with pot plants and grow lights, with all kinds of fancy hydroponic setups. Honestly, she didn't much care, since she viewed pot as basically harmless.

The one thing she wouldn't mention to Randall was that the few times she'd bumped into Jack Meyer, he'd been pretty friendly. All right, *very* friendly. Not enough to invite her into his sanctum, of course, but enough that she knew if she invited him over for drinks or whatever, he definitely wouldn't turn her down.

She had a feeling Randall Lenz might not like that particular tidbit very much.

"Maybe," she allowed. "But that's it for my neighbors. We all kind of keep to ourselves, mostly."

From the way he nodded, she had a feeling he was just fine with that. As was she. At least she didn't have to worry about nosy types paying attention to everyone coming and going from her property.

The conversation flagged after that, and she asked Randall if he was done. He nodded, and they both got up to take their plates into the kitchen. During that entirely prosaic activity, she still found herself acutely aware of him, of the strength in his hands as he set his dish and his glass down on the countertop, of the way her entire body seemed to thrum a little because of his proximity.

Neither of them said anything, though, and once again she found herself walking him to the door.

She didn't want him to leave. She wanted....

Well, she knew what she wanted. Problem was, she didn't know whether he wanted the same thing. She thought she'd seen something in his eyes when their gazes met, but she could have been imagining that flicker because she so desperately wanted it to be real.

Hand resting on the door handle, she said, "So, I'll see you at ten tomorrow to go over the stuff for the gate?"

He nodded. His voice sounded husky as he said, "I'll be here. And thank you for dinner...again."

Joanna opened her mouth to tell him it was

no problem, but she didn't get the chance, because he bent and pressed his lips against hers.

Possibly there was the briefest flash of surprise, but almost at once it got overridden by the desire that surged through her veins, the overwhelming need to be as close to him as possible. She pressed her body against his as she let go of the door and wrapped her arms around him. Everything inside her seemed to be flaring to life, waking up in a way she knew she'd never been before.

How could a single kiss change her so utterly? It was like throwing an oil-soaked rag on top of an open flame.

Randall's arms tightened around her as he deepened the kiss. Oh, yes, this was what she'd wanted—to taste him, to feel as if every inch of her was suddenly, gloriously alive.

A moment later, though, he lifted his mouth from hers and stared down into her face. "I shouldn't have done that."

"I wanted you to do that," she said at once, knowing she needed to disabuse him of the notion that he'd somehow overstepped his bounds.

His jaw tightened. "I don't...."

The words trailed off, and Joanna tilted her head as she stared up into his face. "You don't what?"

"I don't deserve this."

An ache stirred in her, one that had nothing to

do with the need that still surged along every vein. "Don't worry about what you *deserve*," she said fiercely. "Tell me what you *want*."

A long, long moment, during which he continued to gaze down at her, expression tormented. At last he said, his voice only a murmur, "I want you."

That was all she needed to hear. She pulled him against her again, mouth finding his, in another searing kiss that made her realize she could search the world over and never, ever find another man who made her feel the way Randall Lenz did.

A wild impulse seized her, and she took him by the hand and led him to the stairs. For just a second or two, she'd felt some resistance in him, as if he battled with himself as he grew to realize what she wanted. But then he seemed content to follow when she hurried up the steps, pulling him into the bedroom.

Shirts and jeans and boots and belts went everywhere as they hastened to get out of their work clothes. His fingers, strong and deft, unhooked her bra and then moved across her breasts, caressing them. Joanna gasped, body coming even more alive at his touch. Dear God, that felt good.

A moment later, they fell down onto the bed. Her hand moved under his boxer briefs, sensing at once how hard he was, how ready for her. A small groan escaped his lips, and emboldened, she let go of him for a moment so she could tug down his underwear and toss it onto the floor with the rest of their clothes.

Yes, that was better. She caressed him with both hands, reveling in the smoothness of his skin, the heavy hardness of the flesh beneath. It seemed the most natural thing in the world to take him in her mouth, to taste the salt of their exertions earlier in the day. He moaned, much more loudly this time, but he didn't try to stop her, only let his fingers caress her tangled braid as she suckled on him.

Not for too long, though. Only enough to let him know what would be coming next, the thing they both wanted. Maybe this was the time to stop, to reach in her nightstand for the little packet of condoms she kept there—even though she hadn't needed to offer one to a partner for several years—but Joanna knew she didn't want to do that. The McAllister witches had taught her the charm that would ward off unwanted pregnancy, and she kind of doubted Randall had been sexually active enough for his intimate history to be an issue, either.

Besides, she wanted to truly *feel* him.

She shifted so she could straddle him, could sink down and let him fill her. This time, it was her turn to let out a moan, and she knotted her fingers with his as she rode him, both of them finding their rhythm, losing themselves at last in the feeling of being so unbelievably connected.

Of finally not being alone.

When it was over, she sank down next to him. He pulled her close, his mouth finding hers as they kissed over and over. Even when he let her go, he didn't say anything, but seemed content to lie there as she cradled herself against his chest.

She slept then, in a drift of happy dreams.

6

RANDALL AWOKE, BLINKING FOR A SECOND AS he took in the unfamiliar room. Warmly paneled walls, plain dark red curtains at the window...a red, white, and green quilt pushed down nearly all the way to the footboard.

Joanna Wilcox sleeping next to him, hair coming out of its French braid and lying over her shoulders like the finest black silk floss.

As soon as he moved, she stirred, blinking up at him with wide, dark eyes. For just a second, she stared, uncomprehending, and then realization seemed to sweep through her, since a flush touched the warm-toned skin on her cheekbones.

"Good morning," he said.

And it was a good morning. He could beat himself up all he wanted about the foolishness of sleeping with Joanna Wilcox, but something deeper, some instinct even stronger than his conscience, told him that this was exactly where he should be. The sex had been spectacular, and yet it was more than that. He'd slept next to her all night, soundly and deeply, and had never once woken up in the dark, plagued by nightmares and hearing his own ragged breathing as he tried to calm himself enough to go back to sleep.

It was the first solid night's sleep he'd had in more than ten years. What that meant exactly, he didn't know, except that it seemed the universe approved of him being here with Joanna.

"Good morning," she echoed, but something in her tone seemed a little hesitant, as if she wasn't completely certain of how he would act now that everything between them had changed.

To reassure her, he bent down and kissed her. They'd passed out without brushing their teeth or doing anything else to get ready for bed, but he didn't care. She still tasted sweet to him.

At once, a radiant smile touched her lips. She was so beautiful that he wanted to lie there and just stare at her so he could imprint every detail of this moment on his memory so he never forgot it.

Once again, the thought flitted through his mind that he truly didn't deserve someone like her. She was so strong and fierce and independent, so utterly unconcerned about what other people might think. Randall supposed that lack of worry was a good thing, because he honestly had no idea how Connor and Angela—or Addie and Jake, for that matter—would react to him getting involved with a member of their clan.

"Coffee?" he asked, thinking it might be better if they focused on a neutral topic rather than getting drawn into a discussion of what had passed between them the night before.

"God, yes," Joanna responded. She sat up, sheet clutched against her bare breasts. Then a wicked little smile touched her mouth, as if she'd just realized it was foolish to try to hide herself when they'd been lying naked next to each other for hours.

She let go of the sheet and slid off the bed, allowing him a good look at her body as she walked over to the dresser and got out some underwear, followed by a long-sleeved T-shirt and yoga pants. That glimpse only served to remind him of how perfect she really was—breasts not large but high and rounded, hips slim, legs long and muscled. Her skin was the same perfect, smooth light brown all over.

A goddess, just as he'd thought.

While she was occupied with getting dressed, he went ahead and picked up the clothes they'd thrown on the floor in their haste. Unlike Joanna, he didn't have anything clean to change into, so with an inner sigh, he pulled on his underwear and jeans, shirt and socks. His mouth tightened slightly in distaste; he hated to wear day-old clothes, but there wasn't much he could do about it.

"I wish I had something I could loan you," Joanna said, mouth lifting slightly in amusement as she watched him, "but I doubt you'd fit into my jeans."

"Probably not," he agreed. "But it's all right. These will do for now."

They headed downstairs. As they went into the kitchen, a large, outrageously fluffy calico cat gave him some serious side-eye before bolting from the room.

"That's Sassafras," Joanna said. She headed over to the pantry and got out a bag of cat food, and poured some into the companion dish to the water bowl the cat had been drinking out of when they appeared. "She's not much for strangers."

"Apparently not." Randall wouldn't admit he'd been startled to see the cat, because he couldn't recall even noticing her before that moment despite all the time he'd spent at Joanna's house. Obviously, she wasn't exaggerating about Sassafras not liking strangers.

"She'll warm up to you," Joanna went on. "Eventually."

He'd have to take her word for it. What made him absurdly pleased was her intimation that there would be an "eventually" for them. It seemed she didn't intend for this to be a one-time occurrence...and he was damn glad about that.

As she was speaking, she busied herself with getting an old-fashioned cowboy-style coffeepot out of a cupboard, along with a bag of beans. "You okay with mocha java?" she asked. "That's what I have open."

Randall didn't have much of a preference when it came to coffee, as long as it was strong and black. "Sounds great."

"Get ready for a little noise."

She wasn't kidding. The little coffee grinder she was using sounded loud enough to be sawing logs in half. If Sassafras hadn't already beat feet and gotten out of there, the noise would surely have been enough to make her bolt.

But Randall was content to stay there and watch as Joanna measured the freshly ground coffee into the pot, then poured water in and got the thing going. He also had to admire her dedication—he liked good coffee as much as the next person, but he'd never been committed enough to go to the extra effort of grinding his own beans.

"What do you like for breakfast?" she asked then. "I've got eggs and bacon, or I could make you pancakes or waffles."

That all sounded delicious—and he knew it would be, since Joanna was making it. Still, he didn't see the need to go crazy. "Eggs and bacon are fine," he replied.

A wicked little glint he was coming to recognize flashed in her dark eyes. "And hash browns?"

He was a fiend for hash browns. How had she known? Was she psychic on top of everything else? "If it's not too much trouble."

She laughed out loud then, and came over and kissed him on the cheek. "No, it's not too much trouble. If it were, I wouldn't have asked." A sudden thought seemed to occur to her, because she tilted her head to one side and said, "Why don't you do some research on security gates while I'm getting breakfast together? My computer is in the office down the hall."

"Sure you don't want me to stay here and help?"

That question earned him another chuckle. "No. I work better on my own. You'd just be underfoot. Come on—I'll log you in, and then you can do something useful while I'm cooking."

Since Randall figured it was probably better not to argue, he said, "Of course."

Still smiling, she took him down the hall to her office, which he guessed had originally been intended as a bedroom. Now a bookcase covered one wall, and an oak desk stood against the other. On the desk was a newish iMac, looking slightly out of place in its rustic surroundings.

Joanna turned it on and entered her password, then told him, "It's all yours. I'll give a holler when breakfast is ready."

"Sounds good."

She left, and he seated himself on the hard-backed chair in front of the computer. Since she didn't have a real office chair, he guessed that she probably didn't spend a lot of time in here.

At the same time, he realized how much trust in him she'd showed just by the simple act of leaving him alone with her computer. How was she to know whether he'd gone snooping in her personal files, tried to get a peek at her finances or any other sensitive data she had stored on the iMac?

She wouldn't know...and that, he realized, was exactly the point.

Well, he'd make sure her trust in him hadn't been unfounded.

He opened up her Firefox browser and started some simple searches. This wasn't the sort of task that required the expertise of someone like Joanna's computer hacker cousin Jeremy, or even Randall's former assistant, Kelly Dawson. No, he just had to find reputable companies that offered the kind of hardware Joanna had requested.

Delectable smells began to drift down the hallway as he worked, and his stomach growled. About five minutes after he'd been left alone in the office, she reappeared, a mug of coffee in her hand.

"Didn't want you to think I'd forgotten about this," she said, and set it down on the coaster on the desktop. "Finding anything?"

"A few places so far," he replied. "I think we'll be able to narrow it down to something that'll really work."

"Good."

She bent and laid a gentle kiss on the top of his head, then headed back out to the kitchen.

A rush of warmth went through him at the off-hand caress. Randall couldn't remember if he'd ever been with anyone who'd been so immediately easy with him, who'd made him feel so relaxed in their home, he'd almost forgotten he didn't live here as well.

No, he was sure he'd never been with someone like that. If he had, he would have made her a permanent part of his life.

So, what did that mean about his relationship with Joanna Wilcox?

He didn't know if he wanted to answer that question. They'd spent a few days working together, had shared a night he knew he'd never forget, but it was probably a little early to be thinking about anything permanent. For all he knew, she was just amusing herself because the local offerings for male companionship had grown a little stale.

No, that definitely didn't feel right. Some people might have said it was crazy, the way they'd jumped into bed together, but he knew better. For as hasty as it had been, he also knew it hadn't been casual. He'd had a couple of one-night stands in his early days, enough to know what that sort of liaison felt like. This had been entirely different. It had been… intense. Unlike anything else he'd ever experienced.

Was this what it was like when a witch and a warlock got together? A connection so deep, it felt as though that person had been in your life forever?

In a good way, though. Not a relationship where everything had gone stale through too many years of repetition, but one where the sight of that one special person still made you light up inside, made you feel as if forever might not be long enough.

Randall didn't know. He could ask Joanna, but that would give away far too much of what he was currently feeling.

Would that be a bad thing?

For someone else, maybe not. For himself, when he'd spent so many years keeping his thoughts and feelings as locked down as possible, he wasn't so sure.

He continued to work, getting a list of five products and companies that sounded very good, along with a second string of four more just in case the most likely prospects turned out not to be a good fit, for whatever reason. Just as he was copying the last URL to a file he'd opened in the Text Edit application, Joanna called down the hallway.

"Breakfast is ready!"

"Coming!"

He picked up his half-drunk mug of coffee and went into the dining room. Obviously, she'd been busy, too, since the table was set, and in addition to the promised eggs, bacon, and hash browns, there was also a little basket of fresh-baked biscuits.

"I thought you said you weren't going to get elaborate," he remarked as he went to take a seat.

Joanna's slender shoulders lifted in a shrug. "Oh, well," she said in self-deprecating tones. "Once I got started, it just seemed as if I might as well throw some biscuits in there, too. They really didn't take any time."

Although he knew her talent was working with the weather, Randall had to wonder if she had a bit of kitchen witch slipped in there some-where. That would make sense, considering what a talented cook she was.

He smiled. "Well, it all looks wonderful."

And it was. The scrambled eggs were buttery and hot, the hash browns just the perfect golden color. Crispy bacon, and biscuits so light, they tasted as though they could take wing at any second.

He praised the food, and told Joanna what he'd found during his internet search. "There are a lot of good prospects," he concluded. "I think what I need to do next is get some measurements of your gate so we can decide what will be the best fit."

"That sounds good," she said. "After breakfast, I'll shower, and then…." Her words trailed off as she appeared to inspect his expression. "I mean, we'll shower."

While Randall thought sharing a shower with her would be a wonderful thing, he couldn't ignore the day-old clothes he was wearing. "Actually," he said, "I think I'd better go home and shower and change. Then I'll come back, and we can keep working on the gate."

Although she looked a little disappointed, she didn't argue. "Right. Of course you'll want to get some clean clothes." She paused there as she reached for another biscuit. Not quite looking at him, she added, "Maybe you should keep some here."

Well, nothing like charging right in. If anyone else had made such a suggestion, he would have demurred. It was way too early to be leaving clothes here...and a toothbrush and whatever other toiletries he deemed necessary.

Except he definitely wanted to do that. In fact, some crazy impulse told him he'd be all too happy to pack up his few belongings and bring them right over. Strange as it might sound, he felt more at home in Joanna's house than he did in the cottage he'd been renting for the past nine months.

"That's a good idea," he said, doing his best to sound casual. "If you don't mind."

His comment made her shoot him an amused glance. "Of course I don't mind. I wouldn't have offered if I did."

Well, that seemed to settle the matter. "Then I'll go home and get some things together, and come back this afternoon. Sound good?"

Her posture relaxed slightly. "Sounds great."

They finished their breakfast, and he helped clear the table and put away the leftovers. Afterward, Joanna gave him a quick kiss, and he told her he'd be back in a few hours, and that she could go ahead and look at the information he'd left on her computer.

Then he headed out, inwardly glad that her property was so secluded, and that no one could tell his truck had been parked out by the garage all night. No, there was no reason to feel ashamed of what they'd done, but at the same time, he didn't think Joanna's love life was any of her neighbors' business. The less they knew, the better.

The cottage felt smaller than ever after the spacious interior of Joanna's ranch house. Still, he didn't want to disparage the little rental property, not when a Wilcox cousin had so graciously loaned it to him when he desperately needed a place to land. If he decided to move on, he was sure someone else would be more than happy to make it their home.

Looking around only told him how little he'd done to leave his mark on the place. Because it had originally been a vacation house, it was fully furnished when he moved in. About the only change he'd made was the little philodendron that now lived on the windowsill in the kitchen. The plant had been an impulse buy when he was grocery shopping at Safeway, and he'd been nurturing it for months, watching as it grew and thrived. Actually, he'd been thinking he needed to transplant it, but he knew that project should wait until it was a little warmer.

For now, though, he took a long, hot shower, stripping away the sweat of the day before. Since they wouldn't be doing any physical labor, he figured it would be safe to wear one of his newer pairs of jeans, and a dark green henley-style shirt instead of the faded flannels he'd worn to help Joanna with her split-rail fences.

And because she'd basically given him permission to bring over as many things as he'd like, he went ahead and packed a duffle bag with another pair of jeans, several changes of underwear and socks, and his little travel bag of toiletries. Looking at it gave him a small twinge; it was the same cache of personal supplies he used to keep in his "go" bag when he worked for Homeland Security. Back in the day, he'd had to be prepared to leave on a moment's notice, since he never knew when one of Dawson's algorithms might flag a likely prospect for Project Daedalus.

Well, those days were long gone. And good riddance. The entire project had been built on a lie…or, at the very least, an extremely large set of false assumptions. There was no such thing as secret psychics hiding among the world's population, only witches and warlocks. Randall supposed some might argue they were one and the same, but he knew that wasn't exactly the truth. A very strong genetic component existed in the witch population; they didn't just appear from nowhere.

He'd just finished zipping up the duffle bag when a floorboard creaked out in the living room. At once, his nerve endings shrilled with alarm, even as he told himself that the little house made odd noises all the time. Even so, he found himself instinctively reaching for his shoulder...only to realize that of course he didn't have his shoulder holster or the pistol he once wore there. He'd left the shoulder holster behind, and his Ruger was locked up in the small gun safe he kept tucked away on the top shelf in his closet.

Two men entered the bedroom. Randall knew he'd never seen either one of them before, although the sudden, sharp twinge he experienced at the back of his neck told him they must be warlocks, even as the alarm he'd experienced a few seconds earlier turned to something sharper, fiercer. Damn it...he knew he shouldn't have kept his gun locked up.

The men weren't dark enough to be Wilcoxes —one had fair hair, and the other man's was a medium brown, almost the same shade as his own, and they were dressed in button-up shirts and trousers, not exactly standard issue for most of Flagstaff's residents. Those were the only details he was able to note, however, because the fair-haired one said, "We found him," even as the brown-haired man raised a hand.

"Sleep," he said, and it was as though someone had slipped him a double dose of Ambien. His surroundings blurred, and Randall slumped to the floor as his knees gave way.

A snore escaped his lips just before the world turned black.

7

JOANNA GLANCED AT THE CLOCK AGAIN. A quarter to three. Randall had said he'd be back in a few hours, and he'd left a little before eleven. In her mind, "a few hours" meant he should have returned no later than one or one-thirty, but maybe that was her own fault for not setting an exact time.

But she didn't think any dictionary in the world would define "a few" as four hours. She sat in her office, phone in hand, and kept staring down at Randall's entry in her contacts list. The logical thing to do would be to call him and make sure everything was okay. It was entirely possible that he'd gotten hung up doing something, although what that something might be, she had no idea. After all, he didn't have a real job, hadn't mentioned any business he needed to take care of, like going to the grocery store or the bank or whatever.

However, she hesitated because the last thing she wanted was to come off as seeming clingy. What if he'd gotten home, reevaluated the situation, and realized he'd made a colossal mistake? Maybe he'd decided that ghosting her was the best way to make a quiet exit from her life.

No, that didn't seem right at all. Joanna knew she didn't have an intuitive sense about people or anything like that, but she'd have to be colossally clueless to have misinterpreted Randall's behavior earlier that day. He'd been warm and friendly, had kissed her first thing that morning so they could quickly get past any initial awkwardness. If he'd really wanted to slip away, he would have come up with a reason to take off first thing, rather than hang around and have breakfast and look up security gates for her, for God's sake.

"Okay, I'll call," she muttered to herself. Out in the hallway, Sass gave her an inquiring look, and Joanna added, "Yes, I'm talking to myself. Get over it."

Looking singularly unimpressed with this declaration, the cat stalked off toward the kitchen. Joanna blew out a breath and pressed the green "call" button.

The phone rang four times, then switched to

voicemail. "This is Randall. Please leave a message."

Definitely no warm fuzzies from that particular greeting. It was brisk and businesslike, just like the man himself. Or at least, like parts of him. Joanna now knew he could also be warm and passionate, quietly funny.

She had a feeling most people never got to see that side of Randall Lenz.

"Hey, Randall," she said, doing her best to sound casual and breezy, and not at all like a woman who might have just gotten stood up after going to bed with a guy the night before. "I was just wondering if you knew when you would be coming over. It's a little before three, and I have some chores I was going to take care of if it turned out you couldn't make it. Let me know. 'Bye!"

A push of a button to end the call, and she set the phone down on her desk. The list of possible suppliers for her new gate was still up on her computer screen, and she stared at them morosely.

Why would he have gone to the trouble to do that work for her if he really didn't give a damn?

To lull her into a false sense of security?

That didn't seem much like him…but then, if he really was capable of standing her up like this, he obviously wasn't the person she'd thought he was.

Scowling, she scooped up the phone and

shoved it into her pocket, then headed outside. The *crias* were now almost four days old and doing well, so she didn't really need to be checking on them all the time.

But going to take a look would give her something to do, and maybe some fresh air would help to clear her head a bit. The house still smelled faintly of the bacon she'd made for breakfast that morning. Normally, she would have enjoyed the rich aroma, but now it only served to remind her of the man who'd shared that breakfast with her.

The sun shone down brightly, but a brisk breeze blew from the northwest, and she wished she'd stopped to grab a jacket. No matter. She wouldn't be outside all that long.

As expected, the *crias* were fine, trotting along in the sunshine next to their mothers. Joanna leaned on the newly repaired fence and watched them for a moment, still frowning.

Something about this didn't feel right.

She couldn't really say why, because getting stood up after a one-night stand wasn't exactly that unusual an occurrence. And all right, she supposed that technically, it couldn't be called a one-night stand because she'd spent several days with Randall before anything intimate occurred between them, but still.

Her talent was controlling the weather. She'd never claimed to be psychic or to have any kind of precognitive abilities. All the same, some sort of lizard-brain sense was telling her Randall hadn't simply skipped out.

And okay, even if her instincts were right, what was she supposed to do about it? Just show up on his doorstep?

Because that would definitely give off some kind of crazy fatal-attraction vibe if it turned out he really was just blowing her off.

What if something actually had gone wrong, though? Was her worry about coming off like a stalker worth leaving him alone to deal with whatever was going on?

Probably not. If it turned out he really was okay, she'd apologize for disturbing him and leave. She could be cool and adult when she needed to be.

That seemed to settle things.

She grabbed the keys to her truck—it was a restored 1972 C/K, and therefore didn't have anything as fancy as automatic door locks and ignition—and hurried off to the garage. A few minutes later, she was bouncing down the gravel lane that would take her to Highway 87 and back toward town.

As she drove, the sensation of disquiet she'd been experiencing ever since she realized Randall was seriously late kept ratcheting higher and higher. She tried to tell herself that all she was doing was freaking herself out, but she couldn't quite believe all this was her thoughts playing tricks on her and nothing more.

The small house he'd been renting was located in the historic area south of Route 66 near downtown, not too far away from the train station. His was a quiet, tree-lined street with bungalows and farmhouse-style homes on either side, most of them set back from the street with small but tidy front yards of grass and flowers. The grass was still yellow and dead, and hadn't yet bounced back from its winter hibernation, but forsythia bloomed here and there, a reminder that spring was definitely on the way.

As she pulled up to the house, she noticed right away that Randall's black Nissan Frontier truck was parked in the driveway. Seeing it, she didn't know whether to be worried or annoyed. Obviously, her fears that he'd gotten into a car accident on the way back to his house had been unfounded.

Maybe she should leave. It seemed clear to her that he was home and had decided, for whatever reason, that it would be better if he didn't return to her house.

Except....

She sat in the driver's seat of her own truck, irresolute. Would it be better to just drive off and chalk all this up to temporary insanity?

Of course, her vintage truck wasn't exactly inconspicuous. For all she knew, he'd already spied her parked out here. If she drove away without even bothering to knock on the door, she'd look even more desperate, wouldn't she?

If you decide to do something, make sure you're going to follow through with it, her mother had told her on more than one occasion. And Naomi Wilcox hadn't raised a quitter.

Joanna pulled in an exasperated breath and made herself open the door and climb out. At least the neighborhood looked pretty quiet; since it was the middle of the afternoon, most people were probably at school or work. There shouldn't be too many witnesses to her humiliation if Randall opened the door in response to her knock and then sent her packing.

While the truck still shielded her, she ran a quick hand over her hair, smoothing it so it lay sleekly over her shoulders. Then she headed up the front path, past rosebushes that obviously had been recently pruned. Was that something Randall had done, or did her cousin Lorelei have a gardener?

She knew she was distracting herself with random thoughts like that because she didn't want to think about the upcoming confrontation. Despite her distraction, her feet propelled her up the path and deposited her in front of the door.

Before she could hesitate, she reached out and knocked, since there didn't seem to be a doorbell. A few seconds crawled past, and then a few more.

No one answered.

Was he so determined to remove her from his life that he couldn't even be bothered to open the door? That definitely didn't seem like Randall... unless she really didn't know him at all.

She knocked again, and waited.

Maybe he was in the shower.

That possibility seemed plausible enough, although she had to work to banish a sudden image of him from her mind, lean, muscled body covered in water droplets, short-cropped brown hair slicked to his head. Despite her current anxiety, desire flickered through her.

Damn it.

What to do now? Admit defeat and slink off before he realized she'd been here at all? That was probably the logical thing to do, but Joanna knew she didn't want to do that. If she slipped toward the back of the house, she might be able to hear the water running. At least if she could determine that Randall actually was in the shower, she'd have a better idea of what to do next.

A casual glance down the street told her that there still didn't seem to be anyone around. Moving quickly—but not quickly enough to attract notice, just in case any of the neighbors did suddenly appear—she followed the driveway to the back of the house. Beyond the truck was a small one-car garage with a padlock on the door, and a little path that went from the driveway to the back entrance of the house.

She paused there, listening intently. The place was dead quiet as far as she could tell, with the only sound at all the faint hum of traffic from Butler Avenue, the main thoroughfare just a couple of blocks away.

Before she realized what she was doing, her hand had descended to the handle of the back door. It gave a faint *click* as the lock released in response to her witch powers.

Crap.

She almost locked it again. What in the world could she say to Randall if he suddenly appeared and demanded to know just what the hell she was doing? Better to walk away.

Something in her said no. It was a quiet voice, coming from somewhere deep inside. A trickle of unease worked its way along her spine, a little shiver that told her something was definitely not right here.

Okay. If he was home, she could probably talk him out of charging her with breaking and entering.

She hoped.

Her palms felt damp, and she rubbed them on

her jeans before she forced herself to step into the house. Just inside and off to the right was the kitchen, small and neat. No dishwasher, but a few plates and bowls rested on the wooden dish drainer immediately next to the sink.

The place looked scrupulously clean, which was about what she would have expected from Randall Lenz. He definitely didn't give off a sloppy vibe.

Joanna paused for a moment, listening. It was even quieter in here than it had been outside, probably because no street noise penetrated the closed windows.

And definitely no sound of running water.

She stepped out into a short hallway. The house was really very tiny, just that postage stamp kitchen, a bathroom, a bedroom, and a front room that served as a sort of combination living and dining area.

And it was also very empty. Not even a hint of moisture from the bathroom to show that someone might have showered there recently. When she reached out to touch one of the towels, it felt bone dry.

What in the world was going on?

It was one of those houses where there was a place for everything and everything in its place. Randall's toothbrush rested in a brushed nickel cup on the counter in the bathroom; she wouldn't touch the bristles, but she somehow knew if she did, they would be just as dry as the towels.

Unease thrumming along every nerve ending, Joanna made herself go into the bedroom. Like the rest of the house, it was very small, with barely enough room for a queen-size bed, a nightstand, and a narrow highboy tucked into one corner. Here was the first sign she noticed of any occupation—the quilt looked slightly rumpled, as if someone had sat on it recently.

So, did that mean Randall had come home, sat on the bed to change his clothes or whatever, and then gone back out? She supposed that was possible; his house was only a few blocks from Flagstaff's downtown, definitely in walking distance.

Of course, that didn't answer the question of what could have been so urgent that he would have gone out without getting cleaned up first. He'd seemed pretty adamant about taking a shower.

The mystery didn't seem any closer to solving itself, unfortunately. Joanna realized then that she was standing in Randall's bedroom after basically breaking into his house, and if that didn't tell her something had seriously gone wrong with her judgment, she didn't know what would.

Just go, she told herself. *He isn't here, but he could come back at any moment. Do you really want to have to explain just what the hell you're doing here?*

Probably not. She would, of course, if that unfortunate situation presented itself, but better to get out while she could.

As she turned to go, however, she noted one thing out of place in the tidy little bedroom.

Lying on the warm oak of the wood floor was a dark brown sock.

Under other circumstances, she might not have thought that was too big a deal. So what if he'd dropped a sock on the floor while he was sorting laundry or whatever?

But because the entire house was so neat, she found it hard to believe that Randall Lenz would let a dropped sock just lie there.

Which meant…what?

She honestly had no idea, but the sensation of unease within her only grew.

In for a penny, she thought, and crossed the room to the closet.

At first glance, everything looked in order. Shirts hung from hangers, and at one end were a couple of dress jackets, relics of his time with DHS. On the top shelf were a couple pairs of neatly polished shoes, one brown, one black, and a pair of hiking boots off to one side.

But then she realized that several of the

hangers were empty, as if he'd removed the shirts that had hung there for some reason.

So what? Joanna asked herself. *They're probably just in the hamper.*

That seemed like a reasonable explanation…and one she could check easily enough. She'd spotted the hamper in the bathroom, and so she went in there and looked inside. The wicker container held a couple of pairs of jeans and the flannel work shirts she recognized from the days when he'd helped her with repairing the pasture fence.

Three shirts.

She went back to the closet and counted. Seven hangers were empty. Even accounting for the shirt he presumably had on his back, that still meant three shirts were unaccounted for.

Which meant absolutely nothing. He probably had a couple of spare hangers in his closet at any given time. Lots of people did.

Only she had a feeling that Randall was too precise to have extra hangers just rattling around. For one thing, there just wasn't a lot of room in the closet for that sort of extravagance.

Okay, so…he'd packed a couple of shirts to bring back with him to her house. She supposed that an inspection of the highboy would reveal gaps in his jeans and underwear and socks, but that wasn't as easy to confirm. Besides, she felt weird enough being here already. She was not about to go poking around in his underpants.

Even assuming he'd been getting ready to return to the ranch, that still didn't explain where in the world he could be. His truck was still here.

And the garage?

Good question.

She went back outside and headed to the door she'd spotted on the side of the garage. There was no point fussing with the padlock; her witchy powers didn't work on locks like that.

But the side door had just a regular deadbolt, something that was easy enough to get past. As soon as she opened the door, she reached for the light switch next to it and flipped it on.

A single fluorescent fixture glared down from overhead. It revealed a sleek, dark gray car, obviously very fast and very expensive. A quick peek at the badging told her it was an Audi.

She hadn't known that he had a vehicle in addition to the Nissan truck. Probably, he'd brought the Audi with him from Virginia but had realized early on that he needed something a little more practical for Flagstaff's winters.

However, the Audi's presence told her that he hadn't taken off in a second car. Both vehicles were still here...but no Randall.

Something very strange was going on. Exactly what, she didn't know.

Time to call in the big guns. She reached in her purse and pulled out her phone, then pushed the contact button for Connor Wilcox.

~

Randall's eyes opened slowly. Above him was a gorgeously coffered ceiling of dark wood and plaster, unfamiliar.

Where the hell was he?

There had been those two men...two warlocks. No time to react, no time to do anything except go down like a ton of bricks as soon as the first warlock told him to sleep.

And apparently, sleep he had. He took a quick physical survey and realized that he felt almost remarkably well, rested and full of energy. No sign of the kind of knockout drug he'd given Addie when he brought her back to the SED facility in Virginia, which meant the sleep had been a natural one...or at least, a magical one, not something induced by medication.

He sat up and took note of his surroundings. The room was large and furnished with heavy dark antiques, very old and very expensive. A huge Persian carpet covered the floor, and velvet drapes at the windows blocked out most daylight. However, enough trickled in to tell him that it was still daytime.

The place felt familiar. Not because he thought he'd ever been here before, but because the room reminded him of the houses of his mother's friends back in Manhattan, brownstones meticulously maintained and filled with pricey antiques. Some of those women had updated their homes, but others had preferred to keep things as they were, making it a point of pride to fill their houses with the kind of furniture those places would have contained when they were first built in the 1880s or 1890s.

Despite the odd familiarity of his surroundings, he couldn't quite hold back a thrill of worry. He could think of roughly a hundred reasons why someone might have kidnapped him like this, none of them good. Despite his underlying unease, he told himself he needed to focus.

Someone had brought him to New York?

Probably. This sort of house could be found in other cities on the East Coast, of course, but he somehow felt in his bones that he'd been returned to the very place where he'd grown up.

But why? Randall knew he had plenty of enemies, but he couldn't think of anyone who would bother to put him in a fancy bedroom and make sure he was comfortable. For the first time, he realized he was wearing pajamas, the kind of silky cotton kind that he remembered his father lounging around in on the weekend, with a foulard robe on top.

To his relief, however, he saw a change of clothing draped across a nearby chair—dress pants and shirt, expensive-looking wingtips waiting on the floor beneath. He climbed out of bed and went over to the chair, then changed quickly, not wanting to get caught with his pants down, so to speak.

After he was done getting dressed, he walked over to the window and pulled the curtain aside. A street of familiar-looking brownstones caught his eye, with the trees that lined the narrow road just beginning to leaf out, the fresh green a shimmer along their branches.

It definitely looked like New York. In fact, he thought he could probably identify the street. He thought it looked like 77th Street, just around the block from his parents' home on 76th Street.

His worry began to morph into puzzlement. Just what the hell was going on here?

The sound of a door opening behind him made Randall turn abruptly away from the window. Standing a few feet away was an older woman, probably in her late sixties or early seventies, with white hair cut into a chic chin-length bob. The bones of her face told him that she had most likely never been pretty, although she was now a handsome woman, age refining her strong features rather than diminishing them.

"Hello, Randall," she said, voice smooth and unruffled, as though there was nothing terribly strange about the way he'd been kidnapped and brought here. "I've been looking for you for forty years."

8

CONNOR SAT ON THE COUCH IN RANDALL'S living room and stared at Joanna with perplexed eyes. He'd come alone, which in a way was a relief; it had been hard enough to explain the situation to the Wilcox *primus* without having his wife listening to every word as well.

"I still don't really see how you can think foul play was involved here," Connor said slowly, and Joanna gave a helpless shrug.

"I know it sounds crazy. But this just isn't like Randall Lenz."

For a moment, Connor didn't reply. Then he said, his tone almost too gentle, "You know him that well?"

Of course she didn't. She'd started to get to know him...had begun to get a glimpse of the man behind the impassive face he showed to the world.

But then he'd disappeared.

"I really don't think he'd bug out like this," she said. "Anyway, if he really has decided to take off, he couldn't get very far. Both his cars are still here."

"The train station is only a couple of blocks away," Connor pointed out.

"Yes, but we both know that the eastbound Amtrak comes through Flagstaff at o'dark thirty in the morning, and the westbound Southwest Chief doesn't get here until late at night. You think Randall's just cooling his heels at the station, waiting for the next train to come through?"

The *primus* ruffled the hair at the back of his head. Sometime over the past few months, he'd cut it short again, apparently tired of having to deal with his shoulder-length locks. Looking rueful, he said, "No, probably not. I'll admit this does seem kind of strange. But I'm not sure what you expect me to do about it."

Good question. Knowing she sounded desperate—and not much caring—Joanna said, "Can't you...I don't know...try to detect whether any kind of magic was used here?"

"That's not really my power."

"But you're the *primus*."

Presented with that undeniable fact, Connor

gave an uncomfortable smile. "Yes. And when I'm working with Angela, I can do a lot. On my own…I don't know."

"Can't you just try, though?" Joanna asked. "If you don't pick up anything, maybe you can try again with Angela here."

He didn't appear thrilled by that suggestion— she had a feeling he'd come alone because their kids would be getting home from school right around now and Angela would have her hands full —but neither did he say no. With a small hitch of his shoulders, he replied, "Okay, I'll give it shot. Just don't expect too much."

"I won't."

Connor's expression was dubious, as if he'd realized that she was, in fact, expecting quite a lot. However, he didn't contradict her, only got up from the couch, saying, "Let me check out the bedroom. Since that's where you found that stray sock, it makes sense that it might be the place where something happened. *If* anything happened. Wait here."

Joanna didn't like the idea of hanging behind while he did his work, although she didn't argue. Maybe having her around would mess up the vibes, or whatever. She didn't really know how his *primus* powers worked.

Anyway, she sat with her hands folded in her lap and stared at the small bookcase that also served as a TV stand, studying the eclectic assortment of volumes it contained. Everything from John Grisham to Deepak Chopra to Stephen King to Dostoevsky. She honestly didn't know whether those were Randall's books or whether they'd been here as part of the vacation home's furnishings when he moved in. However, the odd collection somehow seemed like him, seemed like the sort of thing someone with his questing mind might gather to fill the solitary hours.

She got a brief image of him sitting on this couch, reading glasses perched on his nose, as he pored over a beat-up copy of *The Stand*. Was that a true seeing, something born of the connection between them, or was she only imagining things?

Either possibility seemed equally plausible.

A moment later, Connor returned to the living room, expression troubled.

"I didn't feel anything," he said, and her heart sank, even though Joanna had already warned herself that he might not be successful in trying to detect whether there'd been a magical incursion here. "Which doesn't mean much," he added quickly. "I can get Angela up here—once we find someone to watch the kids—although I honestly don't know whether that will make any difference. Randall's disappearance looks pretty sketchy, but I don't see why magic has to be involved. After all, the guy's made plenty of enemies over the years. I think it makes more sense that someone he crossed while he was working for DHS managed to finally track him down here."

Joanna hadn't even thought of that. Her stomach tightened with worry at the thought of ruthless mercenaries or gang lords—or whoever else might have been on Randall's trail...she honestly had no idea what he'd done at Homeland Security before he'd gone to work at the Special Enforcement Division—but she told herself she needed to be tough and look at the problem with a clear head.

"That's a definite possibility," she said. "So, how do we go about trying to discover who might be involved?"

Connor rubbed the scruff on his chin. "I don't know. The guy's been as tight-lipped as a clam ever since he came to Flagstaff. It's not like he's been hanging out at Collins Pub, pouring out his life story to anyone who'll buy him a beer."

That mental image was so incongruous, Joanna had to smile. "No, that's for sure. But there has to be some way to get some inside info."

"Jeremy," Connor said at once. "If he can't dig up a piece of information, it doesn't exist. You should really go talk to him."

"Is he at Trident?" Joanna asked, referring to the converted Craftsman house that Jake and

Jeremy used as headquarters for their witch-finding operations.

"It's regular business hours, so I would assume so," Connor replied. "But if he isn't, Jake or Laurel probably will be."

Joanna fervently hoped Jeremy would be working at Trident, and not his older brother. Not that she had anything against Jake Wilcox, but she would really prefer to avoid discussing her relationship with Randall with him. She knew he wouldn't be very happy that she'd become intimate with the man who'd killed Addie's mother. Accidentally, of course, but still.

While Joanna knew they would have to deal with that whole mess eventually, she figured she had enough on her plate at the moment.

"Great," she said. "I'll head over there right now. Thanks, Connor. I guess I should've thought of that first and not made you come chasing up here."

He made a dismissive wave of one hand. "Don't worry about it. Part of the job, and it was worth a shot. Besides, I'm going to stop at the house on the way back to Jerome and take a quick look. We'll be back in Flag in about a month."

Right, as soon as the kids were out of school. Joanna figured Connor and Angela's house in Forest Highlands was just fine, since Jasper had done his own inspection a few days earlier. But she supposed it never hurt to be vigilant, and the place was right on his way.

"Sounds good," she commented, because she figured she needed to say something. "I'll let you know if Jeremy finds anything."

Connor nodded, then said a brief goodbye and let himself out. After he was gone, Joanna performed a quick walk-through of the house, more to reassure herself that nothing else was out of place. But she didn't find anything, and soon enough had pointed her truck north toward downtown and the renovated house that was Trident Enterprise's base of operations.

She hoped to hell that Jeremy would be able to help her…and Randall.

Randall stared back at the strange woman with the silver hair. Roughly a million questions raced through his head, but he asked the one that seemed the most plausible.

"Are you my biological mother?"

At once, she smiled, although something about that smile seemed almost condescending, as though she thought he was presuming a great deal in thinking she was his mother. "No. I am Greta Van Horn, *prima* of the Van Horn clan. Your mother was my younger sister, Alicia."

His aunt was the head of the Van Horn clan? Months ago, when Addie had first told him that he was a warlock, she'd speculated he might be one of the Van Horns, just because he'd been left in a basket on the steps of a fire station in Brooklyn, and the Van Horn family held sway over most of New York. Still, it had never crossed his mind that he could be so closely related to their *prima*...especially when he'd been without any kind of magic for most of his life.

Voice rough, he said, "Where is she?"

Just the barest flicker of Greta Van Horn's icy pale eyes, so similar in color to his own, although he guessed her hair had been much lighter than his when she was young. "She's dead. She died a few hours after delivering you."

Anger...followed by loss...flashed in him, as sharp as it was unexpected. "I thought you witches had healers for that sort of thing."

"We do," she said. Her inflection never changed, but he noted the way her mouth, thin under a coating of expensive lipstick, tightened for just a fraction of a second. "Come, Randall—let's go downstairs and discuss this over tea like civilized people."

He would have preferred a shot of brandy, but he guessed that none would be forthcoming. "So, I'm not a prisoner?"

"That's an ugly word. You're my nephew, and

an honored guest. But I think it would be better for all concerned if you didn't leave this house for a while."

Meaning that yes, he was a prisoner, even if he might not be confined to this dark, luxurious room. Since he didn't know how many other Van Horns might be lurking around, ready to use their magic on him if he tried to escape, Randall decided he would play along for now.

"Why would I want to leave?" he asked, doing his best to sound unconcerned. "You're my family, and I have questions."

Her lips quirked slightly. "I'm sure you do. Come with me."

He followed her out of the room, down a long hallway to a staircase with a lavishly carved mahogany balustrade. An expensive runner covered those stairs.

As they descended toward the first floor, he could tell that every inch of the property appeared to have been lovingly maintained so that it probably looked much as it had when the house was first built in the middle of the nineteenth century. He knew it had to have been maintained and not restored, because the Van Horns must have lived here continuously throughout the decades.

The contrast with the home where he'd grown up was subtle, but obvious enough to him. His parents had bought their own brownstone around the corner in the early 1980s when he was just a toddler. They'd put a lot of sweat equity into the place, but they'd also updated it, removing the Victorian wallpaper and painting the surfaces revealed beneath in washes of subtle color— celadon green and jonquil yellow and sky blue. Even though they'd kept the original woodwork intact, the overall effect was one of lightness and openness.

Unlike the Van Horn manse, which felt oppressive to him. Or possibly that was only because Randall knew he wasn't getting out of here any time soon.

The room where Greta Van Horn led him was a bit lighter in feel, just because the wallpaper was used as accents and didn't cover every square inch of the walls. A floor-to-ceiling fireplace with a mantel wider than he was tall took up most of one wall, and bookcases filled the others. At the center of the space was a leather love seat and matching ottoman, along with a large wing chair.

Greta sank down onto the chair and inclined her head toward the love seat. "You may sit there."

He wondered what she would do if he refused. However, since he didn't want to get into a battle of wills this early on—not when he needed to hear exactly had happened to his birth mother—he sat down as requested. He ignored the ottoman, though, and sat on the cushion, hands clasped on his knee as he looked at her expectantly.

"Soon," she said, clearly seeing his impatience. She reached for a bell that rested on the marble-topped table next to her chair and rang it, an imperious little tinkle that seemed to carry far beyond the room where they sat. A subtle form of magic, possibly.

A moment later, a fair-haired woman who looked to be around Randall's own age appeared, carrying a silver tray on top of which rested a very old set of fine bone china, painted with a delicate rose in the center and a sea-green border edged in gold.

As the woman approached, Randall got the faint twinge at the back of his neck that told him the woman, who he'd assumed had to be a servant, was actually a witch. He looked over at Greta Van Horn in surprise, and she sent him an indulgent smile.

"There are those in the Van Horn clan who are glad to be of service to its *prima*," she said, adding as the woman handed her a teacup, "thank you, Elaine. That will be all for now."

Elaine nodded and went back the way she'd come—although not without shooting a curious glance in Randall's direction as she went. She didn't linger, however, and closed the doors to the library behind her as she went.

"Now, then," Greta went on, "I know you must have many questions. I'll try to answer them as best I can, but even I don't have all the information you probably seek."

As invitations went, that wasn't the most encouraging. But Randall brushed away his misgivings and asked, "Who is my father?"

A disapproving droop appeared in one corner of her mouth. "I don't know. Alicia never said."

He sipped some of his tea. Because he wasn't exactly a connoisseur, he had no idea what he was drinking, but it was fragrant and hot and not bad, even though he would have preferred coffee. "There weren't any likely suspects?"

His aunt raised an eyebrow. "No. My sister never showed a particular interest in anyone. Actually, no one even knew she was pregnant."

It was his turn to lift his brows. True, he'd heard that Sloane Kennedy, an "orphan" witch whom Jeremy Wilcox had found and was now his girlfriend, had a mother who'd managed to conceal her pregnancy because her inborn talent was illusions. However, Randall had a hard time believing that his birth mother also possessed that very same ability. The odds of such a coincidence were pretty damn high.

"How is that even possible?" he asked.

Greta sipped some of her own tea. "My little sister had a very odd gift. I always thought of it as 'don't look at me,' although it was a bit more subtle than that. Basically, she could use it to keep anyone away from her. You wouldn't even think anything was strange about not seeing her for weeks or months at a time, because she was using her power to make sure you were busy enough with your own life that a thought of her wouldn't even cross your mind. And at the time, I truly was busy with my own children—they were five and two—and I suppose I never stopped to think about her...until it was too late."

That did sound like a very odd gift. Randall's time working with orphan witches and warlocks at the SED—even though back then he'd thought they were blessed with psychic gifts and not actual magical powers—had told him that such talents could come in all sorts of shapes and sizes. Even so, he never could have imagined a gift that would make people stay away from you for as long as you needed.

Was his father a civilian? Was that why his mother—Alicia Van Horn, apparently—had kept her pregnancy secret? He could see why an old, very powerful clan might frown on such things, although from what he could tell, every witch family made sure to have some civilians in its bloodlines to prevent the clan from getting too inbred.

"If she hid me from you, then how did you even know I existed?"

Greta—it was too difficult to think of her as his aunt, and so Randall didn't even bother—set down her teacup. "Because she had me listed as her emergency contact. It seemed she was taken to the hospital after you were born because the bleeding wouldn't stop. They rushed her into surgery, but it was too late. She'd lost too much blood."

All this information was delivered in a cool, neutral tone. If her younger sister's tragic passing had affected Greta Van Horn at all, it seemed that she'd managed to put the pain behind her.

Then again, it had been forty years.

When he didn't speak, she went on, "There was an autopsy, of course. It revealed that she'd given birth to a child very recently. Naturally, I did my best to discover what had happened to that child, but all my searches turned up nothing." A pause, and then she added, "I don't know how Alicia managed to hide you so well. How did you come to be adopted by your parents?"

Parents Greta Van Horn knew, since their social circles overlapped. Randall himself had never been to this house before, but he knew his mother and late father had attended charity events held here.

"I was left on the steps of Fire Station Number

226 in Brooklyn," he said, and Greta's eyes narrowed.

"That explains some of it. I hadn't thought to look that far afield, considering how ill my sister must have been after you were born. I have no idea how she could have possibly made it that far from her home in her condition."

Honestly, Randall didn't know how his birth mother could have managed such a feat, either, but he supposed she must have had a damn good reason for wanting to keep her newborn son far away from her older sister. Too bad she'd taken that reason with her to the grave.

"However," Greta went on, "that doesn't explain how you managed to keep yourself hidden from me all this time. I should have been able to detect your powers as soon as they began to develop. In fact, the only reason I found you now was that I felt your presence here in Manhattan over the holidays. And then your mother mentioned to me at the Foundation for the Arts' New Year's luncheon that you'd come to visit her at Christmas, and I recalled that you would be exactly the right age to be my missing nephew… and then I realized something very strange must be going on." She sat back in her chair, and fixed him with a speculative stare. "How did you manage it? Did you inherit your mother's gift of keeping people from noticing you?"

Randall wished he had. It was a gift that would have served him well during his tenure at DHS. At the moment, he could only wonder why his actual gift of luck hadn't stepped in and kept him from being taken by Greta Van Horn's goons. Was there some bigger picture here that he'd missed?

"No," he said, then sipped some of his own tea. How much to tell her? He didn't want to drag the Wilcoxes into this mess, but since he'd been taken from a house in Wilcox territory, that particular cat was already out of its bag. "Funny thing, actually. The reason you never detected my magic—never realized another Van Horn warlock was right around the corner—was that my powers were dormant for most of my life. They only were woken up this past summer."

Greta's eyebrows lifted in surprise before she could quite conceal her reaction. The pale eyes focused on him, appearing as though they wanted to drill right into his brain so they could see the truth there for themselves. "How is such a thing even possible?"

Randall shrugged. "I don't know. Since I didn't even know witches and warlocks were real until around nine months ago, I can hardly claim to be an expert. I was hit by lightning, and that incident appeared to shake my powers loose...so to speak."

"I have never heard of anything like that."

She'd spoken the words in a flat tone, as if her ignorance of the topic was enough to negate its existence. He had no doubt that members of her own clan were disinclined to contradict her when she uttered such pronouncements, but he wasn't her subject…he hardly wanted to admit that he was her nephew…and so he didn't see any reason to mince words.

"Maybe you haven't. That doesn't change the fact that it's exactly what happened."

Her lips pressed together, and she took a sip of tea to hide her annoyance. Randall wondered how many years it had been since someone showed so little regard for her position as *prima*.

A long time, probably.

"I'm wondering how you found me, though," he went on. "I thought I did a pretty good job of covering my tracks."

"To the casual pursuer, probably," Greta responded. "But your mother had already let slip that you had resigned your position at Homeland Security and had relocated to Arizona. It took a little more work, because you'd changed your name and maintained a public address down in Phoenix, but eventually, I was able to determine that the Wilcox clan had a new addition. A little surveillance from my son Karl and his cousin Toby—they're the ones who brought you here—

and they reported that Randall Garnett and Randall Lenz were the same man."

"So, they decided it would be a good idea to kidnap me rather than have a civil discussion?"

She didn't even blink. "Oh, don't be disingenuous, Randall. They were trespassing on another clan's territory. Luckily, it seems that the *primus* of the Wilcoxes"—her lips lifted in a sneer as she pronounced the name; clearly, she had no use for a clan ruled by a warlock—"doesn't have the ability to detect foreign witches and warlocks in his territory, but the longer they stayed, the more they'd be pressing their luck. Besides, you don't belong in Arizona. You belong here, with your family."

"I'm sure my mother would agree with you on that point," he said smoothly, and Greta's brow creased in annoyance.

"Your adoptive mother," she corrected him.

"The only mother I've ever known," Randall responded. "But she's had to come to terms with the reality of me living far away from her, and you'll need to do the same. New York isn't my home any longer."

As he spoke, he thought of Joanna—Joanna, who surely had to be either frantic with worry or pissed off as hell that he'd apparently disappeared on her just when it seemed as though their relationship was heating up. He wanted nothing more than to be with her, or at least to be able to call her and let her know that he was fine, that he hadn't checked out because he'd decided a relationship just wasn't what he wanted right then.

"It *will* be your home," Greta Van Horn said firmly. "I understand that this all may have come as something of a shock to you, but you will adjust."

"Maybe I don't want to adjust," he said. Anger had begun to flare in him, although he kept his tone level. Luckily, he'd had plenty of years at DHS to fine-tune his self-control, to make sure he didn't reveal anything he didn't want to be revealed. "I have a life in Arizona, you know."

Those words elicited a derisive chuckle. "Oh, don't be ridiculous. You were living in a tiny rented house and doing food delivery, of all things. How in the world can that compare to being the nephew of the Van Horn *prima?* You will have the very best of everything here."

Except my freedom, he thought. Those words might have been melodramatic, but Randall also knew they were very close to the truth. He didn't know exactly what Greta Van Horn had planned for him, but he guessed it couldn't be anything good.

But until he had a better idea of what her game exactly was, he figured it was probably better not to be too combative. "I'm not saying I don't want to stay for a while, get to know this side of the family," he said. "But in the end, you have to agree to let me make my own decisions."

At once, her smile turned almost treacly. The overly sweet expression warred with her strong features, and he knew she thought he'd already capitulated.

"Of course, Randall," she said. "No one is going to force you to do anything. But I think after you've been with us for a bit, you'll understand why your place should be here. And just think how happy Barbara will be to have you in New York permanently."

That piece of emotional blackmail wouldn't fly —Randall knew his mother would never interfere with how he intended to live his life—but he saw no reason to let Greta know she was on the wrong track with that particular angle of attack. Instead, he reached for his tea and said, "I guess we'll just have to see."

The words were about as neutral as could be, but the Van Horn *prima's* smile only broadened. Clearly, she thought she had him right where she wanted him.

Well, they'd just have to see about that.

9

Joanna thanked God that she didn't flush easily, because after she'd explained her predicament to her cousin Jeremy, he leaned back in his office chair and shot her a sly grin.

"You and Randall Lenz? Seriously?"

"If you're going to get all judge-y, I can leave," she snapped.

He raised his hands. "No judgment," he said, his tone casual. "I mean, I don't know what Jake and Addie are going to think about all this, but that's between you and them."

"So, are you going to help me?"

"Of course," Jeremy replied, turning back to his computer. "It'll give me something new to do. So, you think Randall was grabbed by someone he crossed during his time at DHS?"

Irritation fought with relief. While she definitely needed her cousin's help, something about his attitude rubbed her the wrong way. Honestly, she didn't know how Sloane could put up with him.

But that was between him and Sloane. Right then, Joanna was just glad that Jeremy had been alone when she arrived at Trident Enterprises. He'd explained that Addie and Jake were off tasting wedding cake samples, or doing something that involved their upcoming nuptials. Jeremy had been kind of vague, probably because he didn't much care one way or another, except that their absence gave him some of the alone time he craved.

On that particular point, Joanna could definitely sympathize.

"Well, that's my theory," she said. "I don't think he has any enemies in the witch world."

"How could he? The guy keeps such a low profile, he's practically invisible."

Which was a good thing, as far as she was concerned. However, his profile obviously wasn't low enough, because *someone* had found him.

Without waiting for her to reply, Jeremy went on, "It's a good thing I did a data dump of all the SED files while I had access to their servers. I can poke around, but in my opinion, I don't know if

I'm going to find what you're looking for there. Reading between the lines will only get us so far, because I doubt we're going to locate anything that directly spells out who Randall Lenz might have pissed off during his time at DHS."

Joanna crossed her arms, irritation ratcheting up a few notches. Maybe she was allowing herself to be annoyed with Jeremy because that way, she wouldn't have to think about how worried she was over Randall's disappearance. "Then what's your suggestion?"

"I think you'd be better off talking to the people he worked with," Jeremy replied. His mouth had a faint quirk at one corner, as if he'd detected her annoyance and was more amused by it than anything else. "They're a lot more likely to know something about any personal enemies he might have made, that kind of thing."

"And how am I supposed to find out who he worked with?"

Jeremy flexed his fingers and typed a few commands. Almost at once, a list of names appeared on the computer screen to his right. The screen to the left displayed scrolling ranks of numbers, and she had no idea what they were for or what they were doing. Anything technical like that made her want to go a little cross-eyed.

"These were his immediate superiors and

subordinates at the SED," he said. "But I think the person you probably want to find is Kelly Dawson. She was Lenz's assistant, from what I can tell."

"Where is she? Still in Virginia?"

Which might as well have been on the moon. Joanna didn't know who the witch clan was in that particular part of the world, but she had a feeling they wouldn't be too thrilled to have a Wilcox show up in their territory, intent on pursuing a personal investigation.

Jeremy typed something, then shook his head. "No, after Project Daedalus fell apart, she was reassigned to the DHS office in Manhattan. She's been there for about eight months." A few more commands, and then a printer off in one corner of the room came to life and spit out a piece of paper. "I just printed out her work and home addresses, and her personal and work cell phone numbers."

No point in asking how he'd managed to do all that so effortlessly. Making data his personal bitch was just part of Jeremy's talent with computers.

And obviously, he expected her to go chasing off to New York in search of this Kelly Dawson person. Otherwise, he would have just supplied her phone numbers, and maybe her email addresses.

However, it was pretty easy to blow off a text message or an email. It was a lot harder to ignore someone who'd just popped up on your doorstep.

"How am I supposed to go to Manhattan?" Joanna asked, feeling exasperated. Not for the first time, she chafed at all the arbitrary restrictions of the witch world. Logically, there was no reason why she couldn't just get her ass on a plane to New York—it was a free country, after all. But you couldn't simply travel to another clan's territory without permission, and while she didn't know much about the other clans dotted around the United States, she knew that the Van Horns, who controlled that part of the country, were a very old, very powerful clan whose *prima* probably wouldn't be too happy to have an interloper drop in and start asking questions... even if those questions were directed at a civilian and had nothing to do with the Van Horn family.

Jeremy's shoulders lifted. He looked like he didn't have a care in the world—which he probably didn't. After all, his life was going swimmingly. It wasn't as if his significant other had just dropped off the face of the planet.

It was probably way too soon to be thinking of Randall as her S.O., but Joanna couldn't come up with another term for him. Boyfriend? Hell, no. Lover? Technically, she supposed the description was correct, although she couldn't imagine herself ever uttering that word out loud.

Person she cared about?

Absolutely.

"I suppose you could get on a plane and fly there," he said. "Or, better yet, see if Connor and Angela can teleport you. That would save a lot of time."

Yes, it would. On the other hand, Joanna couldn't imagine her cousin and his wife going along with this particular scheme.

"And actually," Jeremy went on, "what you should really do is see if they can throw some magic on you to hide your powers from the Van Horns. Then you wouldn't have to worry about them even detecting that you're in their territory."

She stared at him. Was he serious?

He looked serious, but it was Jeremy, so who knew?

"They can do that?"

"Probably," he replied. "I mean, I know when they combine their powers, they can do all sorts of stuff. Also, way back in the day, Damon cast a spell to hide Connor's magical nature from Angela so he could go do recon in McAllister territory. Same thing, basically."

"True," Joanna said slowly, mind churning away. If she could hide who and what she was, then yes, a trip to New York suddenly became a whole lot more possible. But.... "Just because Damon was able to cast that kind of spell doesn't mean Connor can. Their powers are totally different."

"It's not as simple as that," Jeremy told her. He didn't look at all perturbed. "I mean, yeah, Connor isn't as strong a warlock as Damon was, but he'd be working with Angela. And if it's just a question of not knowing exactly how to set up such a spell, all they have to do is take a look at Damon's papers and notes."

"They still have those?" That revelation surprised her. Connor had been such a mess after Damon's death, she'd just assumed he would have destroyed any documents his older brother had left behind. After all, it was his meddling in forbidden magic that had led to the former *primus's* demise.

Jeremy nodded. "Yes, they have them locked up in a safe at their house in Forest Highlands."

"I don't suppose I want to ask how you know that."

Her only answer was a grin, and a dancing light in Jeremy's dark eyes. "It's my job to know things."

Of course it was. She couldn't even give him grief over the way he poked into matters that were supposed to be kept private...not when such knowledge might be the very thing that would help her track down Randall Lenz.

"Thanks, Jeremy," she said, and meant it. At the same time, she began doing a quick mental calculation. Connor had said he was going to stop at the Forest Highlands house on his way back to Jerome. He might be there even now.

She needed to make a call.

"Good luck," Jeremy said, and she flashed him a distracted smile and hurried out of the converted Craftsman house, already reaching for her phone before the door had even shut behind her.

Luck. She was definitely going to need as much as she could get.

Randall sat down in the wing chair over by the fireplace and assessed his options. Greta had led him back up to the room that apparently was to be his for the time being, informing him that dinner would be promptly at six-thirty.

"You'll hear the bell," she said, then added, "The dining room is past the library at the end of the hall. Don't be late."

What she intended to do if he was tardy, he

didn't know. Take his supper away and make him stand in a corner?

Not that he intended to skip the meal. He didn't know who would be in attendance, and it would be a good way to gather more intel about the Van Horn family.

Also, he'd realized as he climbed the stairs to his room that he was ravenously hungry, as though the big breakfast Joanna had made for him had been consumed many, many hours earlier. Which he supposed was entirely possible; he didn't know how long he'd been asleep, but unless Greta Van Horn or some other member of the family possessed Connor and Angela's ability to teleport instantly, he must have been brought here by plane.

And that meant hours and hours had gone by. Probably a whole day, since he would have been losing time as they traveled eastward, and it was clearly afternoon when he awoke in this grand, gloomy house.

Joanna had to be frantic…unless he was flattering himself, and even now she was thanking the universe for so neatly plucking him out of her life.

No, he refused to believe that. What had begun to grow between them was new enough that he didn't want to give it a name, but even so, it was strong. She'd be worried, wondering what could possibly have happened to him. With the way he'd been taken, it probably looked as though he'd disappeared into thin air.

Well, worrying about how worried she must be wouldn't help either one of them. He had to stay focused.

That Greta had some sort of grand plan in mind, Randall was certain. It was far too early to begin to guess what that plan might be, but even their short acquaintance had been enough to convince him she never did anything without a purpose that would benefit her or the Van Horn clan as a whole. He highly doubted it was a mere desire to find a long-lost nephew that motivated her.

What, then?

On his own, he was no one terribly important. Randall had long ago learned to assess himself dispassionately, without bias. He knew he was clever and driven, and possessed certain skills that might be valuable to some people, but he didn't see anything in himself that would make him the object of such a hunt on its own. Maybe if he'd still been working for DHS, his connections would also have had some value. However, that ship had sailed nine months earlier.

Idle speculation wouldn't do him much good. He knew it was better to wait and see what happened.

At least his kidnappers—Greta's son Karl and

this Toby person, whoever he might be—had picked up his duffle bag and brought it along when they took him, and so Randall had his own clothing and toiletries. The amount of scruff on his chin told him that it had definitely been far more than twenty-four hours since the last time he'd shaved, and he got out his electric razor, went into the bedroom's *en suite* bathroom, and got himself cleaned up.

Somehow, he had a feeling that the Van Horn *prima* wouldn't appreciate a scruffy guest at her dinner table.

As he put the razor away, he thought of his mother—his *real* mother, no matter what his genes might say otherwise. Barbara Lenz was just a street over from where he now stood, and he wished he could reach out to her. Not because he thought she could do anything to help him; she was a formidable person in her own right, but he doubted she could go up against someone like Greta Van Horn.

No, right then he just would have liked to hear his mother's voice. Even during the worst of times, like those horrible months after the Twin Towers fell, she'd been a steadying presence in his life, a reassurance that love and life and beauty would go on, no matter what evils might be transpiring in the world.

But there wasn't a land line in his room, and

he'd noted at once that his cell phone was missing. He'd recorded that detail with more a sense of resignation than anything else. After all, taking away his phone was probably the first thing he would have done if he were in Greta's place.

No computer, either. His prison was a luxurious one, but he'd been quite clearly cut off from the outside world.

For the time being, anyway. Randall was sure the opportunity to use a phone or a computer would present itself eventually. He just had to be patient.

From downstairs came the sound of a bell ringing, loud enough to penetrate even the heavy carved doors of his borrowed room. He brushed at his slacks, took one last glance in the mirror to make sure he looked presentable, and headed down the stairs.

Even though he'd left his room as soon as he heard the bell, when he reached the dining room, he saw it was already fully occupied. Greta Van Horn sat at the head of the table, and the fair-haired warlock Randall guessed was her son Karl occupied the seat to her right. Next to him was a pretty blonde woman in her late thirties who was probably his wife.

On the other side of the table were an attractive woman, probably around forty or a bit more, whose features resembled Greta's so closely that

Randall assumed she must be the *prima's* daughter. At her side sat a balding man with a goatee, presumably the woman's husband.

He didn't see any sign of the *prima's* consort. Was she widowed? He realized Greta hadn't mentioned her husband once during their conversation in the library earlier. Well, this probably wasn't the time to ask.

The chair immediately to her left was empty. She gestured toward it, smiling. "Good evening, Randall. Please, come take a seat."

Acutely aware of all the eyes on him, he walked over to the indicated chair and sat down. He nodded at the people grouped around the table, and was met with expressions that ranged from frankly curious—on the part of Karl's blonde wife—to vaguely hostile. That last came from the husband of Greta's daughter, and Randall had to wonder what he'd done to merit that kind of look when he'd never even met the man before. Did the man not like the idea of someone new intruding into their family circle, or was something else going on here?

"It's so nice to have the family all together," Greta said. She smiled, but there was something appraising in her eyes, as though she hadn't missed a single reaction from the assembled company. A bell sat by her place setting—Randall didn't know whether it was the one he'd heard earlier, or whether she had duplicates of that damn thing all over the house—and she lifted it and rang it twice.

At once, Elaine—the same witch who'd brought him and Greta tea in the library—appeared. This time, she held an uncorked bottle of wine, and began to go around the table, pouring a precise measure into each person's glass.

Randall murmured a thank-you to the woman under his breath, even though he noticed none of the other people assembled at the *prima's* table did the same. What, did they think such politeness was beneath them because they were closely related to the head of the clan?

Well, he didn't care who his birth mother supposedly was. His own mother had raised him to show courtesy to people, no matter who they were. He had to keep himself from smiling as a wry thought passed through his mind. Addie Grant might have had a few choice words to describe him, but he doubted that any of them included "rude."

Once they all had their wine, Greta raised her glass. "To Randall, for coming home to his family."

He would have much preferred not to be the subject of the toast. Since protesting would have made him even more conspicuous, he only raised his glass in silence and allowed the *prima* to touch her own goblet to his. Those goblets were made of very fine crystal, cut in an intricate pattern, and the sound they made as they clinked against each other seemed far more melodious to his ears than the bell she used to summon her servant.

All around the table, people murmured, "to Randall," and gently bumped their glasses together. He swallowed a small sip of the wine, which he thought might be a Bordeaux, rich and complex. Wine had never been an area of expertise for him, but he'd picked up enough knowledge over the years so he wouldn't embarrass himself in social settings.

"I suppose I should make the introductions," Greta went on. "This is my son Karl"—she nodded toward the blond man to her right—"and his wife Laura. And that is Victoria, my daughter, the *prima*-in-waiting, and her husband Neil." A pause, and she added, "My husband passed away late last year. I'm sorry you didn't get a chance to meet him."

Well, those words cleared up that particular mystery. Randall murmured, "I'm sorry," and she nodded.

"It was quite a blow to all of us. But the Van Horns do what they must to soldier on."

Since he didn't quite know the best way to respond to such a comment, he asked, "Do you all live nearby?"

Victoria smiled. "Neil and I are just down the street. Karl and Laura have a place in Soho."

"Oh?" Randall replied. "My mother owns a gallery in Soho. It's called Extensions. Do you know it?"

Everyone at the table exchanged an uncomfortable glance. Were they troubled by the off-hand way he'd referred to Barbara Lenz? They certainly couldn't have been expecting him to immediately start thinking of the long-dead Alicia Van Horn as his mother, could they?

Well, considering how clannish witch families seemed to be, maybe they did. However, they'd need to learn that just because he might share some blood in common with the Van Horns, that didn't mean he was going to pretend his adoptive parents had never existed.

To his relief, Laura Van Horn smiled. "Actually, I do know it. Karl and I have bought a few pieces there. Your mother seems like a lovely person."

This friendly comment was met by a faint frown from the *prima,* although she didn't bother to interject. And her son Karl was also giving him the side-eye, although that could have been because of the way his wife had just smiled at Randall. He wasn't one to flatter himself, but he got the impression that the lively interest on her face had something more to it than mere curiosity about this latest addition to the family.

"Is it really true that you didn't have any powers until you were struck by lightning?" Victoria asked. In contrast to her sister-in-law, her expression showed only simple interest in what he had to admit had been a strange set of circumstances. Obviously, her mother had filled her in on some of the details, but not all.

"Apparently," he replied. "My gift is luck. When I went back and analyzed the situation, I realized it had probably been operating at a low level for most of my life. But it wasn't until the lightning strike that things really kicked into high gear, so to speak."

Had he revealed too much? But then, he'd already told Greta about his particular talent, and so he had a feeling everyone gathered around the table already knew. He certainly wasn't going to provide any more details than he already had.

"How did it happen?" Victoria's husband Neil inquired.

"While I was working a case for DHS," Randall said, which was only the truth. They didn't need to know that the lightning bolts in question had been human-directed. But because everyone was staring at him expectantly, obviously wanting to know more, he added, "I'm afraid I can't say anything more than that. The information is still classified."

"How exciting!" Laura exclaimed. She took another sip of wine. "I don't think the Van Horns have ever had a government agent in the family."

"Former agent," he told her. "I resigned from Homeland Security last summer."

"Which is just as well," Greta said. "That's entirely too dangerous a vocation for someone in this clan. We'll think of something else for you to do. Or really, there's no need for you to do anything at all. You have quite a large inheritance waiting for you as the son of my late sister."

That was news. Not that he cared terribly about the money; his months in Flagstaff had taught him that material wealth didn't really count for much in the grand scheme of things. He knew he'd felt happier and more fulfilled while mending split-rail fences with Joanna than he had in a very long time.

Across the table, Karl and Victoria exchanged weighted glances. Randall didn't know for sure what that was about, except that maybe if he'd stayed missing, his part of the inheritance would have been theirs after their mother was gone.

"Really?" he said, trying to sound noncommittal.

"Oh, yes," Greta said. "It's all been held in a

trust. I always hoped that one day I'd be able to find you, so I made sure to keep it safe."

He wouldn't ask how much money was involved. That was a conversation he and Greta could have later in private. He also didn't like the intimation that she would concoct some kind of socially acceptable occupation for him. His life was his own, and he'd make his own damn decisions about it.

However, his earlier resolve to play along for now remained in place. He didn't want to risk antagonizing the *prima*—or anyone else in the family—until he'd had a chance to figure out the best way to make his escape. Too bad he didn't have Connor and Angela's gift of teleportation, or he would have already been gone.

"Thank you," he said, his tone neutral.

At that moment, Elaine reappeared, this time pushing a serving cart with a large standing rib roast and a variety of side dishes. Randall was glad of the interruption, and remained silent while she set down the various platters and dishes, then departed. As he watched her go, he had to wonder what her particular talent was, and why she'd decided that a life of fetching and carrying for the Van Horn *prima* and her family was better than anything she could have provided for herself.

Apparently standing in for his late father, Karl carved the roast and handed off portions to everyone at the table. The ritual of passing the various side dishes—steamed asparagus, potatoes au gratin, some kind of fruit compote, a basket of rolls—commenced then, and soon enough, Randall's plate was laden with the kind of bounty usually reserved for Thanksgiving dinner. Was this standard fare for them, or had Greta put on a show to welcome her long-lost nephew back to the fold?

But at least eating meant he could abstain from conversation for a while, which was a relief. Not that anyone had asked him any probing questions, but he didn't care for the underlying assumption he would abandon everything about his life to become a part of the Van Horn clan. That just wasn't going to happen.

When the conversation picked up again, it wasn't focused on him, thank God. Greta and Victoria discussed an upcoming charity dinner, and Karl and Neil talked about going out on a fishing trip on Karl's boat. If Randall hadn't known better, he would have thought he was out for dinner at the home of one of his mother's friends. The talk was the kind that only members of an extremely rarefied slice of New York society could have, but it was also oddly familiar.

He didn't know what to think about that. In a way, it was disquieting to see how easy it might be to slip back into this milieu, into a life that could have been his if he'd decided to be an investment banker like his father rather than going to work for Homeland Security.

Had that been Greta Van Horn's plan all along?

Possibly. Randall watched and listened…and silently vowed not to fall prey to her schemes.

10

As luck would have it, Joanna just missed Connor at his Forest Highlands house. However, he hadn't quite started down the switchbacks into Oak Creek Canyon when she called, which meant he still had reception.

"You want me to do what?" he asked, sounding annoyed.

"I want you to go through Damon's papers and see if you can find the spell he used to disguise your witch nature," she said, praying she could get him to agree before the call dropped.

"I don't think that's a very good idea—"

"I have to go to New York," Joanna cut in, knowing how desperation added an edge to her words. "And I can't go into Van Horn territory without making sure they can't tell I'm there."

"Joanna, I understand that you want to help Randall, but think about what you're asking here."

She'd already thought about it. Yes, going into another clan's territory without permission was one of the biggest no-nos in the witching world, but she was damned if she was going to let an old nicety like that get in the way of making sure Randall Lenz was safe. Trying to keep her voice level, she replied, "I know, Connor. But I also know that you and Angela are the only ones who can make sure I can do this safely." She hesitated, wondering if she should beg. Instead, she said quietly, "Please, Connor."

A long pause. Then he said, "All right. I'll turn around. And I'll call Angela and tell her to meet me at the house. I don't think this is the sort of thing I can pull off on my own."

"Thanks, Connor."

"Don't thank me yet. We don't even know if this is going to work."

The call ended there. Joanna didn't know whether that was because he'd lost reception, or because he was hurrying to contact his wife before his phone died.

Either way, he'd agreed to help her, which was the important thing. And he also hadn't given her any crap about going to these lengths to help out Randall Lenz, a man who technically wasn't even part of the Wilcox clan.

She'd already been halfway to Connor and Angela's house in Forest Highlands, so Joanna continued on that route. Most likely, she'd get there before Connor, but she could wait in the driveway until he arrived.

Her nerve endings hummed with tension. No, there probably wasn't any way to make all this go faster, but at the same time, she couldn't help fretting over what might be happening to Randall at this very moment. Who could have taken him, and for what purpose? What if he'd been kidnapped by foreign nationals and was off being tortured somewhere?

All right, that scenario wasn't very likely. He hadn't said much to her about his time with Homeland Security, but she'd gotten the impression that most of his work had involved domestic issues, up to and including his hunt for people with special powers. Honestly, it seemed more plausible that he'd been grabbed by someone from one of the witch clans of the orphan witches who'd been returned to their family. Joanna thought it entirely possible that certain individuals in those families had decided it wasn't enough just to have their missing members delivered to them, and had decided to get a much more personal revenge.

Or it could be something else entirely, a person Randall had crossed during his time at

DHS, an enemy he'd made as he was working his way up the ranks. The only way she'd know for sure was if she could find Kelly Dawson and talk to her in person.

Joanna pulled into the upscale development where Connor and Angela's house was located, and followed the winding streets until she reached their house. It sat on more than an acre of land, set a little away from the neighbors, and was a large, handsome structure with several stone fire-places and sharply peaked roofs. The driveway was big enough to accommodate a half dozen vehicles, and so she pulled up and parked over to one side, leaving plenty of room for both Angela and Connor to park there.

He arrived first, which was no big surprise; he'd only had to drive back from the switchbacks, while Angela would be coming all the way from Jerome. His dark green Toyota FJ SUV was the same one he'd been driving ever since Joanna had met him. As *primus,* he could have afforded to get himself a new car every year if he'd wanted to, but clearly, he intended to drive the FJ until it dropped in harness.

As soon as the vehicle came to a stop, Joanna climbed out of her truck and went to meet Connor. He emerged from his SUV looking a little frayed around the edges, but he sent her a smile as he approached.

"Let's go inside," he said. "It's going to be kind of cold—we have the heat turned down because the house has been empty for months. But I'll fire up the furnace for us."

"Thanks, Connor," Joanna said simply, hoping he'd understand that her gratitude went far beyond simple thanks. "I really appreciate this."

"No problem."

The standard reply, and one she wasn't sure was really the truth. She knew he didn't like having to dig around in his late brother's belongings, would have preferred to keep that part of the past firmly locked away.

But he hadn't said no, and that was the important thing.

As promised, the interior of the house was uncomfortably cold. Connor went to the thermostat and adjusted it upward, and at once the furnace came on, blowing welcome warm air through the vents.

"Let's go into the living room," he said. "I'll turn on the gas logs there, and that should help, too."

Joanna followed him into the space, which felt oddly empty, even though all the furniture was in its usual places. But the last time she'd been here had been for the Wilcox Christmas potluck, and with the tree long gone and all the other holiday decorations presumably packed away in their various boxes, the room felt bare.

However, once Connor got the gas fire going, and friendly flames started to leap around the faux logs in the hearth, the place cheered up immediately. "Coffee?" he asked. "Or tea? We've got a Keurig, so I can get you pretty much whatever you want."

"Some hot tea would be great," she replied. If nothing else, she could use the mug as a hand warmer until the interior temperature got a little more comfortable.

"Back in a sec," he promised.

Since there wasn't much else she could do, Joanna sat down on one of the leather couches, although she kept her jacket on. Eventually, the room would be warm enough that she wouldn't need it, but right then she was glad of the extra layer.

A few minutes later, Connor came back, a mug of heavy glazed stoneware in either hand. Judging by the heavy aroma that drifted from the mug he kept for himself, he'd opted for coffee instead of tea. He took a few sips, then said, "I suppose I might as well start going through Damon's papers. I just wanted to get a little hot coffee in me before I started on that."

"Do you want to wait until Angela gets here?"

He shook his head. "No. I mean, I'm going to

need her help with the actual spell, but I'm the one who organized Damon's stuff after he—well, after he was gone. She wouldn't even know where to look."

Something taut in Connor's expression told Joanna he really wasn't looking forward to the task ahead. If there had been any other way, she would never have asked this of him. It had been more than seven years, but clearly, that wound was still far too raw.

But because she knew calling attention to the situation would only make things worse, she just said, "Thanks."

That was all, but he seemed to understand. A nod, and then he headed off toward the wing of the house where the bedrooms were located. Joanna knew they used one of them for a shared office space, and she assumed Connor must keep Damon's papers in there somewhere.

For herself, there wasn't much she could do except wait. She sat quietly, sipping the English Breakfast tea Connor had made for her and feeling the room gradually warm up to the point where she had to set her mug down for a moment so she could take off her jacket. A clock hung on the far wall, ticking away into the silence.

Was this crazy? After all, she didn't know Randall very well. A few days together, one amazing night...was that really enough to ask

Connor and Angela to dig into a painful past, for Joanna to take the risk of traveling thousands of miles into a strange clan's territory?

On the surface, maybe. And yet…and yet, she knew Randall would have done the same for her if their roles had been reversed.

About twenty minutes after Connor had disappeared into the office, a whisper of tires in the driveway told Joanna that Angela must have arrived. She caught a brief glimpse of a big white SUV, followed by the McAllister *prima's* slim form striding up the front walk. A few seconds later, the door opened.

Angela peered into the living room and waved hello at Joanna. "Where's Connor?"

"He's in the office, going through Damon's papers."

The *prima* accepted this information with a brief nod. "Then I'll let him keep at it. Do you need a refill on that tea?"

Actually, she did. Joanna rose from the leather sofa where she'd been sitting and came over to meet Angela at the entrance to the room. "That would be great. Although do you have any decaf, or something herbal? I'm jumpy enough without having any more caffeine."

That request was met with an understanding smile. "I think we've got a few things. Let's go take a look."

The two women headed into the kitchen, which was just as grandly proportioned as the rest of the house. Since Joanna was very happy with her own kitchen, she didn't experience even a single flicker of envy at the gleaming expanse of the granite countertops or the oversized Viking stove and matching stainless appliances.

Everything was immaculate, which made sense, since the family hadn't stayed here since Christmas. Joanna knew that Connor and Angela had someone come in and dust and wipe everything down once a month, so the house would be in perfect shape when they returned toward the end of May.

"Um…I've got cinnamon spice, or lemon for the herbal stuff," Angela said as she rummaged around in the walk-in pantry. "Or there are a couple of pods of decaf green tea."

"The decaf green tea would be great."

She emerged from the pantry and slipped the pod into the Keurig machine. While it was working away, Joanna headed over to the sink and rinsed out her mug. Angela watched her, expression speculative.

Since she could guess what was probably going through the *prima's* mind, Joanna went ahead and said it out loud. "You think I'm crazy for hooking up with Randall Lenz."

Angela's big green eyes widened further. "Did

I say you were crazy?"

"No, but you were thinking it pretty loudly."

That comment earned her a laugh. Angela came over and took the rinsed mug from Joanna, then set it down on the counter so she could pour the newly brewed green tea into it. Once that was done, she popped a cinnamon spice tea pod into the machine and turned back toward her guest.

"I don't think 'crazy' is the right word. I guess I'm just more surprised than anything else. For one thing, it doesn't seem as if he'd been hanging out with the Wilcoxes enough for you two to have even bumped into each other."

"He came over to help me repair a fence," Joanna explained. "Jasper was supposed to do it, but he was busy. And so Randall lent a hand… and I guess one thing just led to another."

"That old witchy chemistry," Angela said, still smiling slightly.

"You really believe in that?"

The *prima* shrugged. "I don't think it's really a question of 'believing' or not. I've seen it happen enough that I know it's real. Why it happens that way for witch folk, I'm not exactly sure. I suppose what surprises me about Randall Lenz is that he'd be susceptible to it at this point. After all, he's not some twenty-two-year-old kid falling for a girl for the first time."

No, that he definitely was not. He hadn't said

anything to Joanna about the women in his past because, frankly, their own relationship hadn't really gotten to that point. But it seemed obvious enough to her that there hadn't been anyone of any true significance. "Maybe it was like his magic…it just recently woke up."

"I can see that." Angela poured her cinnamon spice tea into a mug and blew on it gently. "And you never felt that chemistry with anyone before?"

"No," Joanna replied. "I mean, it's not like I was saving myself for marriage or anything, but I also knew I'd never experienced what I saw in other witches after I came back to live with the Wilcoxes. I suppose I just figured it was different for me because I was half civilian."

Angela's expression was musing. "I don't think it works that way. I mean, I know people with a civilian parent who've definitely felt that kind of chemistry—my cousin Jenny, for one. But maybe you never felt it before because the universe was waiting for you to meet Randall Lenz."

"That seems a little far-fetched," Joanna protested. She wouldn't deny the connection she felt with him, but neither was she willing to admit that theirs might be some kind of star-crossed love for the ages.

"Maybe not as far-fetched as you think," Angela said. She sipped some tea, cradling her fingers around her mug just as Joanna had only a few minutes earlier. "After all, his gift is luck, isn't it? I could see how his talent was operating in the background to make sure you'd be available when your paths finally crossed."

That proposition sounded even crazier...or maybe it was more that Joanna didn't know if she wanted to accept it was possible for someone's magic to be powerful enough to influence everyone around them. "If he's so lucky, why was he kidnapped?"

"We don't know that's what really happened to him," Angela replied, then continued, appearing to relent as she saw the flash in Joanna's eyes, "although I'll admit that seems to be what's going on here. But sometimes it's really hard for those of us caught up in events to see the big picture."

That observation made some sense, so Joanna didn't bother to argue. Although she and Angela were roughly the same age, she knew the *prima* had been to hell and back to secure a happy future with Connor. If anyone knew about the big picture, it was Angela McAllister.

"I thought I heard voices in here," said Connor as he entered the room, a leather binder in one hand. He paused to place a kiss on his wife's cheek, then set the binder down on the butcher-block island in the center of the kitchen. "I think I found the spell Damon used."

Angela squeezed Connor's hand, as if

acknowledging how hard it must have been for him to look through the late *primus's* papers, then said, voice turning businesslike, "Let's take a look."

Connor opened the binder and flipped past a couple of pages. "It's this one."

Joanna sidled around the both of them so she could glance down at the words on the paper. They'd been written in all capital letters, geometrical and precise. "I thought Wilcoxes didn't need to use spells."

"We don't," Connor said. "But Damon's talent was magic, basically. He came up with ways to manipulate it, basically bend it to his will. One of those ways was designing spells that would create the outcome he desired."

His explanation still didn't make a lot of sense to her, but Joanna only nodded. Magic could be a capricious thing, and she realized that Connor and Angela knew a hell of a lot more about it than she did.

"So, what we're going to do is analyze this spell, see how Damon put it together, and then do our best to make it workable with our combined energies," the *prima* put in. "The way we practice magic is very different from how he did it, and so it might take a little tweaking."

"But hopefully not too much," Connor added. "Since Damon already laid the foundation, the hard work has been done." He glanced over at his wife. "What do you think?"

"It's pretty simple, actually," she replied. "That is, the spell focuses on keeping the subject's core of magic intact while preventing its signal, so to speak, from radiating outward. That's how you were still able to use your own power to alter your appearance while Damon's spell was operating and preventing me from discovering you were really a Wilcox."

She sounded so casual as she spoke, as if it wasn't a big deal that the *primus* of the Wilcoxes had basically sent his younger brother to spy in McAllister territory. But Joanna supposed that was all water under the bridge at this point. Connor and Angela were clearly meant to be together, and all of Damon's machinations had ultimately come to naught.

"Let's give it a try, then," Connor said.

Angela nodded, and reached out so they could entwine their fingers. Standing a few feet away, Joanna thought once again of how the two of them always looked so right together, so easy and comfortable in one another's presence...even when practicing new and unfamiliar magic, as they were now.

"What lies within is completely concealed,
Binding a secret that won't be revealed.
Magic soul deep, hidden for now

Revealed to no one, but never told how."

Joanna looked down at herself. "I don't feel any different," she said.

"You wouldn't," Angela replied, now sounding amused. "That's kind of the point."

"We need to test it, though," Connor said. "Obviously, having Joanna go and hang out with the Wilcoxes in Flagstaff won't work, since everyone in the clan has already met her and they wouldn't get their little 'twinge' anyway."

Angela glanced over at Joanna, who returned her gaze. She honestly had no idea whether the spell had worked, because, as she'd told them a minute earlier, she felt exactly the same as she always had.

"We'll take her to Jerome," she said. "You've never been, have you?"

Joanna shook her head. "No. I guess I'm kind of a homebody. I've meant to visit but just never got around to it."

"In this case, that's a good thing," Angela replied. "You won't have met any of my relatives, and so they'll be able to tell me right away whether you give them a twinge or not." A pause, and she added, "You can ride with me."

"We're not teleporting?" Joanna asked, halfway disappointed. Secretly, she'd always wanted to try that instantaneous form of travel.

"Both our cars are here," Connor pointed out.

"We need to get them back to Jerome. Angela and I can only teleport together, which is why she had to drive over here. But we'll teleport you when we're done."

She supposed she had to be satisfied with that. "Makes sense."

"Let me turn off the fireplace and turn down the thermostat," Connor said. "Then we can get going."

Joanna followed him into the living room so she could retrieve her jacket, and after that, all three of them left the house. Angela led her to her Jeep Grand Cherokee, while Connor climbed into his Toyota. Before too long, they were back out on 89A, heading down into Oak Creek Canyon.

This part of the journey was at least somewhat familiar, since Joanna had traveled down into the canyon and into Uptown Sedona a couple of times. But once they were pushing westward on the highway, heading toward Cottonwood and Jerome, the landscape became utterly new to her. Gone were Sedona's red rocks and the ponderosa pines that surrounded Flagstaff. Instead, she watched rolling hills dotted with juniper pass by, the grass freshly green with recent rains. Wildflowers dotted the sides of the highway, and she realized that, at this lower elevation, spring came much earlier than it did in her hometown.

"I'll take you to meet my Aunt Rachel,"

Angela said. She'd been quiet up until then, as if she'd guessed that Joanna preferred to be silent as she observed her new surroundings. "She owns a store in Jerome, so it's not like we'll be barging into her house or something. And if we need even more proof, we can go visit my cousin Kirby. He manages the candy shop."

"That sounds good," Joanna replied. To her surprise, she realized she was almost nervous. This would be the first time she set foot in McAllister territory, and even though she understood intellectually that Jerome and its environs weren't off limits and hadn't been that way for years, it still somehow felt as though she was doing something illicit.

They drove through Cottonwood's charmingly restored downtown, and went on through Clarkdale, somehow even smaller and more quaint. Then the road began to climb upward, heading toward Jerome where it perched on the side of Cleopatra Hill.

Because it was a weekday and they were a little past spring break, the traffic wasn't too bad. Even so, the former mining town's streets were lined with vehicles. Joanna wasn't sure whether it was luck or a little *prima* magic that allowed Angela to find a parking space directly in front of Jerome Mercantile—apparently her Aunt Rachel's shop—but they were able to pull right in.

Connor wasn't so lucky, but he found a space a little ways down the street, in front of a restaurant called Grapes.

"Normally, we'd just go up to the house and park there," Angela explained as she shut off the engine. "But it's kind of a hike, and this will be faster."

"Whatever's easiest," Joanna responded. She undid her seatbelt and got out, taking a minute to get a quick glimpse of her surroundings. The buildings here seemed very old, even older than the structures in downtown Flagstaff, but what she saw looked well-maintained, with cheerfully painted façades and shop signs.

They waited on the sidewalk for Connor to join them, and then the trio walked into Jerome Mercantile. A woman who appeared to be in her late fifties with graying reddish hair was working behind the counter, arranging jewelry in one of the display cases. She looked up as they walked in, and immediately a smile warmed her already cheerful face.

"Afternoon!" she called out. "I didn't think I'd see you today."

"Oh, we wanted to show Joanna around town," Angela replied. "Joanna, this is my aunt Rachel. Rachel, this is Joanna Wilcox."

At once, a flicker of confusion passed over Rachel's features. "Oh, it's very nice to meet you," she said. "Have you been in Jerome before? Maybe that would explain...."

The words trailed off, and Connor and Angela exchanged a look of triumph, even as Joanna experienced a flicker of hope. Was Rachel puzzled because she really hadn't been able to sense that Joanna was a witch?

"No, this is my first time," she said, and shot a glance at Angela. Should she explain, or leave it up to the *prima*?

But obviously Angela didn't want to leave her aunt hanging for too long, because she said, "You couldn't tell that Joanna was a witch, could you?"

"No," Rachel replied. "It's the oddest thing. I've never *not* gotten a twinge from a strange witch before."

"It's because we cast a spell to hide her witch nature," Angela said. "We figured we'd test it out on you because we knew you'd never met Joanna before."

Rachel shook her head in amazement...but then she sent a narrow look at her niece, as if she'd just figured out that Angela probably wouldn't be testing that sort of spell if she didn't have a particular purpose in mind.

And generally, you didn't try to hide someone's witch nature unless they were going someplace they weren't supposed to go.

"Wilcox business," Angela said briefly.

Her aunt released a breath, lips tightening as if she wanted to tell Angela that it didn't matter whether it was Wilcox business or not. But then her shoulders lifted slightly. "Then I won't ask," she said, although the wariness in her tone was obvious enough.

Joanna wondered if she should say anything, then decided sometimes it was better to just keep quiet. Angela might have been the *prima* of the McAllister clan, but it was clear that her aunt was still very protective of her. Since Rachel looked as though she was ready to let it go, no point in stirring things up.

"We're going to take Joanna to meet Kirby, too," Angela added. "I figured it was probably better to test the spell on a few different people, just to be safe."

"Yes, I suppose that's best," Rachel responded, still looking troubled. "And it'll give her a chance to see a bit more of the town."

"It seems very charming," Joanna put in, hoping that was an innocuous enough statement.

"It is," Rachel said. "I hope you'll get to spend a little time here to explore."

That hadn't really been the plan; Joanna only wanted to test the concealment spell, then have Connor and Angela send her off to New York. However, she realized she couldn't go to Manhattan without a little preparation beforehand. At the very least, she'd need to pack an overnight bag, since she didn't know how long she'd be gone. Also, she'd need to see if Jasper or someone else could come out and keep an eye on the alpacas and feed Sass while she was away... however long that turned out to be.

"I hope I get to see some more of Jerome, too," Joanna said.

Connor glanced toward the window. A family of four had clustered outside the shop window and now looked as they were preparing to come inside, and he was probably thinking that this was a good time to head down to Kirby's candy shop.

"Thanks for the help, Rachel," Connor said. "You and Toby will be up for dinner tomorrow evening, right?"

"Wouldn't miss it," Rachel responded, her smile returning. As the bells on the shop door jangled and a pair of kids, probably around eight and ten, came running in, she added quickly, "It was nice meeting you, Joanna."

"Nice meeting you, too," Joanna replied.

They had to wait until the whole family had entered the shop, but afterward, they slipped out and headed down the street. She tried not to look like a complete tourist as she glanced from side to side, sneaking peeks at all the various shops and restaurants. For such a small place, there seemed to be a lot to explore. Now it seemed silly that she'd never taken the time to come down here before this. She and Randall would have to come and spend a day here when they had the chance.

As soon as that thought passed through her mind, it was followed by a ripple of sadness…and worry. She didn't even know where Randall was, or whether he was safe. What if they never got the opportunity to come to Jerome and wander from shop to shop, to eat at Grapes or at that place she'd spied called The Bordello, to taste wine and pause to stare at the awesome view of the Verde Valley you got from almost every stretch of the town's main street?

You're going to find him, she told herself fiercely. *You're going to New York, and you'll find Kelly Dawson, and she'll help you figure out who took him.*

That was a hell of a lot of maybes, but Joanna had to believe it would all be fine. Otherwise, why had she come here in the first place?

Connor and Angela took her to another shop, one much smaller than Rachel's. The warm, heavenly scent of chocolate drifted out as soon as Connor opened the door, and Joanna took in a deep breath, savoring the aroma. This had to be the candy store.

A man around Angela's age—in his early thirties—with light brown hair and dancing gray eyes was just ringing up a purchase as they walked in.

Since the shop was small, they had to crowd off to one side until the couple who'd been buying some candy were done with their transaction and had headed out the door.

As soon as they were gone, though, Joanna followed Connor and Angela to the counter. The man working—who must have been her cousin Kirby—shot an inquisitive look in Joanna's direction. "I don't think I've seen you before," he said.

"Kirby, this is Joanna Wilcox, my cousin," Connor said.

That revelation obviously took Kirby aback, because his eyes narrowed almost the same way that Rachel's had, and he gave her a piercing look. "But...my ears aren't ringing."

"Because we cast a spell to hide her witchiness," Angela explained. "We went to visit Rachel first, and she couldn't sense anything, either. But we figured it would help to test it with someone else, too."

"Well, it definitely worked," he said. Unlike Rachel, he didn't seem inclined to ask any more questions—most likely because he knew his cousin wouldn't give him any real answers. If you were going around hiding someone's witch nature, it probably meant you were working on something clandestine. He glanced back at Joanna. "Some chocolate before you go?"

"That sounds fabulous," she replied. "How about a piece of that double fudge?"

"Coming right up."

He got busy behind the counter, slicing a piece of fudge for Joanna—and also filling up a bag with treats for Connor and Angela...or probably for their kids. From the look of resignation on Angela's face, she wasn't going to argue with her cousin, even if the gift of candy was probably going to send the twins and Miranda bouncing off the walls.

When Kirby was done, he handed over the various bags, and they all thanked him before heading back outside.

"Well, it looks like the spell is a success," Joanna said. "I don't want to delay too much longer, but I need to go home and put a few things together before I go to New York."

Angela glanced around; they stood out on the sidewalk, but no one was immediately nearby to overhear them. "We'll go to the house," she said. "We need to move the cars anyway, and then we can teleport you back to our place in Forest Highlands so you can get your truck. After that, we can meet at your house and take you to New York." She paused, a flicker of concern passing across her features. "Except we don't even know where to take you."

"To Kelly Dawson's building," Joanna

responded at once. She'd already started working out the logistics, so she had a ready answer. "We can look it up on Google street view so you have a clear target. I thought it would be safer to approach her there—it's probably not a good idea to be loitering around DHS headquarters in New York."

"No, probably not," Connor agreed with a grin. "And it'll be evening in Manhattan by the time we're traveling, so she should be home."

Joanna had to hope so. Who knew what kind of hours Kelly Dawson worked? But approaching her at a Homeland Security office felt like a very bad idea, so her apartment it was.

"Anyway, that's my plan," she said.

"It should work," Angela replied. "Let's go and move the cars, then, and go on from there."

The matter settled, they headed back up the street to the spot where the vehicles waited. As she walked, little bag of fudge clutched in one hand, Joanna couldn't quite ignore the flutters of nervousness in her stomach. It wasn't so much anticipation at finally getting to teleport—or to go to New York, a place she'd never dreamed she would end up visiting.

No, it was the worry that despite their plans, Kelly Dawson might not be able to help after all.

And if that turned out to be the case, Joanna had absolutely no idea what to do next.

11

BECAUSE HE'D TRAVELED SO MUCH WHEN working for DHS, Randall didn't have any problem sleeping in a strange bed. Or rather, although he'd been plagued by insomnia for most of his adult life—except, it seemed, when he was sleeping next to Joanna Wilcox—he could at least be somewhat comfortable in surroundings that weren't familiar.

Not tonight, however.

He lay on the king-size bed and stared at the ceiling, thoughts unsettled, darting this way and that. Although he tried to tell himself he wouldn't be much use if he didn't get at least some sleep, he knew better. Far too often, he'd been forced to get through his day on only two or three hours of sleep, so he knew he'd be functional the next morning…if not precisely happy.

Everyone had done their best to make him feel welcome, like he was a part of the family, but Randall couldn't shake the impression that neither of his cousins—*first* cousins, he reminded himself, since he guessed he must be related to Victoria and Karl's spouses as well, if only very distantly— were less than pleased to have him brought back into the fold, so to speak.

The inheritance, he supposed. Greta hadn't gone into any detail, and he hadn't imagined she would, not at the dinner table like that. No, she'd hinted that she would speak with him in private on the subject, and he'd nodded and let it go for the moment. He could already tell that Greta Van Horn was someone who did things in her own time and in her own way.

Would Karl and Victoria be shocked if he told them he didn't care about the money, and that he only wanted to go back to Flagstaff? No doubt if it were up to them, they'd cheerfully put him on the next nonstop flight to Phoenix.

But it wasn't their decision. Greta ruled the roost around here, and so Randall guessed he would have to wait and see what she planned to reveal...and when. It was a good thing he'd culti- vated patience during his time at DHS, because otherwise, he would have already been demanding to return to his life in Arizona.

As much as he worried about Joanna, and

what she must be thinking about his disappearance, he also knew he wasn't quite ready to go back to Flagstaff. He'd learned of his mother's identity, true, but that was only half the mystery.

Who was his father?

The answer to that question had to lie somewhere here in New York. Although he supposed it was possible that Alicia Van Horn had left the city to seek romance elsewhere, everything he knew about witch clans told him that didn't seem very plausible. Witches just didn't travel. No, they stayed in their own territories, for the most part.

Which led him back to the possibility he'd already considered, that his biological father was a civilian. If Alicia had been rebelling at what he guessed was her family's heavy-handed rule, then having an affair with a civilian was a pretty perfect fuck-you. And since her magic involved getting people to stay away from her, she could have maintained such a relationship for quite a while, with the Van Horns being none the wiser.

Still, trying to find one man in a city of roughly eight million people wasn't going to exactly be easy...especially since Randall had absolutely no idea who the man in question could have been. About the only thing he could guess was that his biological father must have been dark-haired. The Van Horns seemed to be uniformly fair, and he was definitely darker than any of them, although he'd inherited their light blue eyes.

And if he'd born in the usual way, in a hospital, then there would have been records that could have been traced. Although Greta didn't seem to know all the details of his birth, it didn't seem out of line to surmise that Alicia had attempted a home delivery, and had been so injured by the ordeal that she'd died of the trauma not long afterward.

So...that appeared to put him back to square one.

He wished he could get in contact with Jeremy Wilcox. Randall had no doubt that all he'd have to do was give Jeremy the few details he had, and then let the Wilcox clan's resident computer genius connect the dots in a way that no one else could.

But was it really true that Jeremy was the only person Randall knew who possessed the peculiar ability to slice through data like a hot knife through butter?

His former assistant, Agent Kelly Dawson, had also been extremely skilled in those sorts of things. And she was a hell of a lot closer....

The notion engaged him so much that Randall sat up in bed, pondering the situation and analyzing the possibilities. So far, he didn't have a very clear idea of how much freedom Greta Van

Horn would allow him. It wasn't as though he'd been locked in his borrowed bedroom or anything close to that, but at the same time, he didn't know if he'd have the liberty to go wandering around New York.

Somehow, he needed to convince her that he wasn't a flight risk.

Well, since he didn't have his cell phone or wallet, he couldn't get very far. But he didn't require either of those things to get around Manhattan, although he'd need some kind of cash for transportation, if nothing else.

Would Greta believe him if he told her that he only wanted to go out so he could refamiliarize himself with the town where he'd grown up, but where he hadn't lived for more than a decade?

Maybe. If nothing else, he needed to visit his mother. He'd have to make it very clear to Greta Van Horn that he couldn't possibly come back to live in New York and be expected to have zero contact with the woman who'd raised him.

Randall settled back against the pillows, now smiling faintly. Probably the first thing he needed to do was let Greta know how very, very pleased he was to learn about his inheritance.

After all, money was something that could tie a person to a place more than anything else.

～

Kelly Dawson lived in an apartment building on East 84th Street, a little less than a mile from her office at DHS. Connor and Angela had teleported Joanna into the nearest alleyway, where luckily, no one was around to witness their precipitous arrival.

"You're sure you're going to be okay?" Angela asked. On the next street over, someone honked, and the response was a volley of more honking. The *prima* winced, obviously not too impressed with the bright lights of the big city.

Not that Joanna could call herself impressed, either. All right, the only thing she'd seen so far was this alley, but what she hadn't been expecting was the enormous, crushing weight of having so many people packed into such a small space. The tall buildings felt as though they wanted to topple over on her, and the air was thick with the scent of exhaust.

How could people live like this?

But apparently they did, and she knew she needed to suck it up and get on with the task at hand. "I'll be fine," she replied. "I've got a hotel room booked not far from Kelly Dawson's apartment, and you know I'll reach out to you as soon as I find anything—or if I need help."

"All right," Angela said, but she still flickered a worried glance at her husband.

Connor put in, "Yes, you need to call if

anything feels off, or if you think you've attracted the wrong kind of attention. The spell will hold indefinitely—or at least until we manually remove it—so you should be okay, but still...be careful."

"I will." Even though she knew she had their spell protecting her, Joanna still thought that walking out of this alley would be a bit like walking naked onto a stage. She felt horribly exposed. "You two go on home. I'm fine."

To her surprise, Connor and Angela crushed her into a brief, awkward combined hug before they disappeared. Left alone, Joanna couldn't do much except go out to the street and then start walking toward Kelly Dawson's apartment building.

She hoped no one was paying attention to her. Not wanting to attract any unwanted notice, she'd ditched her faded jeans and cowboy boots for a newer pair of jeans and the one pair of flats she owned, and topped it off with a sleek leather jacket she'd bought on a whim a while back. Her reflection in the mirror at her house had shown a far more chic Joanna Wilcox than the world usually saw, and she prayed she'd blend in with the rest of the New Yorkers.

Since she didn't seem to have drawn any curious eyes, she felt somewhat safe in approaching the building. There was a doorman, but he sat at a desk a ways off from the locked glass doors to the lobby.

Was she going to have to go through him to get to Kelly Dawson?

To Joanna's relief, she noticed in the next second that there was a directory mounted on the wall next to the door, with a buzzer system. "K. Dawson" was listed as being in Apartment 5D.

Well, here went nothing.

Before she could lose her nerve, Joanna touched the buzzer and waited. Then a woman's voice came through the speaker, softer than she'd expected. "Who is it?"

"Hi, Ms. Dawson," Joanna said. "You don't know me, but my name is Joanna Wilcox. I need to speak with you."

A long pause. "Did you say 'Wilcox'?"

"Yes."

Another silence followed her reply. Joanna waited, wondering what in the world she would do if Kelly Dawson turned her away.

Wait until morning, she thought. *Then ambush her when she leaves for work.*

As plans went, it wasn't a very elegant one. However, Joanna couldn't think of anything better.

Except....

She leaned closer to the speaker. "It's about Randall Lenz."

Once again, she was left to wait…and wait.

Then….

"Come on up."

That was all, but the door buzzed, seeming to indicate that it had unlocked. Joanna hurried inside, then said to the doorman as he lifted his head from inspecting his phone's screen, "I'm going to see Kelly Dawson in 5D."

All she got in response was the barest of nods, but that was okay. He hadn't tried to stop her or ask her any questions, and that was the important thing.

Joanna went to the elevator and got in, then pressed the button for the fifth floor. It began to move upward, and she forced herself to stay where she was and try not to get freaked out by the realization that she was traveling in a little metal box that was only held in place by a thin cable.

Was it sad that she was thirty years old, and this was the first time she'd ever been in an elevator?

Probably. But Flagstaff was pretty short on high-rises, and the multi-story buildings it did contain were hotels and some buildings on the campus at Northern Pines, none of which she'd had any reason to frequent.

To her relief, the elevator stopped at the fifth floor without incident. She got out, looked around, and saw that 5D was the apartment at the end of the hall.

The building was actually very nice, she realized. Not that Joanna would ever want to live someplace with so many people packed in together, but the flat-pile carpet underfoot looked new, and the light fixtures were understated, vaguely Art Deco frosted glass sconces. There had even been a half-moon table with a faux orchid plant on it directly facing the elevator.

She'd just lifted her hand to knock when the door to Kelly Dawson's apartment opened. The woman standing there looked basically like the official photo Jeremy had retrieved as part of his research on Randall's former assistant, but her hair was now a few shades lighter and worn loose on her shoulders rather than pulled back in a severe ponytail, and she even appeared to be wearing a little makeup.

"Come in," she said briefly, and stepped out of the way so Joanna could enter the place.

It was beautifully decorated in soothing shades of cream and blue, like something out of a magazine. And although Joanna already knew she wasn't a fan of New York, she had to admit that the view from the corner apartment was pretty spectacular.

Kelly Dawson closed the door and gave Joanna a worried look. "Is Agent Lenz in trouble?"

It was on the tip of Joanna's tongue to correct the other woman, to tell her that Randall Lenz certainly wasn't a federal agent anymore, and so there was no reason to refer to him in that way. But she realized there was no point in being pedantic.

"I don't know," she said simply. "Maybe. He's disappeared."

Agent Dawson's lips pressed together. "He's living in Flagstaff, isn't he?"

The way she'd asked the question, it was more as though she was trying to confirm an internal suspicion rather than because she had any concrete data on the subject. Joanna knew he'd done his best to muddy the waters by changing his last name—and probably taking a few other measures that she didn't even know about—but she had a feeling that someone like Kelly Dawson could have located him if she'd really wanted to.

And anyway, she'd come here to get Agent Dawson's help, so beating around the bush and trying to hide information from her didn't seem like a very good idea.

"Yes," Joanna said. "He disappeared earlier today. He was supposed to come back to my house to help me with something, and he never showed up. There weren't any real signs of a struggle or anything at the place he's been renting, but both his cars are there, and yet he's gone. I think someone took him." She stopped there, watching Kelly's reaction. The other woman's lips had thinned slightly, but she wore an almost abstracted expression, as if her mind was already going a mile a minute. "I was hoping you could tell me if he had any enemies who might be out for revenge."

"'Enemies'?" Kelly shook her head. "That is, he stepped on a few toes while he was working at DHS, but that's not uncommon. I don't think any of it would have amounted to enough to have someone go across the entire country to kidnap him. Although...." Her words died away, and her mouth tightened again. When she spoke, though, it was to ask something entirely prosaic. "Do you want something to drink? Water, or tea?"

Since it was already past eight o'clock local time, Joanna didn't think drinking anything with caffeine was a very good idea. "Some water, please. Thank you."

Kelly went into the kitchen—which was as nicely appointed as the living room, with quartz counters and stainless appliances and cabinets painted a soft gray-blue—and got some water from the door in her refrigerator. "We should probably sit down," she said, then handed Joanna the glass of water before walking over to one of the velvet-upholstered armchairs that faced the couch across a sleek table of marble and brushed bronze.

Sitting down sounded like a good idea, so Joanna followed her and took a seat on the long sofa, placing herself precisely in the middle. "You said 'although' and didn't finish. Did you think of something?"

Kelly shook her head. "I'm not sure. I mean, when Project Daedalus fell apart—do you know what that was?"

"The project you and Randall were working on," Joanna replied. "The one where he was collecting people with special talents."

"Yes." She paused there, again giving Joanna one of those probing looks. Her eyes were a soft blue gray, with the only makeup accenting them a light coating of brown mascara on some surprisingly long lashes. "Do you want to tell me what was really going on with you Wilcoxes?"

Again, Joanna reminded herself that she was here asking for help, and trying to conceal the truth of her situation probably wouldn't help either one of them. Even so, the rules against revealing the witch community's secrets to outsiders were pretty strict.

Those rules stated that she needed to lie. Unfortunately, lying wasn't something she did very well. She had a sneaking suspicion that Kelly Dawson, DHS agent that she was, would probably be able to tell she wasn't telling the whole truth about exactly what Randall Lenz had been doing in Flagstaff, or why Joanna herself had felt compelled to come to his aid. And if the other woman guessed she was lying, then she probably wouldn't be too inclined to offer any sort of assistance.

Damn it.

She sipped some of her water, hoping doing so would help to center her a bit. The cool taste of the liquid on her tongue seemed to ground her at least, telling her she knew what she needed to do.

Joanna said, "All those people in Project Daedalus?"

"Yes?" The word came out with a rising inflection, as if she knew there was a lot more to the question.

"They weren't psychically gifted. Or at least," she hurried on, as the other woman opened her mouth to comment, "they had psychic talents, but it wasn't because they were genetic freaks or something. It's because they were witches and warlocks."

As soon as those words left her mouth, Joanna could tell Kelly had shut down. Her expression went blank, and she said carefully, as though she was trying to avoid upsetting a madwoman, "Witches and warlocks aren't real."

"They are," Joanna replied. Oddly, she felt

almost cheerful, as though she'd already done her worst and now just had to keep trudging on. "I'm a witch, and so is Addie Grant. Jake Wilcox is a warlock…as is Randall Lenz."

A disbelieving laugh escaped Kelly Dawson's lips. "Randall Lenz is a warlock. Of course. And I'm the Wicked Witch of the West."

Privately, Joanna thought the other woman would look better in Glinda's costume, but she only said, "No, you're just a civilian. That's what we call people who aren't witches and warlocks. And Randall didn't know he was one until Addie woke up his powers. But that's why he had to free them all."

Kelly sat in silence for a moment, realization dawning in her expression. "Now it starts to make sense," she murmured. "I could never figure out why he was all right with letting everything crash and burn…why he didn't fight harder to try to keep the project going." Her gaze sharpened as she stared back at Joanna. "If you're a witch, what's your power?"

"Weather," Joanna responded immediately. Kelly Dawson lifted an eyebrow, looking skeptical.

"The same talent Addie Grant has?" she said. "That's convenient."

"Maybe it's convenient," Joanna said. "But it's the truth. My power isn't as strong as hers, though. I can't summon lightning bolts or anything like that.

Mostly what I can do is coax a rainstorm to come a little closer, that sort of thing." She paused, reaching out with her talent to touch the clouds that floated above Manhattan. They didn't seem inclined to do much except drift across the city, but she thought she might be able to make them rain a little if she tried hard enough. "Do you want me to show you?"

Agent Dawson didn't even blink. "Sure."

Joanna focused. Yes, a push on the wind, to make the clouds blow in this direction, and just a bit of a nudge to make the moisture within them coalesce and form into raindrops.

A moment later, rain began pattering down the windows.

Kelly Dawson's eyes widened. She got up from the sofa and went to look outside, at the water as it began to streak its way down the glass. "You did that?"

"Yes."

A long pause. Then the other woman turned and resumed her seat. She settled against the back of the couch, suddenly looking very tired. For the first time, Joanna realized that Agent Dawson probably wasn't any older than she...if even that. "Randall had to let it all go, didn't he?"

Joanna nodded. "It was the only thing he could have done. He brought everyone from Project Daedalus to Flagstaff, and then one of our own people who's really good with computers managed to track down the witch clans they belonged to. They're all scattered around the country now...well, except for Ethan Sitko and Natalie Delacroix. They stayed in Flagstaff and are married now. They're expecting their first child soon."

To Joanna's surprise, Kelly smiled at that revelation. "I'm glad to hear that," she said. "I got the impression that something was going on between those two...or at least that they wanted something to happen. They would never have had that kind of freedom if they'd stayed in the program." Her manner turned brisk, though, as she went on, "I suppose there's a possibility that someone who worked for the SED or was higher up in the chain of command might have decided to go gunning for Agent Lenz, especially if they were up for a promotion or a better posting, and their history with Project Daedalus torpedoed it. That's something I know I can look into."

That suggestion sounded promising, although Joanna told herself not to get up her hopes too much. Still, who better than a fellow agent to break into Randall's home and catch him unaware?

On the other hand....

"Being passed over for a promotion doesn't

seem like a sufficient reason to commit a federal crime, though."

"I know," Kelly said. "And maybe I'm reaching on this one. But it seems like a logical place to start." She paused there, her manner turning hesitant, as if she wanted to say something but didn't quite know how to phrase it. "So...you and Randall...?"

The question hung there, not quite finished, but Joanna thought she knew exactly what the other woman was asking.

"We're...." She had to stop for a second, wondering exactly how she could even explain her relationship with Randall Lenz. It wasn't anything formal; they hadn't even exchanged any endearments. But Joanna knew in those few days she'd spent with him—and a night that had changed everything—something had begun to grow between them, a budding romance that had been cut short by his disappearance. "There's something, I suppose. I'm just not sure exactly what it is."

She paused for a second or two. Did she dare to ask? But knowing what kind of relationship Kelly Dawson had shared with her superior would make it a lot easier to proceed from here.

"You and he weren't...?" The words trailed off as she realized exactly how awful the question must have sounded.

To her relief, Kelly laughed—a small, uncomfortable chuckle, but it was enough to let Joanna know her fears on that subject had been completely unfounded. "Oh, no," she said quickly. "Randall Lenz is way too professional to ever have a relationship with a fellow agent—especially one who was his subordinate. And he's far too old for me, anyway."

He'd said the same thing to Joanna not too long ago, although she'd dismissed those concerns. What difference did ten years make when both the people involved were adults with their own lives and their own careers? Maybe she would have felt differently about the situation if she'd met him when he was thirty and she was twenty, but as things stood, the separation in their ages really wasn't an issue.

Still, she was relieved Kelly had tacked that little disclaimer onto the end of her comment. If her only argument had been that he was too professional to get involved with a coworker, Joanna would have worried that Randall's former assistant might still have harbored feelings for him. As it was, that didn't seem as if it would be a problem.

Kelly was watching her with a speculative look in her eyes. "I'm kind of surprised he got involved with anyone," she admitted. "He never seemed to have any time for that sort of thing."

"Well, his life has changed a lot over the past nine months," Joanna replied, and Kelly nodded.

"I suppose you're right. I'm curious, though— why didn't you just call me? Why come all the way here?"

On the surface, those seemed like valid questions. However, traveling across a continent wasn't that big a deal when you had a *prima* and *primus* who could zap you there instantaneously. But because Joanna didn't know if she should quite reveal the extent of her clan leaders' powers, she figured she'd better leave that concern aside for the moment.

"Because I thought I'd have a better chance of getting you to believe me if I talked to you in person," she said, which was partly the truth. "Also, phone calls and emails are a lot easier to trace, aren't they? An in-person conversation just seemed safer."

"True." Kelly paused there before adding, "Although rooms can be bugged, of course. But this apartment is clean—I sweep it a couple of times a week just to be safe."

Joanna stared at her, probably more shocked than she should be. "That's really a thing?"

"It can be. I mean, the position I hold now isn't all that sensitive, so there probably isn't any real reason to bug my apartment. But it's always a concern."

What must it be like to always be looking over your shoulder, wondering if someone had decided you had access to information valuable enough that it was worth invading your privacy to get at it? Joanna really didn't like that idea at all, although Kelly seemed almost blasé about the prospect, as if she'd lived with that possibility for enough years that it didn't faze her at all.

"I'll start poking around," she went on casually, possibly noting the stunned expression on her guest's face. "Where are you staying?"

"At the Courtyard by Marriott on 92nd Street," Joanna replied.

An approving light entered Kelly's eyes. "Oh, good. So you're close at least. That will help. Give me your phone number so I can get in touch if I find any leads."

Joanna told her the number, and the other woman recited it back to her.

"I don't want to put it in my phone or write it down, for obvious reasons," she explained. "But I've got it in my head now. I can't really take any time off work at the moment, so I'll just have to squeeze this in among my other duties. I'll call you if I find anything."

That seemed like the best plan, although it left Joanna feeling a bit at loose ends. "So…what am I supposed to do in the meantime?"

Her plaintive question made Kelly smile.

"You're in New York, Joanna. Go and see a show —or three. Visit the Empire State Building...the Statue of Liberty...a museum. Go shopping, go out to eat. I'm sure you'll figure out something."

Considering there were apparently an infinite number of activities she could pursue to keep herself busy, Joanna didn't bother to argue.

However, she didn't know how she could possibly enjoy herself while her worry about what might be happening to Randall loomed over everything she did.

12

To his relief, Randall's breakfast was left for him on a tray outside his room. A discreet knock was his only warning that the food had been deposited there; since he'd gotten up early and was already dressed and showered, he had no problem going to the door to see who was outside.

But whoever had delivered his meal—although he guessed it had been the silent Elaine, Greta Van Horn's servant witch—they seemed to be long gone by the time he opened the door.

Which was fine. He really wasn't in the mood for conversation right then anyway.

His breakfast included some of the best eggs benedict he'd ever had, along with cottage potatoes and a cup of sliced honeydew melon. Everything was as elegantly presented as though he'd ordered it from a five-star restaurant, and he found himself wondering whether Elaine was the cook as well, or if the Van Horn *prima* had a chef on staff as well. It seemed like the sort of thing she would do. Certainly he couldn't really imagine Greta Van Horn in the kitchen whipping up an omelet.

The food tasted as good as it looked, and he ate with a decent appetite, figuring he might as well get his day started right. Exactly what that day might hold, he couldn't begin to guess. Soon enough, he'd need to start testing his limits here, letting Greta know that just because he'd turned out to be her long-lost nephew didn't mean he intended to be under indefinite house arrest.

Especially since he currently had no access to his phone, a computer, or even a television. Was her plan to keep him completely divorced from the outside world?

A few minutes after he'd finished brushing his teeth, the imperious ringing of her bell drifted upstairs. The sound made a flash of annoyance go through him. So, she thought she could summon him like one of her servants?

Even though he wanted to hear what she had to say, he purposely dawdled, straightening the velvet coverlet on the bed until it hung just so, lingering by the window for a minute or two so he could look at the day outside. It had grown cloudy and appeared to be threatening rain.

Not that it mattered, he thought sourly, since it didn't look as if he would be going anywhere soon.

After approximately five or so minutes had passed, he left the room and headed in a leisurely way down the stairs and toward the library where he'd met with the Van Horn *prima* the day before. When he entered, she was standing by the fireplace, an irritated expression on her angular features.

Good.

"The Van Horns don't appreciate tardiness, Randall," she snapped as soon as he entered the room.

He lifted an eyebrow. "It's hard to know if I'm tardy when I don't have a phone, a watch, a computer, a television, or even a clock in my bedroom."

She appeared almost taken aback, as if she hadn't expected him to go immediately on the attack. Well, it probably was a rare occurrence when someone stood up to her—if everyone's behavior at dinner the night before was any indication—but he thought she'd better get used to it. He didn't like people ordering him around.

"Well," she said, her expression softening just a bit, "I suppose I can see if we can get a television in there for you."

How magnanimous. As if he didn't know she

had enough money to buy a warehouse full of TVs.

"In the meantime, though," she went on, becoming brisk, "please sit down. We have a few things to discuss."

Only a few? he thought wryly, although he went ahead and sat on the same love seat he'd occupied during their discussion the day before. He'd dressed in the jeans he'd packed in his duffle bag, along with a long-sleeved knit shirt, and the disapproval in Greta's eyes was clear enough as she took in his outfit.

"I see we will have to get you some suitable clothing," she said with a sniff. "I can't have my nephew going around Manhattan looking like a lumberjack."

If she thought he looked like a lumberjack now, she probably would have had a fit over the faded plaid shirts he'd worn while working on Joanna's fence. Almost at once, though, the thought of Joanna muted his inner amusement, and once again he wondered what she was doing right then, if she was worried about him. He had to hope she was, even while he acknowledged that he didn't want to cause her any anxiety.

Not that he was responsible for his current situation. No, the blame for that could be laid squarely on Greta Van Horn's bony shoulders.

"Am I to assume by your comment about

'going around Manhattan' that I'm free to move about the city?"

Her nostrils flared in annoyance. "Of course you are. I hope you don't think you're a prisoner here."

"Well, I wanted to think that I wasn't, but I couldn't be sure."

She crossed her arms, although she didn't slide backward in the wing chair where she sat. Randall got the impression she was of the generation who'd been raised to believe a lady's back never touched the back of her chair.

"New York is the domain of the Van Horns," she intoned, voice deepening somehow. "We are all free to do as we please here—and you even more than some of the others, since you are directly related to me. In fact, that is what I wanted to speak with you about."

"Yes?" he said. He kept his expression as neutral as possible—and since he'd had years of practice doing that very thing, he knew Greta wouldn't be able to read anything in his face. It was probably a good idea to keep her guessing as to whether he was all that eager to learn about his supposed inheritance.

Annoyance glinted in her eyes, but she only went on, "As I hinted yesterday, your mother left behind a sizable fortune. It has been held in a trust all these years, with the clan's financial planners managing and investing it. I'm happy to say that it was grown quite a bit."

Randall got the impression she was dragging this out the way the host of reality show might drag out the big reveal. It wouldn't have completely surprised him if she'd added, *"And you'll find out right after the break!"*

He only responded, "Oh?"

Her mouth began to look a little pinched. "The fund is now worth approximately fifty million dollars."

It took everything in him not to blink at that revelation. Yes, her hints had let him know that they were talking about a fairly substantial sum of money, but he'd thought that probably meant two or three million dollars, maybe five or six at the most.

But fifty million dollars? What in the world was he supposed to do with that kind of money?

His lack of reaction must have annoyed her even more, because she said, "You don't seem pleased."

"I suppose I'm just surprised," he responded, figuring that was a safe enough response.

It also happened to be the truth.

"I don't know why you would be," Greta said. "You had to guess that the Van Horns possess a great deal of material wealth."

The house where they were now sitting had

been one giveaway, true. Because he had grown up not far from here—and because the Van Horn *prima's* home was far grander than the one his parents owned—he'd already estimated that this place was probably worth twenty or thirty million at the very least. But if a younger sister could leave behind that kind of fortune, how much did the rank and file Van Horns have?

He had a feeling quite a lot.

"Most witch families do seem to be fairly prosperous," Randall said carefully.

Greta sniffed again. "'Prosperous'?" she repeated in contemptuous tones. "I doubt they're anywhere close to what we have. Remember, Randall, that our family has been here for hundreds of years. We've lived in Manhattan since before America was even its own nation. All that time, we've guarded our investments carefully."

"It would seem so."

Her fingers tightened on the sleeves of the silk jacket she wore. A band of large, intensely radiant diamonds sparkled from her left hand. Apparently deciding to ignore his noncommittal tone, she said, "There is also the matter of the house."

"'The house'?" he repeated.

"Yes, your mother's house. That was where she was living when she had you. I've employed a series of caretakers over the years to make sure it's been maintained and ready for you, but it's stood empty all this time."

Randall really hadn't been expecting a house, and wasn't sure what to do with that information. At the same time, though, he experienced a stir of excitement. What if his mother had left behind some kind of clue that might lead him to his mysterious father?

He tried to tell himself such a possibility had to be a long shot; just because the house had been unoccupied for the last forty years didn't meant Greta or other members of the Van Horn clan hadn't gone through the place and removed every bit of personal property his birth mother had left behind.

But what if they hadn't?

"Where is it?" he asked.

"You're a very practical person, aren't you, Randall?" Greta asked. Now she seemed almost amused, as though she appreciated his cut-to-the-chase sort of attitude.

"I try to be."

"The house is in the West Village. Fifteen Bank Street. I can give you the keys...not that you'll need them, I suppose."

No, because the peculiar witchy power of being able to open ordinary locks without the help of a key was another gift that had gotten awakened by Addie Grant's perfectly aimed lightning bolt. Even so....

"I think having the keys would make it more official."

A thin smile touched Greta Van Horn's lips as she rose from her chair and went over to the antique desk near the opposite wall. She opened one of the side drawers and drew out a small manila envelope, then brought it back over to Randall.

"Here they are," she said. "The house will need some updating, of course, but I think you will find it quite comfortable. I can have my driver take you there whenever you like."

The sooner, the better. He couldn't deny that Greta had provided some fairly elegant hospitality while he was here...but he also couldn't deny that she'd kidnapped him and taken him away from the life he'd built for himself. Even the best eggs benedict in the world couldn't erase that particular misdeed.

"You should also stop by the bank," she went on. "Chase Bank, on East 79th Street. I've already set it up so that all you need is to show your identification, and your accounts will be signed over to you."

He reflected it was a good thing that he'd kept his original Virginia driver's license, although he'd been using the fake Arizona one with the false identity of Randall Garnett ever since Jasper Wilcox had provided it for him. Most likely, Greta could have made another call to the bank to change the name on the accounts, but this would be simpler.

"I will," he said. A pause, and then he added, "Thank you. I honestly hadn't expected any of this."

For the first time, something that looked like a genuine smile lifted the corners of her mouth. "It's the least I could do for my only nephew. After all, you're the only thing I have left of my sister."

"Still." Because it seemed as if their interview was over, he got to his feet. "I'll go ahead and pack my things, and head over to the house."

She nodded. "Do let me know if you plan to come back for dinner."

"Will it be the whole family?" he asked. Although he'd do what was necessary to get along —for the time being, anyway, until he could get his bearings and decide what to do next—he would prefer to avoid another of those uncomfortable gatherings if at all possible.

Greta's smile returned, although this time, it was a knowing one, as if she could guess all too well what he was thinking. For all he knew, she could see his thoughts. She'd never once given a hint as to what her own magical talent might be, although he realized that, as *prima*, she had access to many more gifts than the one she'd been born with.

"No, just me," Greta replied. "The others all have children of various ages, and they don't like to spend too many evenings away from their families."

He got an image of her sitting alone at that huge table, but even so, he couldn't quite find it within himself to feel sorry for her. Cautiously, he said, "I'm not sure yet…it depends on what I end up doing at the house. Six-thirty again?"

A nod. "Yes, six-thirty."

"I'll let you know."

There was no way in the world he could imagine hugging such a formidable woman, even if she happened to be his biological aunt. He settled for inclining his head as well, and then left the room.

It seemed he had his freedom. Now he had to decide what to do with it.

"This is all yours?" Barbara Lenz asked, looking around at the living room of the house in the West Village with astonishment.

Apparently it was. After stopping by the bank and ascertaining that yes, he had access to several checking and savings accounts that contained the

FDIC assured maximum, and brokerage accounts which held much, much more, Randall had taken a taxi to the house that had once belonged to Alicia Van Horn.

It was much smaller than the *prima's* grand brownstone, but still large and handsome, with a little over three thousand square feet, and four bedrooms and four bathrooms contained on four floors. He'd expected to find everything horribly out of date—after all, no one had lived there for more than forty years—and yet the furniture appeared to be antiques of about the same 1890s vintage as the house itself, and not some terrible relics from the 1970s. While he might not have chosen the pieces himself, he had to admit that the place was perfectly serviceable as-is.

Well, except for the bathrooms and the kitchen. At least the countertops were tile and didn't have avocado green Formica or something equally hideous, but the appliances and fixtures were still woefully out of date.

"Yes, it's mine," he said. "I got the deed from a safe deposit box at the bank. All legal."

His mother shook her head. When Randall was a little boy, he'd always thought her the prettiest woman in the world, with her bright blonde hair and big blue eyes. The hair was a little more ash-toned now, and worn in a chin-length wavy bob rather than the blonde ponytail she'd had for most of his youth, but age had never been able to fade her prettiness.

"I can't believe you turned out to be a Van Horn!" she exclaimed for the third time since hearing the news. "You know, I actually met Alicia Van Horn a few times, although she was never as involved in charity work as her older sister."

It seemed somehow insane that his birth mother and adoptive mother had known one another, even though he reminded himself that their circle had always been fairly small, and it wasn't so odd that they might have crossed paths a time or two. "What was she like?"

"She was a very pretty girl—much prettier than her sister, although Greta always knew how to command a room," Barbara said. "But I remember Alicia being very quiet. One of those people where you never quite knew what they were thinking."

This revelation didn't surprise Randall very much. After all, it appeared that Alicia Van Horn had kept a great many secrets from everyone during her short life.

"But the few times I met her, she seemed to want to stay in the background," his mother continued. "As far as I could tell, she seemed happy to let her sister dominate things."

"And their parents?" he inquired next, realizing that Greta had never mentioned anything about the former *prima,* or her consort. Naturally, they must have passed away some time ago, since Greta herself was in her late sixties or early seventies, but he supposed there was a chance Barbara might have met them at some point.

Her forehead creased as she clearly tried to sort through memories decades old—proof that, unlike many of her contemporaries, she'd seen no need for Botox. "I honestly don't recall. Except… maybe I do remember Greta having to bow out from being on the committee for the American Cancer Society charity dinner because of a death in the family. That has to have been more than twenty-five years ago now—I don't think you were even in middle school yet."

Randall acknowledged this information with a nod. Asking had been something of a long shot, but he'd thought he might as well try. "I can always ask Greta, I suppose."

"I'm sure she'd be more than happy to give you any information you need about the family." If she was at all troubled by his sudden acquisition of a biological family, Barbara Lenz didn't show any sign of it. Then again, she'd always said she wished he could find his birth parents, and was sorry there really hadn't been enough information about them to make even beginning a search for them at all feasible. "She must be so thrilled to have found you!" A pause, and then she asked, "How *did* she find you, anyway?"

"Private investigator," he said briefly, and left it there. As much as he wished he could tell his mother the truth about himself, that he wasn't quite an ordinary man, he still wasn't sure whether that would be a wise thing to do. He loved her, loved the way she could walk into a room and be instantly comfortable with whomever she met...but he also knew her easygoing ways included a tendency to discuss matters that probably should have been kept private. As much as it pained him to admit it, he wasn't sure whether he could trust her to keep such a secret.

She absorbed the revelation about a private investigator with a slight nod. When she spoke again, however, it wasn't to ask for more details of Greta's search for him, but instead to inquire about something much closer to home. "So...does this mean you'll be staying in New York?"

The hopeful note in Barbara's voice was impossible to ignore. Obviously, she wanted her only son close by. She hadn't argued when he'd moved to Virginia, because he was pursuing his career and he needed to go where his work sent him. But now that career was apparently over, and she clearly couldn't understand why he'd want to remain in Arizona when all his connections were on the East Coast.

He'd made his own connections in Flagstaff, though, even if they might have seemed tenuous to an outsider. Everything had been coming at him so quickly, he hadn't yet stopped to analyze what all these developments might mean for him long-term. If it weren't for Joanna, he probably wouldn't hesitate. He'd become a part of the Van Horn clan—and thank Connor and Angela and the rest of the Wilcoxes for their hospitality—and move into this house, and embark on a new phase in his life. After all, by living here in Manhattan, he could have both his biological family and his mother nearby. Wasn't that the sort of thing he'd secretly wished for in the past, even if he would never have uttered such a hope out loud?

But there was Joanna. Randall still hadn't quite been able to assess exactly what he felt for her, although he knew he'd never had anyone else come close to affecting him the way she had. Even now, with everything else going on in his life, he missed the sound of her voice, the glint in her big dark eyes as she teased him about something or other.

In all his forty years, he'd never met anyone who'd evoked such a reaction in him. And because these feelings had come to him so late, he had no reason to believe he would ever have this sort of chance again.

"I haven't decided yet," he said, knowing the

long pause before he spoke had already informed his mother that something more was going on here than met the eye. "There are a few things I need to work out."

He'd spoken in as vague terms as possible, but apparently not vague enough to put his mother off the scent.

"You met someone in Arizona?" she asked, tone sharp with interest. Even though he was more than halfway to his forty-first birthday, she still hadn't given up hope that one day she might be a grandmother. "Who?"

Since denial would be useless, he tried to answer as noncommittally as possible. "We just started seeing each other."

"But obviously you like her, or you wouldn't be wondering whether to stay in New York or not."

Well, that summed up the situation fairly neatly. He shrugged, then said, "She's a good person."

"Who is she?"

"Her name is Joanna," he replied, figuring it was probably safe enough to supply her first name. After all, his mother only knew he was living in Arizona, not that he was up in Flagstaff. Out of an abundance of caution, he'd avoided mentioning the Wilcoxes to her, so there was no way Barbara could possibly guess at Joanna's surname. "She owns a ranch."

His mother's eyes lit up. They were blue as well, but a bright, cheerful blue, not the glacier-pale shade he'd apparently inherited from the Van Horn clan. "Oh, that sounds so western! What kind of ranch?"

Although he hadn't performed any kind of research to determine how many alpaca ranches existed in Arizona, Randall had to guess that there were far fewer than those dedicated to cattle or sheep or horses. "Oh, she raises a lot of different kinds of animals," he said vaguely. "She's a very hard worker."

"This Joanna sounds interesting," Barbara responded. "Not your usual type."

He honestly didn't think he had a "type." The only two women he'd ever gotten even partly serious with had been a lawyer and a community college professor, and other than both being professionals, had basically nothing in common with one another. However, he had to admit that at least Susan and Trish had been born on the East Coast and were highly accomplished women with advanced degrees, whereas Joanna....

She'd openly admitted that she'd never finished college, but he still had to think of her as very accomplished. The way she ran her ranch—a small business in its own right—and the way she kept everything in her world humming along smoothly indicated that she definitely knew what she was doing.

"Maybe not," Randall allowed. "She's a very special woman, though."

Even those words felt like he was damning her with faint praise. But if he began enumerating all her charms—her beauty, her wit, the way she didn't expect anyone to work harder than herself —then his mother would definitely start envisioning weddings and china patterns and baby showers and....

Well, it was just way too early for any of that.

"If you think it's serious—"

"It's not serious," he cut in. "Like I told you, we just started seeing each other."

"That doesn't always matter if the chemistry's right," Barbara replied cheerfully. "But I can see you don't want to talk about it. Which is fine. Let me take you out to lunch, and then we can go shopping for new appliances. I know you probably want to hold off on any major renovations, but the things in that kitchen now were installed before you were even born. They have to be a health hazard, if nothing else."

He opened his mouth to protest and just as quickly closed it. If it would make his mother happy to spend a few hours looking at new stoves and refrigerators and dishwashers, then he would go along for the ride. While they were out, he could pick up a burner phone and try to get in contact with Joanna. Surely Greta must have known he would buy himself a phone almost as soon as he had the opportunity. The only reason he hadn't done so already was because he'd hadn't seen any electronics stores near the bank, and he'd wanted to come to the house immediately afterward.

And he also hadn't intended to reach out to his mother so soon, but as luck—that strange force in the universe his gift seemed to bend according to whim—would have it, she'd been walking into the bank just as he was leaving, and so their reunion had taken place sooner than he'd planned.

All those activities would put off his search for any personal papers Alicia Van Horn might have left in her house, but Randall told himself that if they'd been hidden there for forty years, they could wait a few more hours. Sooner or later, he'd be left alone to try to uncover the mystery of what had happened in those months before he was born, and would finally have the opportunity to uncover the secrets that had been hidden for so long.

Maybe at last he could begin to get at the truth.

13

THE NEXT MORNING, JOANNA DUTIFULLY
ventured out of her hotel room, figuring she
should take Kelly Dawson's advice and do some
exploring. To be honest, New York was even more
overwhelming when viewed up close, and after a
few hours spent at Times Square and its environs,
she was ready to head back to her hotel room and
wait there until she heard from Randall's former
assistant.

Doing so seemed like a cop-out, however, and
although she didn't feel like catching a matinee—
either of a movie or a musical or a play—she'd
asked her Uber driver's advice on good places to
shop that wouldn't break the bank. He'd sent her
to the Shops at Columbia Circle, and she'd whiled
away another hour or so there. While she never
would have thought of herself as the shopping

type, Joanna reflected with an inner grin that maybe it had been more because she'd never had the opportunity to spend money in a place like New York. She blew almost a thousand dollars during her spree, buying designer jeans and fun jackets and tops, and even splurged on a pair of dark brown embroidered cowboy boots that were on sale.

Why anyone in New York would want cowboy boots, she didn't know, although she supposed they could be a fashion statement if nothing else.

Eventually, she was loaded down with enough shopping bags that she needed to head back to her hotel room. Once there, she went ahead and put on the boots and one of her new pairs of jeans, along with a gorgeous little wine-colored jacket that she couldn't pass up, even though she had no idea where she would ever wear it.

Maybe to dinner with Randall, she thought, although she knew that wasn't going to happen unless she and Kelly Dawson were able to find him.

No calls from Kelly at all. Of course, the other woman had warned her that she would have to squeeze in this new investigation around her other work, and so it was probably expecting a bit much to think she would have any information to offer this early in the game.

Still, the radio silence bothered Joanna. She hated the thought that she'd been participating in all these frivolous activities while Randall could be in trouble somewhere.

Her phone rang, and she immediately reached for it, picking it up from the bedside table where she'd left it to charge. She didn't recognize the phone number, but she thought it might be a New York area code, so she went ahead and touched the screen to accept the call.

"Hello?"

"Joanna."

Randall's voice, sounding relaxed and unruffled, and not at all like the voice of a man who'd disappeared into the blue only twenty-four hours earlier.

"Randall!" she exclaimed. "Where are you? Are you all right?"

"I'm fine," he said. "I'm in Manhattan."

Something she'd suspected, but relief rushed through her as she realized how close to each other they actually were. "So am I."

"You're in New York?" he asked, shock clear in his tone. "Joanna, what are you doing here? It's not safe."

"It's fine," she assured him. "Connor and Angela cast one of Damon's spells on me to hide my Wilcox nature. Any Van Horns in the area will only think I'm another civilian."

A brief pause. Then he said wryly, "It sounds as though we have a lot to talk about. Where are you staying?"

"At the Courtyard by Marriott. Oh, and I met with Kelly Dawson last night. She's helping me to track you down...although I suppose that isn't really an issue anymore." As she spoke, Joanna realized she'd need to reach out to Kelly and let her know she didn't need to continue with her digging...if she'd even started yet.

"How in the world did you manage to get in contact with Dawson?" Randall asked.

Joanna noted at once the way he referred to his former assistant by her last name only. Well, she supposed that was how he'd interacted with her in the past. He probably had fallen back into those old patterns without thinking. "Jeremy," she replied briefly, and Randall chuckled.

"Right. You can't keep much hidden from that one."

He really did sound fine. Maybe it was possible that he was being held somewhere and doing his best to act natural, but Joanna didn't think so. After all, why would his captors allow him to make such a phone call in the first place, and then reveal where he was?

His next words reassured her further. "I have a lot to tell you. Why don't you come over to my place?"

"'Your place'?" she echoed, not sure what he could possibly mean by that.

"It seems I've inherited a house. Let me give you the address."

It appeared he hadn't been joking when he'd said he had a lot to tell her. Joanna reached for the pad of notepaper and pen the hotel had thoughtfully left on the bedside table. "All right."

He gave her the address of the house. The street name meant nothing to her, since the only thing she thought she knew for certain about New York was that it seemed impossibly large and definitely wasn't the kind of place she could even begin to figure out in a week, let alone a single afternoon.

"It's probably a twenty-minute cab ride or so from where you are," he went on. "I'll be waiting."

"I'll see you then," she replied.

The call ended there, and she sat for a moment, staring down at her phone. What in the world was going on?

Only one way to find out, she supposed.

She stepped into the bathroom to give her hair a quick brushing, and found herself glad that she'd been amusing herself by playing dress-up in her new purchases. At least that way, she would be looking her best to meet Randall.

Beyond her relief that he seemed to be fine, she was dying to know how someone could be kidnapped one day and end up with a new house the next.

Had it been a mistake to invite Joanna over? Possibly, but Randall tried to tell himself that he'd done the right thing. Having her meet him at the house that had once belonged to his mother seemed to be the most concrete way of proving he really was a Van Horn. And, like it or not, they would both have to face that reality and decide what to do next.

His mother had tried to get him to come home with her, suggesting that he should stay for dinner, but he'd demurred. He had quite a few things to get figured out, and she'd accepted that explanation with some disappointment, even as she smiled and told him they could get together another time.

If it weren't for his need to contact Joanna, he probably would have had dinner with his mother instead, since he'd already called the Van Horn residence—oddly, the number wasn't unlisted—and left a message with Elaine to let Greta know he couldn't make it at six-thirty for dinner after all. It had been a long time since he and Barbara gone out for a family meal, and he knew he should be trying to maximize his time with her while he was in town.

But even more than wishing to fulfill his filial duty, he wanted to reach out to Joanna and let her know he was all right. That she'd turned out to be in New York as well had floored him for a moment, although he quickly recovered. There was no reason to believe Connor and Angela's spell wouldn't hold, and that meant even if someone from the Van Horn clan spied him in Joanna's presence, they wouldn't be able to tell that she was a witch. They'd have to assume she was an acquaintance of his adoptive family, or possibly someone he'd once known from work.

He reflected that sometimes it was handy to have a history in a place...if it could be put to work for you.

Since the house was immaculate, he really didn't have much to do to get ready for Joanna's arrival except open a few windows and let in some fresh air. Greta had kept all the utilities on, so there was power and water and heat. Not much he could offer Joanna except a glass of water, although he figured they would go out to dinner when the time came.

As he waited, he realized he was nervous. Why, he couldn't exactly say. It wasn't as though he and Joanna didn't know one another. They'd been intimate, had a history...albeit a short one.

But this time he'd be facing her as Van Horn, as a warlock from a witch family with a long and powerful lineage. Would that knowledge change the dynamics between them? Or would Joanna be able to roll with this particular punch?

The doorbell rang, and he walked from the living room, where he'd been waiting, to the foyer. He was too well trained to have his heart rate speed up at all at the thought of seeing her again, and yet a shiver of anticipation moved through him anyway.

She stood on the stone front step, looking absolutely stunning in a well-tailored wine-colored jacket and a pair of jeans that fit her far better than the slouchy Levi's she wore while working around the homestead. Those new jeans made her slim legs look yards long.

Somehow, he managed to drag his eyes upward to her face. She was smiling faintly, as if amused by his reaction, although at the same time, he could see the relief in her wide dark eyes as she took him in, assessing his appearance as well and apparently reassuring herself that he seemed to be fine.

"Come in," he said, and she entered the foyer, taking another of those appraising glances at her surroundings. It was a beautiful chamber, octagon in shape, with gleaming wood floors and antique tables whose vases should have been filled with flowers but were empty now, just as they had been for the past forty years.

"So, what happened?" she asked.

That was Joanna. Cut right to the chase. For a second, Randall wondered if he would have preferred to have her fall on him and hug him, and exclaim her relief that he was all right.

No, not really. He preferred women who were brisk and businesslike…like him.

"It seems I'm a Van Horn," he said. "This was my mother's house."

For a second, Joanna didn't say anything. Her gaze moved around the foyer, traveled to the glimpses of the rooms just visible beyond. "'Was'?" she asked, now sounding almost hesitant.

"She died right after I was born."

"I'm so sorry."

From most people, that would have been an automatic response. With Joanna, Randall guessed she truly meant the words.

He wouldn't shrug—that would seem callous —but he also wouldn't bother to get too emotional. How could he, when Alicia Van Horn had never been a part of his life? He hadn't even known her name until yesterday.

"I was hoping to hear something different," he said, and left it at that. "But come—we can go sit down in the living room. I can't offer you anything except water, though. The house has been empty for years."

"Water's fine," Joanna said.

They headed into the living room, and he excused himself to go to the kitchen and fill a couple of glasses with tap water. Luckily, what came out of the tap looked clean. Maybe the place had a whole-house filter.

The glasses were also sparkling, evidence that whoever Greta had hired to keep the place clean all these years, they were extremely thorough. Randall went back out to the living room and handed one of the glasses to Joanna, then decided it was probably safe enough to sit down next to her on the couch.

She accepted the glass from him, although she didn't drink. Instead, she asked, "So, the Van Horns took you?"

"Yes," he replied, and allowed himself a cautious sip of his water. It tasted decent enough. If he'd been thinking, he probably could have slipped out of the house and gone to the bodega down the street for a couple of bottles of Perrier—or, better yet, a bottle of wine—but he'd lived away from New York for so long that he'd lost the rhythms of city life.

Joanna's head inclined slightly, but she still looked puzzled. "Why the cloak-and-dagger stuff, though?"

"Greta—she's the Van Horn *prima*—didn't really give me a good answer on that," Randall said. "But I think she didn't want any entanglements with the Wilcoxes. She probably thought it was better to just have her people come in and get me. In this case, those 'people' were her son and one of her nephews. The son's power is sleep."

"So he knocked you out?"

"Basically. But with no ill effects—it was like waking up from the best night's sleep I'd ever had."

Despite the situation, Joanna appeared almost impressed. "That's a pretty slick talent."

"It did come in helpful for Greta." He paused, then decided he might as well provide the whole truth, or at least as much of it as he knew. "Apparently, she's my aunt."

"Well, that would explain the house." For the first time, Joanna lifted her own glass to her lips and took a sip. Since Randall didn't see her grimace or react in any other way, he assumed the water passed muster. Her fingers tapped against the tumbler, which was etched with a delicate star pattern. He couldn't help noticing the way she seemed to stare down at the glass, as if unwilling to meet his gaze. "I guess this means you're kind of a big deal."

"No," he said quickly. "That is, my aunt is the

Van Horn *prima,* but I don't see why that should change anything between us."

Now Joanna did look up. Her expression was almost wistful, as if she desperately wanted to believe what he'd just said but didn't know whether she could. "You can say that," she said quietly. "But look at this place." She waved a hand at their surroundings, where the perfectly placed antiques and original oil paintings on the walls stood silent testimony to the sort of wealth he'd just inherited. "The Van Horns are like—like royalty in the witch world."

"Oh, come on," he began, wanting to disabuse her immediately of that notion, but she only shook her head.

"No, I've heard the stories," she said. "The Van Horns were here in America before any of the other witch families. The Wilcoxes—hell, even the Castillos, who've been in New Mexico for hundreds of years—are upstarts compared to them. And now you're telling me you're the nephew of the *prima,* and we're sitting in your dead mother's house, and I don't know what to do with that."

Many times, actions were better than words. Randall calmly plucked the glass from her fingers and set it down on the coffee table, and put down his own glass as well. Thus unencumbered, he took her hands in his and pulled her close so their mouths touched.

Sweet fire in his veins reminded him of why he'd needed to reach out to Joanna, to reaffirm the connection between them. Her lips parted, and he tasted sweet water on her tongue, even while a few strands of her long, silky hair brushed against his fingertips as they leaned toward each other.

Part of him wanted to press her down against the sofa cushions and show her then and there why he didn't give a damn about being one of the Van Horns, didn't care about anything except being with this woman who could make him forget everything except his need to be with her. However, an echo of rationality in the back of his mind told him it probably wasn't a good idea to have sex right then and there on the couch. It felt vaguely disrespectful, even though his birth mother hadn't inhabited this house for decades.

Eventually, he lifted his mouth from Joanna's and let go of her, although he didn't try to move away. Her already full mouth looked even more lush from their kisses, and her dark eyes glittered with desire.

"You didn't have to stop, you know," she murmured, her voice husky.

"When I make love to you again, it's not going to be on a sofa," he replied.

She sent him a rueful grin upon hearing that remark. "I guess I can see your point."

"Still worried about me being a Van Horn?"

The smile slipped away. "Maybe. This—this thing between us—felt easier when you were just Randall, without any clan entanglements to worry about."

"I'm still 'just Randall,'" he told her. As he spoke, he realized that statement was nothing more than the truth. While he wanted to learn more about his birth mother, and hopefully discover who his father was, he didn't think learning he was a Van Horn had changed anything fundamental about how he viewed himself or his place in the world. Maybe if he'd learned all of this when he was still a kid, the knowledge would have ruffled him more. "No more, no less."

Joanna reached out and took his hands in hers. The faint calluses on her fingers didn't feel harsh at all, but instead served to remind him that this was a woman who did her own work. He knew he couldn't imagine her ordering around a fellow witch the way Greta Van Horn did.

"Okay," Joanna said. "I'll take your word for it. So...what now?"

"I learned who my birth mother was...Alicia Van Horn," he said, relieved that she wasn't going to push the subject and appeared to stand back and see how things unwound, at least for the time being. "But Greta doesn't seem to know anything about who my father could have been."

"Your mother wasn't married?"

"No. Nor engaged or even seeing anyone, from the things Greta said. But she could have been hiding a great deal." Briefly, he explained Alicia's gift for keeping away those she didn't want to see, and Joanna nodded in understanding.

"I suppose that would go a long way in helping a person hide whatever they wanted to be hidden."

"Exactly," Randall said. "I was actually planning to start searching the house to see if I could find anything that might yield a clue."

Joanna looked nonplussed by that statement. "Do you really think anything would be left here after so many years? Wouldn't Greta Van Horn have gone through her late sister's effects?"

"It seems plausible that she would, but I won't know for sure unless I look." He got to his feet and brushed at the gray wool slacks he wore, then extended a hand to Joanna. "Want to help?"

14

IT WAS STRANGER THAN STRANGE TO BE IN this house that had once belonged to Randall's birth mother, going through the items she'd left behind. However, he was the heir to all this, and so Joanna supposed he had every right to undertake a search of the premises.

Also, she had a feeling that he wanted her at his side while he performed what amounted to an inventory of everything he'd inherited. He hadn't said so out loud, but she got the impression that he was still a little off-balance from this turn of events, and so it helped to have a familiar face nearby as he came to terms with such a sudden change in his fortunes.

And a huge change it was. Joanna didn't pretend to know anything about New York real estate except that it was hideously inflated. Even so, she guessed this house had to be worth millions—and that was just the house itself, not even including the expensive furniture and rugs and art.

Downstairs didn't yield anything of a personal nature at all, except the books in a cozy room toward the back of the house that appeared to be a combination study and library. Instead of matching sets of stuffy, leather-bound classics and reference books—the sort of thing she would have expected to see in a place like this—those shelves were instead crowded with a jumble of mismatched hardbacks and paperbacks, everything from Stephen King to Danielle Steele.

Joanna wasn't widely read enough to pinpoint the exact dates of publication of all those volumes, but she'd hazard a guess that none of them had been published later than the late seventies.

Randall, being his usual methodical self, had picked up the books one by one, carefully riffling through the pages of each volume before he replaced it on the shelf. She didn't know what he was looking for—maybe a note from the lover Alicia Van Horn had kept hidden from her family, maybe even something as innocuous-seeming as a phone number scratched on the back of a matchbook cover. Whatever it was, he didn't seem to locate it.

His expression was almost too blank as he

crossed over to the desk placed up against the wall opposite the bookcase, then quietly went through each of the drawers. As far as she could tell, it didn't look as though he'd found anything more interesting than a couple of ballpoint pens and an ancient bottle of Wite-Out that had probably dried up before she was even born.

"Nothing here," Randall said, somewhat unnecessarily.

"Well, I always kept my diary in my bedside drawer," Joanna offered, hoping her comment might help to cheer him up a bit.

As she'd hoped, his clear blue eyes took on the amused glint she'd come to recognize. "You had a diary?"

"Oh, yes," she replied. "My mother gave it to me on my eleventh birthday. It had one of those teeny little locks and everything. Except I realized after dutifully writing in it right before bed every evening that there really wasn't enough interesting in my life to sustain putting down an entry every day. I don't think I wrote anything in it after the first month. But that doesn't mean Alicia Van Horn would have done the same," she added hastily, as Randall's expression abruptly sobered. "I mean, it sounds as though she probably had a lot more to write about than my eleven-year-old self."

"Here's hoping," he said, his tone as neutral as

his face. "Let's go upstairs and take a look around."

They mounted the stairs to the second floor, although she noticed the house also appeared to have an elevator. How many floors did this place have, anyway?

The balustrade of the staircase was carved oak, and a stained-glass window done in warm tones of green and gold and amber illuminated the landing, showing off the intricate pattern of the runner that covered the wooden steps. It really was a beautiful house, if not exactly to her taste. Joanna had never had much patience for anything fussy, but she could appreciate the architecture and the pieces that had been used to decorate it, even if she wouldn't have chosen them for herself.

The second floor was bisected by a hallway with three doors on either side. Two of those doors opened on bedrooms in varying sizes, including the master, with the remaining three doors revealing a large hall closet, a bathroom, and what seemed to be another study of some sort.

Like the ground floor, all the rooms except the closet were beautifully furnished. Joanna supposed that was one upside of purchasing antiques and decorating in the style of the time when a house was built; it lent the place a timeless look rather than being a monument to the godawful gaudiness of 1970s or '80s design. At least Randall wouldn't have to worry about gutting the place to make it socially acceptable.

Assuming, of course, that he planned to stay here at all.

He hadn't said one word about what he intended to do with the house. Joanna had to believe that Greta Van Horn wanted him to move in and stay in New York for the rest of his life, or why would she have gone to the trouble of bringing him here at all?

Troubled, she followed him into the master suite. And it really was a suite, with its own private bathroom and a pretty sitting area with a chaise longue upholstered in dark rose-colored velvet. The colors in here were too frilly for her taste—pale pink on the walls and a coverlet in shades of rose and mauve to coordinate with the chaise and the large floral rug on the floor under her feet—but she supposed she could see why someone in her early twenties might have made that design choice.

"Could you look into the nightstand on the left?" Randall asked as he headed for the right-hand bedside table. "I'm sure Greta has been through all this, but I would have had to make an inspection at some point anyway."

"Sure." Joanna went to the nightstand as requested and opened the top drawer. It was empty except for a little hand-painted china dish that had probably been intended to hold rings or earrings, although it was just as bare as the drawer itself at the moment. The second and third drawers were completely unoccupied, leading her to believe that someone must have cleared them out years and years ago. "Nothing in here," she said as she closed the bottom drawer.

"Same here," Randall replied. He straightened and headed over to the dresser that faced the bed, a large cherrywood piece that matched the other furniture in the room, with an inlaid top and a carved mirror hanging on the wall above it. Methodically, he went through the drawers from right to left, but didn't seem to find anything. "All empty," he added, although Joanna had been watching him the whole time and knew he hadn't found anything.

"Closet?" she suggested, even as she had the feeling they wouldn't find anything in there, either.

Which proved to be the case. A few padded hangers hung on one of the rods in the walk-in closet, but everything else had been removed. It had all probably been donated to charity decades ago. While it might have been interesting to inspect a time capsule of late '70s clothing, slinky disco wrap dresses and all, that sort of project didn't seem to be in the cards this time.

"Greta has obviously been in here," Randall said, now sounding slightly annoyed, even though a few minutes earlier he'd commented that she'd probably already cleared out her late sister's house. "I doubt we're going to find much."

"Maybe," Joanna allowed, then went on, "Or maybe not. If your birth mother was hiding something from her sister, then she probably wouldn't have left it in the master bedroom. That would be way too obvious. Let's check the other rooms."

His expression brightened a bit at that suggestion, although he didn't reply, only gave her a brief nod and headed into the bedroom next door. It appeared to have been set up as a guest room, with a daybed with a lovely curved frame and a friendly-looking armchair and footstool in the little alcove to one side, a space afforded by the curved turret on the corner of the old house.

But the drawers of the furniture here were just as empty as those in the master bedroom, and the closet couldn't even boast the few abandoned hangers they'd found in Alicia Van Horn's former room.

The same thing greeted them in the other rooms. Randall even went up on his toes and swept an arm across the topmost shelf in the hall closet, but all he got for his trouble was some dust on the sleeve of his shirt.

"I guess the cleaners aren't quite as thorough

as I thought," was his only comment, but Joanna could tell he was disappointed.

"We haven't checked the bathroom yet," she pointed out, even as she thought of the rooms on the floors above them, and he sent her a rueful smile.

"You really think we're going to find something in the bathroom?" he asked, and about all she could do was shrug.

"I don't know," she said honestly. "But we're here. We might as well look before we go up to the next floor."

The bathroom had a floor done in a black-and-white checkerboard pattern, and white subway tile covered the walls. There was a free-standing clawfoot tub as well as a glass-enclosed shower, and a long vanity with dual sinks.

Randall dutifully checked inside the medicine cabinet and opened the vanity drawers so he could look underneath. But he straightened following this inspection and shook his head. "Nothing."

"Let me look," Joanna suggested, and he lifted a skeptical eyebrow.

"What's the point?"

"Two sets of eyes are better than one."

Before he could say anything else, she got down on her knees, glad that the bathroom floor was cleaner than the closet shelf. This was important, but she still didn't want to mess up her new jeans.

At first glance, the cupboards under the vanity looked completely empty, just as Randall had reported. However, as she leaned in, head now actually inside the cabinet, she thought she saw something wedged in the U-bend of the plumbing under the sink, fastened by what appeared to be ancient yellowing clear tape.

And that "something" looked like a very small brown paper packet.

It could have been a piece of hardware a plumber had left behind...or it could have been something else entirely.

She reached for the packet, felt her fingers close on the paper wrapping. It crinkled beneath her fingertips, brittle as dead leaves.

No wonder. It had probably been stuck under there for at least forty years. The tape practically broke apart at her touch, and she caught the little bundle before it could fall to the bottom of the vanity, which was covered in equally ancient—if immaculate—contact paper.

Randall's voice. "You found something."

"Yes. Coming out now."

She backed out of the cabinet, precious packet clenched in one hand, and then climbed back to her feet. As soon as she was upright, she extended the little bundle to Randall, who took it from her and stared down at it, brows knitted.

"Do you think Alicia Van Horn put it there?" Joanna asked.

"I don't know who else would have."

Carefully, he unwrapped the packet. A few pieces of crumbling brown paper flaked away at his touch and fell to the floor. He pulled the rest of it away, and carefully emptied its contents onto his palm.

Lying there was a ring of silvery metal—probably white gold or platinum, although Joanna knew she wouldn't have been able to tell the difference—studded with a series of small but brilliant diamonds that glittered like crazy in the afternoon sunlight streaming in through the window.

Was that…?

"It looks like a wedding band," he said, sounding mystified.

"Was Alicia married?" Joanna asked, doing her best to go through the few bits and pieces he'd told her about his mother. As far as she could remember, she didn't think he'd said anything about a husband.

Well, of course she wasn't married, she thought. *Otherwise, Randall would know exactly who his father was.*

"Not that I'm aware of," he replied. "Although

if she managed to hide her pregnancy from the rest of the family, then I suppose she could have hidden a marriage, too."

So many secrets. And ones that apparently Alicia had wanted to be kept, or else she wouldn't have gone to so much trouble to hide the ring. The only reason Joanna had spied it was because she'd been purposely looking for anything out of place. Whoever had been cleaning the house—or whoever had emptied this bathroom of the toiletries or whatever other items Alicia Van Horn might have left behind —would never have noticed it.

Randall flicked on the fixture above the mirror, even though the light coming in through the bathroom's one frosted window provided perfectly adequate illumination. Then he lifted the ring toward the light, squinting at the inner circumference of the band.

"Do you see something?" Joanna asked.

"Yes," he said, rotating the ring ever so slightly to get a better look. "It says 'AVH & TNW, 3-1-79.'" A pause, and he frowned. "That would have been six months before I was born."

"So…Alicia was married after all?"

For a moment, Randall didn't say anything. He kept staring at the interior of the ring, as if those cryptic initials there might reveal the truth he'd been looking for if he just gazed at them long enough. "Maybe. I have to assume that 'AVH' means 'Alicia Van Horn,' although I have no idea who 'TNW' is."

"Well, it's more information than we had a few minutes ago," Joanna said, hoping those words of encouragement might erase the frown that had drawn a harsh line between his brows. "It's something you can have Kelly look up, right?"

He gave a distracted nod. Most likely, he was inwardly reeling at the knowledge that apparently his mother had had a husband, that his father hadn't been a random hook-up or Alicia Van Horn's means of rebelling against her family.

Or maybe he truly had been her way of getting back at the Van Horns. After all, they didn't yet know who the man was. He could have been a civilian. Actually, that seemed like the most logical explanation for the whole situation.

When Randall spoke, his voice sounded firm, though, all abstraction dismissed. "Yes, I can give Agent Dawson the initials and the date. She should be able to start combing through the wedding records from March 1979 and see if she can find anything that matches up."

"Would it be on a computer, though?" Joanna asked. "After all, that was a long time ago."

Randall sent her a pained look, and she realized her gaffe. Before she could say anything else, he remarked dryly, "Yes, that's going back a bit, but most of the records all the way back to the 1960s and even earlier in some cases are now stored electronically. She should be able to find something."

"Good." Joanna added, smiling a little, "You know, you can call her Kelly now. It's not like you're still working at DHS."

"I know." His expression didn't flicker, although she wondered if she'd misstepped again by pointing out that particular fact. He might have resigned of his own volition, but that didn't mean the circumstances of his leaving Homeland Security couldn't still be painful. However, he sounded brisk enough as he added, "I'll reach out to her right away. With any luck, we could have the information we need by the end of the day."

Joanna hoped it would be that easy…and she also hoped Randall wouldn't be upset by whatever Kelly found.

It had felt odd to talk to Dawson—Kelly, he reminded himself, although calling his former assistant by her first name felt awkward to the both of them, if the note of surprise in her voice when he addressed her that way meant anything —but she was glad to hear that he was all right.

"I can actually get on this right away," she said. "I just handed off a big project, and although I have something else I could move on to, I know my supervisor won't be too upset if I slow down a little for the rest of the day."

"Thank you, Kelly," he told her. "I appreciate that."

"It's not a problem."

That task handled, Randall realized he needed to get the rest of his things out of his borrowed room at Greta Van Horn's mansion. He had to assume that, because she'd given him the keys to the house in the West Village, she had no intention of keeping him as a guest indefinitely.

However, bringing Joanna along on that particular errand didn't seem like a very good idea, so he suggested that she go back to her hotel for the interim.

"And I'll meet you there when I'm done," he finished.

Something about the tilt of one dark, graceful eyebrow told him she wasn't particularly thrilled by his plan, but she didn't protest. "All right. I suppose it would stir up way too many questions if I went with you, even with my magic concealed."

"Probably," he agreed. "If anyone sees us in passing on the street, that's one thing. But Greta would wonder why I was bringing a civilian friend to her house."

"'Friend'?" Joanna echoed, and he bent and kissed her—a good kiss, full on the mouth, although he knew better than to press things further than that. Time enough for intimacy later.

He hoped.

"That's how I would introduce you," he said, knowing that she'd been teasing him and nothing more. "The situation is complicated enough without trying to explain to Greta who you really are."

"Fair enough." Joanna went on her tiptoes and kissed him on the cheek. "Just come on by when you're done. I'm in Room 322."

No more questions, no more teasing. He appreciated that about her—she could be just as no-nonsense as he, which was a rare quality. "And I'll take you out to dinner afterward."

"Deal. I'm sure you know all the best places to go."

Randall wasn't quite as confident about that—restaurants came and went in New York with astonishing rapidity, and he hadn't lived there for years—but he could always fall back on Ludovico's, an old standby that his mother loved. Besides, they knew him there, and he guessed he could probably get a table even without having reservations already in place.

"I'll do my best."

They headed downstairs, Joanna already with her phone out so she could use the Uber app to have a car sent over. He wished he could drive her himself, but since he also didn't have a car at the moment, a ride-sharing company seemed the easiest solution.

Once he'd seen her on her way, he went ahead and ordered a car for himself. Only a half hour later, he was on the doorstep of Greta's grand mansion on 77th Street.

It seemed beyond rude to simply let himself in, and so he rang the bell and waited. A moment later, Elaine, the fair-haired witch who appeared to act as Greta's housekeeper, looked out at him.

"Oh, Mr. Lenz," she said. "Greta's out at the moment."

"That's all right," he replied, thinking the *prima's* absence was probably a good thing. This way, he could avoid any questions, just in case he'd misinterpreted her motivations and she hadn't planned to have him leave so soon after all. "I'm just here to get my things."

Elaine blinked, but then she stepped out of the way so he could enter the foyer. "You're moving into your mother's house?"

"Yes," he said simply. Better to leave it there; if he added any qualifiers like "for the time being," Elaine might wonder what exactly he was planning…and would very likely pass that information along to Greta. He didn't bother to ask how Elaine knew about the house in the West Village in the first place. The Van Horns might have their secrets, but he doubted many of them could be kept from a woman who seemed to be around all the time.

Having delivered that reply, Randall nodded at her and went upstairs to the room where he'd awakened barely twenty-four hours earlier. In the back of his mind, he'd wondered whether his belongings would even still be there. For all he knew, Greta might have hidden them away in an effort to keep him close that much longer.

But it seemed that now she'd found her long-lost nephew, she was allowing him to do as he wished. Most likely, she thought his settling back here in New York and becoming one with the Van Horn clan was a foregone conclusion. To someone who'd ruled over such a prominent witch family for so many years, the possibility that such an outcome might not be entirely desirable had probably never even crossed her mind.

Honestly, he wished he had a clearer idea of what he wanted to do. Seeing Joanna in the house in the West Village earlier had made a great many thoughts pass though his mind. She hadn't seemed as out of place as he'd feared, had almost made him think that maybe—just maybe—she might be all right with making a life here with him.

Which he knew was getting way ahead of himself. That she'd come here at all in search of him seemed to prove that the connection between them was far stronger than their brief acquaintance might have indicated, but even so, he didn't think it was quite time for them to go to Saks and start choosing silverware patterns.

If nothing else, the discovery of that wedding band beneath the bathroom sink had added an extra dimension to the mystery surrounding his birth. It was a very expensive piece—the diamonds themselves were extremely high quality, and besides the engraving, the inside of the band had been stamped "PLAT" for platinum.

Not the sort of thing some kid off the street could afford.

Randall supposed Alicia Van Horn could have bought the piece herself, rather than the unknown "TNW." Still, that didn't erase the very real possibility that she'd been a married woman when she died. The date on the ring seemed to indicate she'd been three months pregnant at the time of the wedding. Had she gotten married because she didn't want to have an illegitimate child? Or had she only wanted to make official a relationship that had been going on for quite some time?

Like so many other questions, these ones

would have to remain unanswered for now. He hoped Kelly Dawson would get back to him soon —her ability to dive through databases to get the necessary information to illuminate any given situation had always seemed magical to him, even though she didn't possess any particular gifts beyond a keen mind…and the will to use it.

Because he didn't have much to pack, he was ready to go within five minutes. As he descended the stairs, he halfway expected to be interrupted by Greta's sudden arrival home, but the house remained empty and quiet. He didn't even see any sign of Elaine, although the place was big enough that she could have been anywhere.

However, she popped up just as he laid his hand on the doorknob, coming out of the parlor off to one side of the foyer, a microfiber dusting cloth in one hand. "Going so soon?"

"Yes," he replied politely. "Please tell Greta I'm sorry I missed her, but I'll be in touch either later tonight or tomorrow to check in."

"I suppose you have a lot of work to do, getting your mother's house put together," Elaine said. Something in her tone was almost wistful. Was she imagining what she might do with a home of her own?

Seeing her up close like this, he could see the faint lines around her eyes, although overall, her skin was smooth and clear. He guessed that they were probably approximate in age, although he didn't detect any signs of gray in her fair hair.

Did she still entertain notions of getting married and possibly starting a family? It wasn't completely unusual for a woman these days to have her first child in her early forties. Or had Elaine given up, realizing she would always be a servant in the *prima's* house, whether that *prima* was Greta Van Horn or her daughter Victoria?

That would be far too personal a question to ask, so he only said, "The house is in great shape, but yes, there are still some things that need to be done. I made a start this afternoon, but it's going to be a project."

Elaine smiled. "Then I won't keep you from it. Have a good afternoon."

"You, too, Elaine."

He went out the front door and down the steps, then pulled out his phone so he could summon an Uber to take him to Joanna's hotel. The exchange with Elaine bothered him more than he wanted to admit. While he understood the logic of having witches and warlocks as servants so there wouldn't be any worry about civilians seeing or hearing things they shouldn't, he still thought it was pretty rough luck for anyone trapped in such a position. Was she at least being paid well for her work? Greta could definitely afford to pay Elaine a handsome salary, but that didn't mean much.

Maybe if he stuck around, he'd figure out a way to convince Elaine that her life didn't have to be this way.

And that was a big "if."

For now, though, it was time to meet Joanna.

15

SHE KNEW IT WAS SILLY TO THINK RANDALL wouldn't show up, that he'd abandon her and leave her on her own here in New York. There was absolutely no reason to believe he wouldn't be over just as soon as he was done with his errand at Greta Van Horn's house.

And yet, Joanna had worried the whole time —not because she didn't trust him, but because she didn't trust the Van Horn *prima*. What if he'd gone over there, and she'd detained him somehow? After all, if she was willing to stoop to outright kidnapping, what other tricks might she pull?

But then someone had knocked on her hotel room door, and Joanna had peered through the peephole's fish-eye glass to see Randall standing out in the corridor. Relief flashed through her, even as she opened the door and let him in. He held a duffle bag in one hand, and so she assumed his errand had been a success.

"Any problems?" she asked, and he shook his head.

"No. Greta wasn't even home."

Maybe the universe was watching out for them after all.

Or maybe avoiding the Van Horn *prima* was only more of Randall's luck at work.

"So...what next?"

"Dinner, as I said." He paused there, cool blue eyes studying her face for a second or two. "You were worried."

Was she that obvious? Probably; unlike Jeremy's girlfriend Sloane, Joanna knew she would have been a terrible poker player. "A little," she confessed.

Randall bent and kissed her on the cheek, and a thrill went through her. It was sort of amazing how she reacted to even his slightest touch, although she definitely wasn't complaining. "I suppose I was a bit as well," he told her. "But no one except Elaine—she's sort of the housekeeper, I guess—was even around."

"Good. So, where are we going for dinner?"

"A place called Ludovico's. It's always been a favorite of my family. But if you don't like Italian, we can go someplace else."

"I love Italian," Joanna said firmly, which was nothing more than the truth. In fact, she'd been known to whip up a mean pan of lasagna in her time. But she was happy to go out for Italian food, especially since she guessed that any place Randall or his family enjoyed had to be good.

Neither of them mentioned the wedding band they'd located earlier, or the clue they'd found within it. Right now, about all they could do was wait until Kelly got back to them with whatever information she'd been able to unearth.

They headed out. This time Randall didn't bother with Uber, but just hailed them a cab. It felt better to be riding with him in the back seat, rather than having to go their separate ways in different cars, even if she had to admit that the Uber vehicles had seemed a lot cleaner than this beat-up taxi.

But that was all right. They didn't speak, but only sat next to each other, bodies closer than they needed to be, as if they'd both shared the unspoken admission that they didn't want to be too far away from one another. She liked having him that close; the warmth of his body reassured her in what otherwise would have been completely alien circumstances. A full day spent here had only confirmed her first impression.

She really didn't like New York.

The restaurant, however, was lovely, a

surprisingly airy space on a corner about ten minutes away from her hotel. Joanna hadn't thought to look at the street signs as they passed, and so she really didn't have any idea exactly where she was. That was all right, though; Randall knew this city and wouldn't allow her to get lost in it.

They were guided to a quiet table toward the back, guarded by a lush fiddle-leaf fig plant. Joanna appreciated the privacy, since it meant they'd be able to talk somewhat freely as long as their waiter wasn't nearby.

Everything on the menu looked wonderful. She decided on pasta carbonara, while Randall ordered osso bucco for himself and a bottle of Montepulciano for the two of them. Once the waiter had poured their wine and departed, Randall lifted his glass.

"To going on a real date," he said with a glint of amusement in his clear-hued eyes.

"Even if we had to go all the way to New York to do it," she replied as they clinked glasses, and he chuckled.

"I suppose it's one way to get out from under the watchful eyes of the Wilcoxes," he said.

Joanna hadn't thought of it that way. "But what about the Van Horns?" she asked.

His expression went still, and he shot a quick glance past their table and out to the restaurant's main area. "I didn't sense anyone here," he said. "Did you?"

"No," she replied quietly. "I suppose it's easier to avoid other—well, *others*—in a city this size. How many Van Horns are there?"

"I have no idea. Greta didn't exactly lay out all the clan demographics for me. But I assume it can't be more than a thousand or so at the most. And that isn't much when you're talking about a city the size of New York."

No, it wasn't. More like the proverbial drop in the bucket. Joanna supposed there was a very small chance that one of the tables on the far side of the room might have had a witch or warlock sitting at it, since her powers of detection didn't reach that far. However, she guessed that was a very long shot.

Anyway, she told herself, *Randall's power is luck. If there really were any Van Horns at this restaurant, I have to believe that his gift would have steered us elsewhere.*

That inner reassurance made her feel much better. She took her first sip of wine, enjoying the rich, earthy flavor, while Randall also drank. For a moment, they were quiet as he offered her the basket of bread and she took one of the rolls from within. It was warm and delicious, as good as anything she could have baked, which seemed to bode well for the rest of the meal.

Just as she was about to ask him how his family had found this restaurant—New York was so huge, she had no idea how anyone could decide on where to go out to eat—his phone rang from within his pocket. As he hesitated, she said, "Go ahead and answer. It could be Kelly."

A quick nod, and he pulled down the phone and gave a quick glance at the screen. Immediately, the phone was at his ear. "Kelly, this is Randall."

Just as Joanna had suspected. She sat silently and watched him as his brows drew together, and his expression went...quiet. Still. That shuttered look she guessed he'd cultivated during his time at DHS, and which she hated to see settle on his face.

Bad news?

"Thank you, Kelly," he said. "I appreciate you putting in the time on this one. I will. Thanks."

He ended the call there and slipped the phone back into his jacket pocket, then reached for his glass of wine and sipped from it. Across the table, Joanna waited. Questions were fairly bubbling on her lips, but she somehow knew she needed to let Randall volunteer the information in his own time.

Another swallow of wine, and then he said, "Kelly's fairly certain that 'TNW' was a man named Thomas Nathan Winfield. Records from

Litchfield County, Connecticut, show that he married a woman named Alicia Marie Van Horn on March 1, 1979—just like the inscription on the ring said."

As soon as the name "Winfield" escaped Randall's lips, Joanna had to keep herself from startling. It wasn't possible...it had to be a coincidence....

But it wasn't that common a name.

He must have noticed some change in her expression, because his fingers tightened on the stem of his wine glass and he said, "What is it?"

Suddenly, a swallow of wine sounded like a very good idea. Joanna helped herself to some, then replied, "Winfield. That's the name of one of the clans in Connecticut."

Randall's eyes narrowed a fraction. "You mean my birth mother married a warlock from a different clan?"

"It sounds that way." She paused, then made herself go on. "I can see why Alicia would want to hide the relationship from her family—I'm sure she was expected to marry one of her acceptably distant cousins."

"Because that's how it's done in our families."

Joanna didn't miss the way he said "our." Did he truly feel that way, or had he used the word because it was far safer than saying "witch" out loud, even at their secluded table?

In the end, it probably didn't matter. "Most of the time, yes," she allowed. "But that's not all. The Winfields are the clan that the Wilcoxes broke away from in the 1870s. We've gone our separate ways for a long time now, but...."

"But there's still a distant connection," Randall finished for her.

She nodded.

"So...." He paused there, icy eyes a little too sharp. "That means we're related?'

"Very, very distantly," she said. Stretching across a century and a half, the connection was tenuous at best. "But yes." She stopped there, because his expression had turned unreadable again. "There's something more, isn't there?"

He picked up his glass of wine and took another measured swallow. "Kelly found something else. Apparently, Thomas Winfield was killed in a traffic accident on March 5, 1979."

"I'm so sorry," she said. With both parents gone, he would have a very difficult time reconstructing what had happened between Alicia Van Horn and Thomas Winfield all those decades ago.

Maybe the barest lift of his shoulders. "It's unfortunate. But it also explains why Alicia was so alone when I was born. This is the barest speculation, but I have to think that she was planning to leave New York and go live with her new husband. Of course, I don't have any idea why they weren't together immediately after the wedding, and yet that scenario makes the most sense."

Considering what little Joanna had heard about the Van Horns, she was inclined to agree with that assessment. As to why Alicia hadn't stayed in Connecticut once she was married, that was harder to say. Maybe she had matters she needed to settle in New York first. Also, Joanna had to remind herself that Randall's birth mother had been very young at the time. She'd done something that would have directly challenged the power of her clan's *prima* and was probably struggling with how to handle the consequences of her actions. It seemed possible that she'd gone back to her house to get her head together, thinking that she and Thomas still had plenty of time.

The universe, unfortunately, had other plans for them.

Their waiter appeared then with their food, and so they had to fall silent for a moment while all that was handled. Her plate of pasta carbonara smelled delicious, and Joanna made herself reach for her fork, even though her appetite wasn't quite what it had been when they first sat down.

Randall picked up his own fork, then said in a low voice, "It's all right, you know. That is, I can't say all this isn't disappointing, but at least now I have some answers."

Yes, answers to the most basic of his questions. Even so, there was so much more that needed to be told. How on earth had Alicia Van Horn even encountered Thomas Winfield in the first place? It wasn't as if members of witch clans went freely roaming around in other families' territories. Had his clan known about their connection, or had they been equally in the dark?

Had anyone other than Thomas known that Alicia was pregnant?

An idea began to form in Joanna's mind, one that she was pretty sure Randall would shoot down. Or maybe not. He hadn't been brought up in a witch clan, and even though he knew the rules, he certainly wasn't as hidebound regarding them as a lot of other people were.

After taking a bite of pasta carbonara, she said, "We should go to Connecticut."

He'd been in the middle of swallowing some osso bucco, and so he had to wait a few seconds before he could reply. "We can't do that," he said flatly.

"Why not?" she responded. Now that she'd made the suggestion and gotten it out in the open, it felt easier to defend her idea. "I've still got Connor and Angela's spell working on me, so no one's going to know I'm not supposed to be there. And if your father is a Winfield, then their *prima* shouldn't be able to tell that you're an interloper."

Randall's expression grew pained, and she added hastily, "That is, I know you wouldn't *really* be an interloper. All I'm saying is that your blood would give you every right to be there."

Now there was the faintest of smiles playing around his finely sculpted lips. "Is that how it works?"

Joanna allowed herself to shrug. "I guess so. No one's really gone into the mechanics of it with me, but obviously there must be some kind of genetic marker or resonance or whatever that allows a *prima* to sense when someone's in her territory who shouldn't be there."

"Won't my being part of two different clans muddy the water, so to speak?"

"I don't think so." She set down her fork and reached for her water glass. A swallow of water sounded like a very good idea right about then. "But I honestly can't say for sure. We've started to have a lot of kids from mixed clans in Arizona, but they're all way too young to have started developing their powers yet, and so they wouldn't give off a witchy bat signal anyway."

God, what a clumsy explanation. Obviously, Randall wasn't too impressed by it, because he didn't say anything, only took a bite of osso bucco. Joanna went back to her own neglected meal, knowing she needed to give him time to process all this. While she might have thought in her heart of hearts that the only way he was going to get more answers would be by going to Connecticut, in the end, it was his decision. This was his history, his biological parents.

Once again, he reached for his wine and took a measured sip. Then he said, "You'd really do that for me?"

I'd do just about anything for you, passed through her mind, although she knew she wasn't brave enough to utter those words aloud. "I wouldn't have offered if I didn't mean it."

His gaze caught hers. She made herself sit still and look back at him, trying to let him see how much she wanted to help him...how much she wanted to allow him to get the closure he needed.

And maybe see just a little of what she couldn't keep hidden in her heart.

"All right," he said at last. "Tomorrow? I'll need to rent a car. I know we could take the train, but I'd feel better being more mobile."

Now he sounded calm and businesslike, probably the same way he had when he was planning an operation back in his Homeland Security days. In a way, his brisk delivery reassured her. While she couldn't agree with some of the things he'd done while working for DHS, no one could really deny that he'd been a very effective agent. And that meant he'd approach this current problem with the same diligence and ferocious pursuit of his goal.

"That's a good idea," Joanna responded. "I'd also feel better if we had a car rather than being at the mercy of trains and Ubers or whatever."

Randall nodded. "Then I'll get that managed, and we'll head off to Connecticut tomorrow."

The matter handled—for the moment, anyway—he seemed inclined to leave the subject of their foray into Winfield territory aside for now. Instead, he asked her about what she'd been doing while waiting to hear from Kelly, and seemed more amused than offended that Joanna wasn't too enraptured by the Big Apple.

Even when she blurted, "I know living in New York is a dream for a lot of people, but to me it seems kind of like a nightmare," he only lifted an eyebrow.

"It's probably a shock when you've only known someplace like Flagstaff for your entire life."

A shock. Yes, that was probably a good way to describe it. Sure, she'd seen movies set in New York and read books that took place in the city, but none of that could have possibly prepared her for the scope of the place, the sensation that there were millions upon millions of people packed into a very small geographic area. Maybe you could get used to it after a while, but Joanna really didn't want to.

And while she knew there was always a danger in speaking bluntly, she figured it was better for Randall to know where she stood on the subject of New York. Yes, it was early to be thinking about a future with him, but managing expectations was always a good thing. If he'd been considering asking her to stay with him in the house in the West Village, then he'd know exactly where she stood.

His was a face that wasn't always easy to read, but she couldn't see anything in his expression to indicate he was disappointed by her comments. No, he only remarked that New York could be an acquired taste for a lot of people, and left it at that.

After they had finished their meal and Randall settled the check, they rode back to her hotel, since he'd left his duffle bag in her room. The situation seemed like the perfect setup for her to invite him to stay. Only...did she have the courage?

"You don't have to go back to that big empty house, you know," she told him as he went to retrieve the duffle bag.

He turned back toward her. His expression was still neutral, so she couldn't really tell what he thought of her suggestion. Right then, he looked almost impossibly elegant in his dress slacks and crisp button-up shirt, so different from the man in the faded jeans and the flannel shirt who'd worked beside her as they repaired a series of split-rail fences.

But he was the same person. She needed to remember that.

Before he could say anything, she added, "I mean, do you really want to sleep on a forty-year-old mattress?"

That question made him crack a smile. "Well, when you put it that way...probably not."

Might as well go for broke. "Also, we'd get an earlier start if we both left from here."

Randall came back over to her and took one of her hands in his. The fingers that wrapped around hers were warm and strong. "You don't have to give me reasons to stay with you, Joanna. Don't you know that's the only thing I know I want?"

Relief flooded through her, even as he bent and pressed his mouth against hers. She tasted wine, and the rich chocolate-coffee flavor of the tiramisu they'd shared at the end of their meal. Need pulsed along every nerve ending.

Although neither of them spoke, they both seemed to understand what had to happen next. Her fingers worked at his belt buckle, even as he unbuttoned the jacket she was wearing. He removed her clothing with care, however, draping it over a chair rather than tossing it to the floor the way he had the first time they'd made love. Obviously, he understood that she would prefer him to be careful with the pieces she'd bought earlier that day.

But soon enough there was no time to think about anything other than the touch of his warm flesh against hers, the cool crispness of the hotel sheets beneath her naked body. The way he knew to make love to her with his tongue, to bring her to shuddering orgasm with the deftness of his touch.

And then it was their bodies joining again, fingers entwined, mouths seeking to complete the embrace so they seemed to meld into one person, one shared, shining moment of utter passion. Afterward, he pulled her into his arms, and she laid her head against the firm muscles of his chest.

In that moment, she knew only one thing.

She was in love with Randall Lenz.

16

EVEN WITH HAVING TO RENT A CAR, THEY were still out of New York and headed into Connecticut by ten-thirty that morning. The drive would take around two hours, putting them in Litchfield just in time for lunch. They'd agreed that sounded like the best thing to do—they'd go have a meal, just like a couple of regular tourists visiting the town...and then they'd see what happened next.

Randall reminded himself not to get his hopes up. There was every chance they wouldn't encounter a Winfield at all. From what he'd been able to tell, not every *prima* could sense whether a strange witch or warlock had entered her territory —and, as Joanna had pointed out, there was every chance that he wouldn't even register as one, considering his father had been a member of that clan.

Supposedly. Winfield might not have been the most common name in the world, but it wasn't exactly uncommon, either. There was always the possibility that his father had been a civilian. Not a very strong possibility, considering the Winfield clan was centered in Litchfield and Thomas Winfield's marriage to Alicia Van Horn had been recorded in the county of the same name, but still.

Joanna began to perk up almost as soon as they were out of the city and the countryside around them began to grow more open, greener. Her words from their dinner the night before still resonated in his mind. She wouldn't be happy in New York. Hers was a soul that needed open spaces and blue skies, miles of forest.

Her little pack of alpacas, and a warm, friendly home on a property with just enough land to be comfortable.

Honestly, he thought he was all right with that. Greta Van Horn could expect whatever she wanted of him, but the truth was, she couldn't force him to stay in Manhattan. If he wanted to sell the house he'd unexpectedly inherited, then he'd go ahead and do so. To avoid any ruffled feathers, he could always sell it to another Van Horn for a low price. It wasn't as though he hadn't inherited enough money to buy twenty such homes, if he wanted.

Not that he actually wanted such a thing. No, after taking a brief glance at Joanna, her beautiful profile outlined by the increasingly green landscape outside their rented car's windows, he thought that he had pretty much everything he wanted right here with him.

Besides, if it turned out he truly was half Winfield, then that clan would have just as much claim on him as the Van Horns.

Would Joanna be happier in Connecticut?

Probably. She did look much more cheerful now, a faint smile on her beautifully curved lips as she surveyed the passing countryside. Because they hadn't known who or what they might encounter on this expedition, they'd both dressed casually but nicely, he in jeans and a button-up shirt, Joanna also in jeans but with a pretty embroidered cardigan over a tank top. Had she bought those items on her shopping expedition the day before? They didn't look like anything she would have purchased in Flagstaff.

He supposed it didn't matter. What did matter was that they both appeared presentable and very nonthreatening, two qualities he guessed would be important when venturing into a strange clan's territory.

Joanna had found a place called Meraki that

sounded good for lunch—and which was right on the main drag—so Randall parked half a block down the street in the first available space. The air that greeted him as he got out of their rented Camry was fresh and cool, a welcome change from the haze of auto exhaust that always seemed to hang over Manhattan. Once upon a time, he probably wouldn't have even noticed, but spending the greater part of a year in Flagstaff had given him a keen appreciation for fresh air.

The restaurant was small, with only a few tables, but luckily, someone was wiping down a table that had just been vacated, and so he and Joanna were able to snag that one. The menu was written on a large chalkboard behind the counter; she told him she wanted a cubano sandwich, and he got up to order for both of them, getting the same sandwich for himself, along with a couple of glasses of iced tea. He brought those back with him to the table, and handed one to her.

"This is probably the cutest town I've ever seen," she said. "Makes me wonder why the Wilcoxes left in the first place."

"Why did they?" Randall asked, frankly curious. That was a piece of Wilcox history he hadn't really heard about—not that he'd gone around asking questions, either. Most of the time he'd been in Flagstaff, he'd kept his head down and tried his best to stay out of the way.

She glanced around, but no one seemed to be paying any attention to them. The people behind the counter were busy taking a to-go order from a man and woman in their late twenties who'd entered right after Randall and Joanna, and the groups at the other tables were chattering loudly and seemed entirely focused on their own conversations.

"I guess Jeremiah Wilcox had his own way of wanting to do things," she said quietly. "I honestly don't know all the details, either. But he and his brothers and sister broke off from the Winfields and settled in another town in Connecticut. Problem was, they weren't being discreet enough for the other clans in the area, and eventually they got chased out because it was feared they were attracting too much attention from the civilian world."

A valid concern, considering how careful the witch clans tended to be about keeping their powers hidden. Had Jeremiah's pursuit of power been worth giving up his life here?

Apparently so, since the clan had obviously prospered since settling in Flagstaff. Still, Randall was glad to know that Joanna liked it here. Maybe they could work out some sort of compromise.

If he even was a Winfield…and if they would even want him, half Van Horn that he was.

Their order was called, and he got up to fetch

their sandwiches. It seemed that Joanna's intuition —or maybe her careful reading of Yelp reviews— had been right, because the food was excellent. They'd had room service that morning, but he'd consumed his morning meal almost five hours earlier, and he was hungry.

Joanna also ate with a good appetite, as if she understood that she might as well fortify herself now in preparation for whatever happened next. However, she paused after getting a little over halfway through her sandwich and said, "So... what happens after lunch?"

"We explore, I guess," he replied. "If we're out and about, that gives the Winfields more opportunity to locate us. And I think I'd like to visit the cemetery."

That comment made her raise an eyebrow, but she didn't say anything, only gave a brief nod before she returned to her sandwich.

The thought had come to him as they'd driven into town. Yes, Kelly had given him the particulars of his father's death, and yet Randall still thought he'd like to see the grave for himself, if only to confirm that the man really had died before he was even born. Also, seeing generations of other Winfields buried there would help him to get more of a sense of the family, yet more confirmation that this truly was their place.

His clan's place.

Possibly.

Since he'd paid up front for their meal, they didn't have to wait for a check when they were done. He left a ten-dollar bill on the table for the busboy, and he and Joanna got up and walked out to their rental car.

Someone was waiting for them on the sidewalk next to the Camry—a tall man with brown hair and clear blue eyes, probably in his middle or late thirties. As they approached, Randall felt the twinge at the back of his neck that told him the stranger was another warlock.

Joanna must have experienced much the same thing, because a flash of shock passed over her features before she tried to smooth it away.

No reason to be surprised, though. Not really. This was what they'd come here for, after all.

"New in town?" the strange warlock asked. He sounded pleasant, but his eyes had narrowed slightly, as if he was trying to figure them out. The spell blocking Joanna's witch nature might have thrown him off, which seemed understandable.

"Just visiting," Randall replied. "I thought I might have family around here."

The warlock nodded, a light of comprehension flickering in his eyes. "We were wondering if it might be something like that. Unusual, but…." He paused there, now looking almost hesitant as his gaze moved to Joanna.

"It's all right," Randall told the man. "You can trust her."

"I'm one of you," she put in, and now the strange warlock's expression was one of confusion.

Randall said, "We can explain."

"Good. I'm Joe Winfield, by the way," the warlock said. "Our *prima* would like to talk to you."

"I expected she would," Randall replied. Good. So it seemed they wouldn't have to wander around town in the hope that they'd bump into one of the Winfields; the clan's *prima* had obviously sensed their presence right away. Had she told Joe to wait until they'd finished their lunch before making contact? If that was the case, it seemed pretty civilized of her.

"You can follow me," Joe said, then pointed to a Range Rover parked directly in front of their rental car. "That one's mine. It's not too far."

"Of course."

Randall and Joanna got in their Camry, while Joe headed to the Range Rover and climbed in. A moment later, he pulled away from the curb, headed east.

"Well, that was easy," she said, then glanced over at Randall. "Nervous?"

"I don't get nervous."

Maybe that was a slight overstatement. While he knew he wasn't a robot and therefore experienced anxiety just like anyone else, he also knew how to keep his nerves in check and prevent them from governing his words or his actions. At the moment, however, he thought he was feeling anticipation more than anything else. He'd found some answers already on this trip...but he wanted more.

The *prima's* house truly wasn't far from the restaurant, barely a five-minute drive. Their destination was a large Colonial home with a mansard roof, set far back from the road in a neighborhood of similarly well-kept houses. They followed Joe along the curved driveway and past a border of hedges to park in front of a detached garage with four bays.

He stopped there, and so Randall parked next to him. They got out of the car and met Joe where he waited at the head of a path that wound its way through green lawns to the rear entrance of the house.

"This way," he said, and led them along that path to a spacious back porch, ready for spring with white-painted wicker furniture already set out in anticipation of warmer weather yet to come.

Because he'd grown up in New York and had spent summers visiting friends with homes in Connecticut and Massachusetts, Randall was familiar with this style of house, with its wide downstairs hallway, elegant staircase, and white-painted woodwork. Joanna, however, was looking around with some curiosity; Colonial-style homes were probably in short supply in Flagstaff, Arizona.

Joe took them into the living room, a large chamber with seafoam green paint on the wall and simple, elegant furniture, most likely original to the house. Sitting in a wing chair opposite the couch was a pretty woman probably a few years younger than Randall, with the same brown hair and clear blue eyes as the warlock who was acting as their guide.

As soon as they entered the room, she got up from the chair and came to meet them, a warm smile on her friendly mouth. "I'm Blair Winfield, the *prima* of this clan," she said.

"I'm Randall Lenz, and this is Joanna Wilcox," Randall replied.

At the name "Wilcox," surprise flared in Blair's big blue eyes. "But—"

"A spell," Joanna put in, obviously deciding that it was better to tell the truth about the situation and why she currently seemed undetectable as a witch. "Just to be safe, since I was traveling outside my territory. But I don't mean any harm."

"I know you don't," Blair replied. "I sensed that right away. Just as I sensed that you, Randall, are somehow one of us Winfields. But how is that possible?"

"I was hoping you could tell me that," he said.

Her brows lifted, but she only said, "Let's sit down. I had some tea waiting, just in case."

Sure enough, a pitcher of iced tea and several glasses rested on a silver tray on the inlaid coffee table in front of the sofa. Did Blair Winfield have some sort of precognitive ability? That would be a powerful gift for a *prima* to possess.

He and Joanna sat on the sofa, while Blair returned to the wing chair where she'd been waiting for them to arrive. Apparently, Joe wasn't to be included in this conversation, because he inclined his head toward his *prima* in a casual farewell before disappearing down the hallway. A moment later, the front door shut.

Randall reached for a glass and poured some tea for Joanna, and then another glass for Blair. After getting his own glass—although he didn't pause to drink any—he said, "I think my father was Thomas Winfield. You wouldn't have known him—he died in 1979."

At the name, a flash of sorrow passed over Blair's features. "No, I never met him," she said. "He was my mother's youngest brother, though."

That revelation added another piece to the puzzle. No wonder Alicia and Thomas had kept their relationship hidden—it wasn't just that she was the *prima*-in-waiting's little sister, but he'd been his own *prima's* younger brother.

A real Romeo and Juliet situation, apparently.

"And so, you're my cousin?" she went on. "But...how? My mother never said anything about Uncle Thomas being married or even in a serious relationship with anyone. He'd just barely graduated from college when he died."

In silence, Randall reached into his pocket and drew out the diamond wedding band Joanna had found under the sink in the West Village house. "We discovered this in a house that belonged to my mother," he said. "You can see the engraving."

Blair took the ring from him and peered at the inscription on the interior of the band. "'AVH'?"

"Alicia Van Horn," he said. "My mother."

At once, Blair's eyes widened. Their particular shade of blue reminded Randall of someone, although right then, he couldn't say exactly who. They definitely weren't the same color as his eyes. He had the clear aquamarine eyes of the Van Horn family, almost silvery in bright sunlight.

"That's not possible," Blair replied, her voice now almost a whisper. "We've never had any contact with the Van Horn clan."

Next to him, Joanna shifted on the couch. "Well, there had to be some, because we found a marriage record from Litchfield County showing that Alicia Van Horn and Thomas Nathan Winfield were married in March of 1979."

"They got married here?" While she didn't sound precisely aghast, Randall could tell she was shocked that such a thing could have happened right under her family's nose.

"Maybe not in Litchfield itself," he said. "The records aren't that granular. But somewhere in this county. And apparently, my late mother had an odd talent—she could make people ignore her, make it seem as if she almost didn't exist. So, that makes me think she could have come here to be with Thomas, and the Winfields would suddenly have found themselves very busy with other matters and wouldn't have paid any attention to her at all."

"I've never heard of that talent," Blair murmured, almost to herself. Then her shoulders lifted, and she went on, "But the Van Horns are an old and powerful clan, so I suppose I shouldn't be too surprised that they might have some gifts among them that the rest of us don't."

Randall assumed that theory was entirely possible. He'd never performed an in-depth study of the various witch talents, but he knew they could vary widely, even while some were common enough that you could reasonably expect to see them in just about every witch family. Still, while that subject possibly merited further research at a later date, it wasn't what concerned him at the moment.

"I know this was all before your time," he said, "but is there anyone in the Winfield clan who might have been close to Thomas back in the day? Someone he might have confided in?"

For a moment, Blair was silent, as if she was searching through her own private database of the family to see if there was someone who might fit that description. But then she gave a single shake of her head, saying, "Not that I'm aware of. I mean, my uncle Andrew is still alive, but I'm sure he would have told me if he'd known anything about Tom being tangled up with a Van Horn witch." Almost at once, color showed in her cheeks, and she added hastily, "Oh, that came out wrong. I'm sure your mother was a lovely person. But I think that must have been a secret Tom kept very close, for a variety of reasons. My mother definitely didn't know anything, or I know she would have said something to me. She always said she couldn't have any secrets from me because I would be *prima* one day, and I'd need to be armed with as much knowledge about our clan as possible."

It had been a long shot, so Randall refused to allow himself to be too disappointed. At the same time, though, he wondered what Thomas Winfield's endgame had been. Surely he couldn't have expected to keep his marriage secret forever. Had the couple only been waiting until Alicia's pregnancy was more obvious before they presented themselves to the Winfields? He didn't quite see the point in that sort of maneuver, although maybe it was simply that Thomas had believed his family wouldn't reject a woman who was carrying his child.

Before he could reply to Blair, however, she went on, eyes lighting up as an idea seemed to occur to her, "But I do have a couple of boxes of his papers and other personal items up in the attic. I guess my mother had to help clear out his apartment after he passed, and she brought all those things home with her. I have no idea whether there's anything in there that will help, but it's worth a look, don't you think?"

Hope sparked inside him, and he glanced over at Joanna, who was now smiling. "I think that's a great idea," she said. "And you won't mind us poking around up there?"

"Not at all." Blair paused then, her expression growing more thoughtful as she appeared to consider Randall. "I don't know why I didn't notice it at first, but you do look a lot like the pictures I've seen of my uncle Tom. His hair was a little darker, and your eye color isn't really the same, but the rest of it...." She trailed off before continuing, "Actually, I have a photo of him in the family room. Let me go get it."

After setting down her glass of iced tea, she rose from the chair and hurried from the room. Randall looked over at Joanna, and she extended a hand so she could give his fingers a quick, encouraging squeeze.

"It sounds like we might have a lead," she said, and Randall allowed himself a cautious nod.

"Maybe," he replied. "Or maybe all we're going to find is boxes of old school photos and report cards."

Her nose wrinkled. "Don't be a Debbie Downer. You didn't think you were going to find much in your mother's house, but we found that ring, didn't we?"

True. He was generally inclined to be cautious because that made life simpler, but they'd definitely had a lucky break in locating that ring. Maybe that same luck had followed them here.

After all, luck was his gift, right?

And even if they didn't turn up anything useful, at least now he'd met a few of his Winfield relatives. Somehow, it was grounding to know they existed, that he could put faces to both sides of his biological family.

Besides—while it felt sort of petty to even think such a thing—he had to admit that the

Winfields seemed to be much nicer people than the Van Horns.

Blair returned, holding a photo in an antique brass frame. She handed it to Randall and said, "I think the resemblance is very strong. Don't you?"

He gazed down at the picture. For some reason, he'd thought it would be in black and white, although he realized that was a foolish notion. After all, this picture had probably been taken in the late 1970s, not back in the '30s or '40s.

The man in the photo couldn't have been more than twenty-one at the most. Staring at the image, Randall was assaulted by a strange sense of déjà vu, although he knew that wasn't quite it. No, the dissonance he experienced in this moment was probably caused by the realization that he couldn't possibly be the man whose face looked back at him now, even though they were nearly identical.

Not quite, though. As Blair had already pointed out, this man's hair was darker, his eyes a deeper blue. But the straight brows and longish nose, thin, well-defined lips, determined jaw... they all belonged to a face Randall knew all too well, because it was his own.

If nothing else, the photo appeared to provide some fairly clear-cut evidence that Thomas Winfield had in fact been his biological father. It was an odd sensation, this recognition, especially after so many years of his life spent wondering what his birth parents had looked like.

He didn't have to wonder any longer.

In silence, he handed the photo to Joanna. She took it from him, dark eyes wide with wonder. "It's amazing," she said quietly. "The coloring is a little different, but otherwise, he looks so much like you that it's kind of uncanny."

There wasn't much he could do in reply to her comment, since he'd already recognized that truth for himself. He nodded, then allowed her to set the photo down on the coffee table. After clearing his throat, he asked Blair, "Could we see the attic?"

Apparently sensing that he didn't want to discuss the photo any further, she said at once, "Of course. Let me show you."

They all stood, then followed her up the stairs to the second-floor landing. From there, the attic was accessed by a drop-down ladder that extended from an opening in the ceiling.

"It's probably a little dusty," Blair said, now sounding apologetic. "I try to get in there and tidy up about once a year, but I don't usually do my spring cleaning until sometime in April."

"No worries," Randall told her. "We'll be careful."

"I'll just wait downstairs, then."

She offered them a smile, and headed back down to the ground floor.

"Go ahead," Randall told Joanna, who was eyeing the ladder with some skepticism.

"I knew I should've worn flats," she remarked, but she didn't offer any protests, instead nimbly ascending to the attic without asking for any assistance.

He should have known she would manage just fine. Without commenting, he climbed up after her, and emerged in a large space that seemed to extend over the entire top floor of the house. Joanna had already turned on the overhead lights, so he could see his surroundings clearly enough. Judging by the trunks, boxes, cast-off furniture, holiday decorations, and other odds and ends scattered around the place, generations of Winfield *primas* and their families must have been storing their junk in that attic.

"Whew," Joanna said after taking a quick glance around her. "Looks like there's enough stuff for a couple episodes of *Hoarders* up here. Where do you want to start?"

Randall surveyed the motley collection. "Well, Blair said that Thomas Winfield's belongings were put in a couple of boxes, so I suppose we should start with those. Here's hoping these things are labeled properly."

There were several stacks of boxes; he selected

one at random and leaned closer to take a look. To his relief, the boxes did appear to be marked with their various contents; the handwriting varied from box to box, telling him that they had been packed by a number of different people. He saw everything from school papers belonging to Winfield relations he'd never heard of to spare Fourth of July bunting for the front porch, but he didn't see anything that had been labeled with Tom Winfield's name.

Then again, the materials he was looking for had probably been sitting up here for decades, and the boxes he sought were most likely somewhere near the bottom of the pile. Joanna worked away gamely at her own stack of boxes, pausing to read the writing on each one before she set it aside and continued to the next one. Some of them were probably heavy—at least, he knew that several of the containers he'd hefted were filled with something a lot heavier than spare bedding, but she never asked for any assistance.

And then—

"I think they're over here," she said, stepping out of the way so Randall could view the boxes in question.

At once, he stopped what he was doing and went over to her. Sure enough, there were two large boxes near the bottom of her pile, both of them clearly marked "Tom Winfield, May 1980" in Sharpie that still looked strong and black even after all these years.

The tape holding them closed wasn't in as good shape, however, as it peeled back at his touch, even though he'd planned to use the knife on his keychain to open them if necessary. Once opened, the box revealed what looked like stacks of papers—the school records he'd speculated about earlier, but also what looked like various letters, from his acceptance to Trinity College to a manila envelope containing various certificates from a music school he'd apparently attended for most of his youth.

While all of that might have been interesting on a forensic level, Randall didn't see anything dated later than his birth father's senior year of high school. The two lovers had been very young when they died, but they'd still been older than that.

"Anything?" Joanna asked, and he shook his head.

"Not yet. But there's still the other box."

He went ahead and opened it, and saw that its contents were a little more interesting—some more framed photos, ones that clearly were of Tom Winfield and his family—his parents, another young man a few years older, a young woman who appeared to be older than both of the men and was probably the late *prima*. While

Randall would want to study those further...he'd have to ask Blair if it was all right for him to take some of his late father's personal effects...again, he wasn't finding anything that linked Tom Winfield to Alicia Van Horn.

At the bottom of the box were some books, mostly college texts, as far as Randall could tell. Although he doubted he would find anything of interest in them, he dutifully picked up each book and leafed through it, hoping he would find something that might offer even a single piece of useful information—a receipt, a note, anything at all.

From inside a book on music theory, a business card slid out between the pages and fluttered to the floor. At once, Joanna bent and picked it up, then handed it to him. "Anything interesting?"

The card was a plain white one, although now yellowed with age. "Margaret Latimer," it said. "Midwife." Those words were followed by a phone number with a New York area code and prefix.

Randall told himself not to get too excited—after all, it had been forty years since Alicia Van Horn had needed the services of a midwife, and he somehow doubted this "Margaret Latimer" still had the same phone number.

Or was even alive.

Still, it was a clue, and one they'd have to follow up on.

"Maybe," he said, and handed the card back to Joanna so she could take a look at it for herself.

Her reaction wasn't nearly so reserved. "This is perfect," she said, and she smiled. "Looks like we're going back to New York."

17

ALTHOUGH JOANNA WASN'T COMPLETELY THRILLED to be heading back to the city after spending some time in Connecticut's green spaces, she still was excited for Randall's sake. He'd tried to downplay the discovery of the business card, but it was an important clue, and one that might provide some more information surrounding the circumstances of his birth.

Blair had been excited for them as well, and urged Randall to be in touch and let her know what he found out. "Because it's my uncle, I want to know more," she said. "I want to know why he felt like he had to hide his relationship with your mother from my grandparents. They died when I was fairly young—my mother was nearly forty when she had me—but they always seemed like nice people. I can't really imagine them laying down the law and saying that my uncle couldn't marry a Van Horn."

Maybe that was true...and maybe it wasn't. Family could be very strange sometimes. Joanna had kept silent as Randall told Blair he'd let her know if he discovered anything else. He'd also asked if he could take some of the family photos with them, and the Winfield *prima* had immediately told him that of course he could.

"I want you to have something from this family," she said with a smile. "And I hope once your business in New York is wrapped up, you'll come back to visit us. I know that your Winfield relatives will definitely want to meet you."

He'd said he'd do what he could, and he and Joanna left soon afterward. She could tell he was reluctant to make too many promises, since everything in New York was so up in the air. On the drive back, he informed her that he'd gone shopping with his mother the day before and had already ordered some new appliances for the West Village house.

"But that's something that would have had to be done whether or not I planned to stay in New York or decided to put the house on the market," he added, as if he'd noticed the dismay that flared in her eyes upon hearing that bit of news. "Besides, it made my mother almost deliriously happy to be out shopping with me. After disappearing to Arizona for the last nine months, I figured it was the least I could do."

This last was delivered in a dry, almost ironic tone, as if he poked fun at his mother for being so excited by such a silly consumer activity. But Joanna thought she could see past the sarcasm, and recognized how much he cared for the woman who'd adopted him as a newborn. Alicia Van Horn might have been the one to contribute to his genetic makeup, but Barbara Lenz would always be his real mother.

While they were driving, he'd called Kelly Dawson to let her know what they'd found and to set her tracking down Margaret Latimer, who'd been a midwife in 1970s New York. This search seemed to take her a lot less time than the one for Thomas Winfield, and she called back just as they were passing the toll gate on the Henry Hudson Bridge.

"Margaret Latimer retired in 1995," Kelly said. Randall had patched the call through their rental car's Bluetooth system, so Joanna could hear the entire conversation. "And she passed away in 2004. But it looks like her daughter Susan took over her practice. She has a website and appears to still be working in that same field, although she calls herself a doula and not a midwife."

"I don't care what she calls herself as long as I can get in touch with her," Randall commented, and Joanna tried not to smile. That was such a Randall remark.

"I'll text you her contact info," Kelly replied without missing a beat. She might not have been working for him any longer, but it seemed like their business relationship was picking up pretty much right where they'd left off.

"Thanks, Kelly," he said. "I appreciate you handling this for me."

"Not a problem," she told him. "Susan Latimer was pretty easy to find. I hope she has some answers for you."

Joanna hoped so as well...but that probably depended on how much Margaret Latimer had told her daughter about her past clients. You'd think some sort of confidentiality clause would be in play, but maybe that sort of thing didn't apply to midwives the same way it did to doctors and nurses.

"I hope so, too," Randall said. "I'll let you know."

He ended the call there. Without taking his eyes off the road, he asked Joanna, "Do you want to go to my house, or to your hotel?"

Good question. Her hotel room felt like far more neutral territory, but they'd have more room to work at Randall's house. Besides, she needed to accept that the West Village home was part of his present. Maybe it wouldn't be his future, but she couldn't exactly pretend that the Van Horn side of his heritage didn't exist.

"Oh, probably your house," she replied, hoping she sounded casual about the whole thing. "Although we might want to stop at the store and get a few snacks and some other stuff if we're going to be spending much time there."

"We can go to the bodega down the street," he said, the slight curl at the corner of his mouth telling her that he was slightly amused by her request.

True, they'd had a big lunch, but that was hours ago. And digging up the past was hungry work.

"Deal," she said, and they were both quiet after that.

This time when they approached the house, they came in through the alley so he could park the rental car in the garage. Like the house, that garage was large but not ostentatious, with enough room for two vehicles and maybe something smaller, like a motorcycle or a very under-sized car.

Or storage, she reflected, realizing the garage was just as empty of any personal belongings as the house. If Alicia Van Horn had stored spare Christmas decorations or gardening equipment or anything else like that out here, it was long gone.

Since they'd already agreed to head to the

bodega, they didn't even go in the house, but instead walked down the alley to reach the street, and went on from there. Randall claimed that he didn't much care what they got and said he trusted her judgment, so Joanna chose some crackers and interesting cheese, a loaf of French bread, a couple of bottles of Perrier, and a bottle of pinot noir.

He lifted an eyebrow at the wine but didn't say anything, and only handed three twenty-dollar bills to the clerk to pay for their purchases.

It was a short walk back to the house. Joanna said, "I'll put this stuff away. I know you're dying to call Susan Latimer."

"I don't know about 'dying,'" he replied. "But it's past four, and I want to catch her before she heads home for the day."

Did a doula even have regular working hours? After all, babies came when they wanted to. Still, she understood why Randall wanted to get moving.

"Right," she said. "Go on—I'll be out with some Perrier and cheese and crackers in a bit."

He nodded, then headed out of the kitchen and down the hall to what probably used to be a parlor of some sort but had obviously been used as a family room when Alicia owned the house. There was still a big console TV taking up half of one wall, and Joanna wondered what on earth Randall was going to do with it. A monstrosity like that wasn't exactly the sort of thing a thrift store would want to take, unless people collected those things out of nostalgic whimsy.

Well, money could solve a variety of problems, and she guessed he'd end up calling a junk dealer to haul the television away.

If he even planned to stay here.

She reassured herself that, even though they might be using the house as a base of operations for now, she didn't have to worry about him wanting to sleep here, not on those ancient mattresses. No, they'd handle their business and have a snack—and maybe make plans to go see this Susan Latimer, if Randall could get in touch with her—but eventually, they'd end up back at Joanna's hotel room.

Which was fine by her. She hoped they'd have a repeat of the previous night. They worked easily together, but she could never forget that beneath everything, her blood still ran hot for him, and her body ached for his touch.

When she entered the family room, tray in hand, she saw that Randall was already engaged in conversation. He sat at the edge of the prim Victorian-style sofa, phone pressed to his ear, eyes intent but expression neutral.

"No, that would be fine," he was saying. His gaze caught Joanna's, and he inclined his head toward her in acknowledgment as she set the tray with their snack down on the coffee table. "Six o'clock works. Thirty-third and Madison. Got it. We'll see you then."

He put down the phone, face still not betraying much of anything. Even so, Joanna could tell he was pleased.

"That was Susan?" she asked.

"Yes," he replied. "She has appointments up until five-thirty, but she said she can see us at six. None of her clients' babies are even due this week, so she's fairly certain that we won't be interrupted."

"Sounds perfect," Joanna said, a little thrill going through her. Everything seemed to be going smoothly so far. More of Randall's "luck" working for them? "And that gives us plenty of time for a snack, right?"

He nodded, now looking amused. "Yes. Susan's office is actually only about fifteen minutes from here, so there's not a lot of travel time involved."

That did sound great. Joanna sat down next to Randall and poured some Perrier into the glasses she'd brought. Maybe wine would have been better to celebrate this next step in their search for his past, but she doubted he'd want to go into such a meeting even a little bit impaired.

After handing him a glass, she said, "Did she tell you anything?"

He swallowed some water, then shook his head. "No. She said her mother had left her extensive records, but this wasn't the sort of thing she wanted to discuss over the phone. Odd thing was, as soon as I told her who my mother was, she seemed to remember the case right away, as if her mother had made sure to tell her the details in case I ever surfaced."

"Maybe she did," Joanna responded. "I mean, it sounds as though it was a tragedy all around. I could see how she might have been carrying the guilt over what happened to your mother for decades. She might have wanted to give her daughter the chance to make it right, since she couldn't."

"I suppose that's a possibility." He didn't say anything else, however, but only reached for a cracker and some of the smoked Gouda they'd bought at the bodega.

When Randall got silent like that, it meant his mind was probably working furiously, but he didn't want to discuss what he was thinking. Which was fine; Joanna always hated it when people started poking at her, trying to get her to reveal what was going on in her mind, so she certainly wasn't going to do the same thing to him.

Since she was hungry, she went ahead and helped herself to some cheese and a cracker as well. They were both quiet for a few moments as they ate. After Randall drank a few more swallows of Perrier, he said, "What did you think of the Winfields?"

"That they seem a lot nicer than the Van Horns," she answered at once, and he actually grinned, ice-blue eyes crinkling in amusement.

"The thought had crossed my mind as well," he said. "And it seemed that you liked Litchfield."

"From what I saw, it was adorable." Which was only the truth. Litchfield probably had its downsides, just like every other town in the world, but they certainly weren't immediately visible.

"Would you ever consider living there?"

For a second or two, she could only stare at him. Was he asking what she thought he was asking?

No, that wasn't possible. He'd probably only been pondering hypotheticals.

In response to her dumbfounded silence, he said, "I'm moving too fast here, aren't I?"

Somehow, she managed to find her voice. "I don't know," she replied. "I didn't think…that is, I know we've gotten close over the past few days, but…."

His smile vanished, and that cool, neutral expression was back on his face. "But?"

You let yourself think it last night, Joanna told

herself fiercely. *This isn't the time to be a chickenshit.*

Still…was she strong enough to tell him what she'd kept hidden in her heart?

"Last night, I realized that I was in love with you," she said. "But I don't know whether you feel the same way."

One long, horribly silent moment, during which she could hear her heart thudding away in her ribcage and she wondered if she'd completely blown it.

"Well, that's good," Randall said, his voice cool and no-nonsense. "Because I know I'm in love with you, and it would be kind of awkward if you didn't feel the same way."

Joanna didn't know which one of them moved first. Not that it probably mattered, because in the next second, their arms were around one another, and their mouths met in a kiss deliciously flavored with smoked Gouda. His hand ran down the length of her hair, and she pressed herself against him, body aching with need.

Except…as much as she wanted him, she wasn't sure she wanted to have sex on a sofa that had once belonged to his mother.

Almost as soon as that thought ran through her mind, Randall lifted his mouth from hers. He was smiling.

"It's all right," he said. "I'm not much into sofa sex, either."

About all she could do was chuckle. "Rain check until we can do this properly in my hotel room?"

"Deal."

They both reached for their glasses of Perrier and swallowed some. Joanna was still warm all over from the embrace...and also the realization that Randall Lenz cared for her just as much as she cared for him.

Whatever they found out next, they'd face it together.

He spoke then, his tone musing. "I suppose I was asking about Litchfield because I liked it very much, too. And Blair Winfield made us feel welcome, which is more than I can say for Greta Van Horn."

Since Joanna hadn't met the woman in question, she had to take Randall's word for it. However, she trusted his judgment about people, and so she guessed he was only telling her the unembellished truth. She nodded, and he continued.

"I wouldn't want to take you away from everything you know and love," he said. "But at the same time, I suppose I just wanted to put Litchfield out there as an option."

Her hand stole into his, and she squeezed his

fingers, doing her best to reassure him that what he was asking wasn't outside the bounds of possibility. "It's a good option. I mean, I have my life in Flagstaff, but it's not as if my entire identity is bound up in being a Wilcox. After all, there's a big chunk of my past where I had to do everything I could to hide that part of myself. It's not as if I've really been an active member of the clan for my entire life."

"True. I hadn't thought about that."

Joanna leaned over and kissed him on the cheek. "We'll figure it out, one way or another. But I suppose we should finish this up and then head over to meet Susan Latimer."

He glanced over at the clock on the mantel. "Yes, it's about time."

They gathered up the remnants of their snack, and Randall put the leftover cheese in the refrigerator while she stowed the box of crackers in the otherwise empty pantry. A brief break to get tidied up—Joanna needed to replace her lip gloss after that scorching kiss—and then they headed out to the garage and got in the car.

Because of the time of day, traffic was thick. Joanna stared out at the choked streets around them and wondered how people could live with that kind of congestion day in and day out. Even the backups on Milton Avenue in Flagstaff were enough to drive her crazy, and they were an order of magnitude less than the crush of cars she saw around her now.

But she realized New York and its issues really weren't her problem. Randall loved her, and whatever they ended up doing, it seemed pretty obvious to her that he wouldn't ask her to live in New York. Could she pull up stakes and move all the way across the country to start a new life?

She supposed she'd have to see how her alpacas would fare in Connecticut before she made such a decision. Then again, if they could handle Flagstaff, they could probably handle just about anything.

Randall's luck—or just plain old parking karma—landed them a space just a few doors down from the two-story brownstone where Susan Latimer's office was located. It was a cute area, kind of funky, with a clothing store on one side and what looked like a medical marijuana dispensary on the other. The people who passed on the street definitely looked bohemian enough to have been hanging around in downtown Flagstaff.

These surroundings reassured Joanna. She didn't feel at all at home in the more upscale part of town where her hotel was located, but this spot seemed a lot more down to earth.

Susan Latimer's office was on the second floor. Randall and Joanna climbed the stairs, and then he pressed the buzzer next to the door.

Almost at once, that door opened, and a woman who appeared to be five or six years older than Randall looked out at them. She had curly brown hair and warm brown skin just a few shades lighter, and wore a long dress in a rich maroon color.

Something about her seemed almost immediately relaxing, and Joanna could see why women would like to have Susan Latimer's soothing presence nearby when they were in labor.

A smile, and she said, "Come on in. I have some tea ready."

They entered the office. It was set up more as a little sitting area, with only a table with an iMac sitting on it as a nod to its business functions. Sure enough, a chubby brown teapot and matching cups sat on the little table in front of the couch, and a warm, spicy aroma filled the air.

"You're Randall Lenz?" Susan Latimer asked.

"Yes," he replied. "And this is my girlfriend Joanna Wilcox."

Just hearing him say that simple word made another rush of warmth go through her. Maybe it was silly to make such a big deal about something that, on the surface, wasn't all that important, but she knew Randall wouldn't have referred to her that way if he hadn't wanted her to know the place she occupied in his heart.

"I'm glad to meet you, Randall," Susan said.

"And you, too, Joanna. After so much time had gone by, I honestly didn't think I would ever hear from you—but once my mother told me the story, I hoped I would. What happened to your mother was the biggest regret of her life. But please—sit down and have some tea."

Joanna took a seat on the couch, and Randall settled himself next to her. However, judging by the way he perched near the edge of the cushion, he had no intention of making himself comfortable. She had a feeling that Susan's words about "regret" had put him even more on edge.

However, he accepted a cup of tea with apparent equanimity, then said, "Can you tell me what happened? I've heard a little from my aunt—Alicia Van Horn's older sister—but she came to the whole situation after the fact, so her story has a lot of blanks in it."

Susan's features were a bit too cherubic for her to look completely downcast, but it was obvious from the way her mouth drooped that she didn't look forward to telling the tale. She glanced over at Joanna, who'd picked up her own cup of tea and taken a sip. Sweet cinnamon, exactly the comforting note she needed right then.

After a heavy pause, Susan said, "Alicia Van Horn came to my mother when she was almost seven months pregnant. She told her the child's father had died several months before that, and she'd been keeping the pregnancy from her family because they wouldn't approve. That sounds old-fashioned, but even my mother had heard of the Van Horns, and she had no reason not to believe what Alicia was saying. Alicia also confessed that she hadn't gone to the doctor, except for an early visit to Planned Parenthood that confirmed the pregnancy."

"Why stay away from a doctor?" Randall asked. "I can understand her not wanting to go to a family physician, but it's not as though there's a shortage of doctors in the greater New York area."

Susan gave a sorrowful shake of her head. "I honestly don't know. She told my mother she'd been taking prenatal vitamins and eating healthy and doing moderate exercise, and it seemed she was doing fine. My mother examined her, and it appeared she was progressing naturally. Her due date was in early September, and when she went into labor on September second, she was right on time—which doesn't always happen with a first pregnancy."

"So...what went wrong?" Randall's tone sounded even enough, but it contained a sharp edge Joanna knew was a warning sign.

Not that she could blame him. If Susan's mother had gotten Alicia Van Horn to the hospital on time, she might still be alive today.

A sorrowful little breath escaped the doula's

plum-glossed lips. "Alicia wanted to have the birth at home. My mother warned her it could be a difficult labor, but she insisted."

"'A difficult labor'?" Randall demanded, his voice still controlled, but with a definite bite to it.

And Susan obviously heard, because she winced slightly, even as she straightened in her chair and met his pale, sharp gaze. "Your mother was very slender, even at full term. Delivering twins is almost always difficult for someone built like that."

For one endless second, absolute silence reigned in the room. The blood thudded in Joanna's ears, even as she made herself sit very still. For some reason, she couldn't quite make herself look over at Randall to see how his expression must have shifted.

Then he said, voice now not much more than a rasp, "Are you saying I'm a *twin*?"

"Yes," Susan replied. She seemed almost relieved, as if she'd feared delivering that news for years and now at least could say the moment was safely behind her.

"Your twin sister was born ten minutes after you."

18

THE ROOM WANTED TO SWIRL AROUND HIM, but Randall held himself still, willing the dizziness away. He didn't know why the news should be so unexpected, because in that moment, something within him recognized there was far more to the story than he'd ever believed.

"Tell me what happened," he said, and now he knew he sounded more controlled, the harshness from a moment earlier gone. He'd heard the news about his twin sister—and he'd go back to pick up that thread soon enough—but he wanted the narrative finished. It was entirely possible that Susan Latimer didn't know all of it, but she needed to tell him everything her mother had related to her.

Susan's hands clasped on her knee. Her fingernails were painted a deep iridescent plum to match her lips, an irrelevant detail he noted because he'd been trained to notice everything, even in moments of crisis.

"Both of you babies were healthy, but my mother couldn't stop Alicia's bleeding." She stopped and appeared to gather herself, then continued. "She wanted to call an ambulance, but Alicia kept saying no, that if she went to the hospital, her family would find out. Then she fainted. That was when my mother called 9-1-1. Alicia came to just as they arrived and went into hysterics—told my mother that she had to hide the babies, that her family couldn't get their hands on them. She said something about them belonging to another clan, but that didn't seem to make any sense."

Randall felt Joanna's gaze on him, and he allowed himself the slightest glance in her direction, saw the tightness in the set of her lips and the worry in her wide, dark eyes. Her concern for him felt like an almost tangible thing, like the beating of the pulse in his throat.

But he didn't want to be distracted by her. Not now. No, he needed to focus on the implication that his mother had feared her sister—or the Van Horn clan as a whole—and had always intended that her children should be raised among the Winfields instead.

Apparently nonplussed by his lack of a

response, Susan went on, "My mother promised she would take care of it. Alicia fainted again as they were putting her in the ambulance, but not before my mother had taken the newborns into another room and cleaned them up, made sure they were healthy. It was her plan to bring them to the hospital once she'd determined they were strong enough to be taken there. She never got that far, though."

"Why?" Joanna asked, after sliding another sidelong glance in Randall's direction and apparently determining that he wasn't going to say anything.

No, he only wanted to keep listening.

"Because Greta Van Horn showed up," Susan replied. "How she knew to appear just then, my mother didn't have any idea. You were already sleeping in the crib your mother had prepared for you"—she nodded toward Randall—"but your sister was smaller and wouldn't stop crying. Greta told my mother that Alicia wanted her to take the baby. This was the exact opposite of what Alicia had actually said, but my mother didn't know what to do. Greta was family, after all."

Joanna's brows drew together, her expression troubled. "So…she took Randall's sister?"

Susan nodded. "Yes. My mother said that Greta didn't bother to look around the place, so she had no idea Randall was sleeping in the next room. She just took the baby and left. Frightened, my mother called the hospital, thinking she'd get a message to Alicia so she could find out what to do next."

"And she discovered Alicia had died," Randall said. He was able to say the words calmly enough, even though his gut wrenched at the thought of his mother dying miles away from the children she'd just birthed...at the thought of his sister taken away from him before he was even aware enough to realize he had a sibling.

A breath, and Susan said, "Yes. And...my mother panicked. I mean, there she was in the house of a woman who'd died moments earlier—a woman who was also a Van Horn—looking after a baby who'd just lost his mother and had hostile relatives that his mother obviously had done a whole lot to avoid."

"So your mother scooped me up and took me to that fire station in Brooklyn." He did his best to keep any condemnation out of his tone, but he wasn't sure how successful he'd been.

Probably not very, because Susan's expression grew clouded. She said quietly, "My mother beat herself up about that for years, even though she knew that Alicia wanted her children kept far away from her family. She still kept wondering if she should have said something. But she also said she got a bad vibe off Greta, and I believe her. She had very good instincts about people."

Considering that his interactions with the Van Horns hadn't exactly been models of familial warmth, Randall couldn't argue with that assessment. And Susan was looking so guilt-stricken—even though she was discussing her mother's actions and not her own—that he felt compelled to say, "It turned out fine. My adoptive parents were wonderful people, and I had a great childhood…far better than I would have had if I'd been raised by Greta Van Horn. I wouldn't have asked for anything different, honestly."

"And Randall's sister?" Joanna asked then. Her beautiful dark eyes were troubled, as though she was imagining all sorts of terrible fates for the child Greta had snatched up so many years earlier.

Susan spread her hands in a helpless gesture. "I don't know. I mean, my mother did her best to keep track of Greta Van Horn, which wasn't that hard because she was in the society pages of the newspapers all the time. They never mentioned anyone other than a son and a daughter. Nothing about a niece, or even a second daughter, if she was trying to pass off your sister as her own."

The son and daughter were obviously Karl and Victoria. "Maybe she gave my sister to another family member to raise," Randall suggested, and Susan's shoulders lifted slightly.

"Maybe," she said. "All I know is my mother could never figure out what had happened to that little baby. She worried about it until the day she died."

That was a lot of guilt to carry through one lifetime. But Randall supposed that for someone who'd given their life to helping others and making sure children entered the world safely to loving families, having one of those children taken away and effectively disappeared would be more than a little upsetting.

Something was nagging at him, though. For some reason, Blair Winfield's face flashed into his mind, although he couldn't say why. She was only peripherally connected to this mystery.

Something about her eyes. Blue eyes, a deeper shade of blue than his.

Winfield eyes, apparently, since his father's eyes had been almost the same color.

He'd seen those eyes before.

But where? The answer hovered at the edges of his mind, an important piece he couldn't quite fit into the puzzle.

Like one of Addie Grant's lightning bolts, it came to him, and his fingers clenched the edge of the overstuffed sofa where he sat. Joanna sent him a look of alarm.

"Randall, what is it?"

He didn't want to believe what he was

thinking could possibly be true…but the pieces fit together. Their apparent ages matched.

"I think I know who my sister is," he said, and both Joanna and Susan stared at him in shock.

"Who?" Joanna asked.

"Elaine Van Horn," Randall replied. "The woman Greta's had working in her house as her servant for years."

He didn't know why Greta would have subjected her niece to that kind of cruelty, unless it was some form of punishment in absentia for the worry Alicia had put her through, the shame she'd brought to the Van Horn clan. Revenge could take on some very twisted forms…and familial revenge could be the worst of all.

Joanna's expression was still one of consternation. "You're sure about that?"

"Not completely," he replied. "I just know when we met Blair—my father's niece," he elaborated for Susan's benefit, since she was looking even more confused. "She reminded me of someone, and I couldn't think who. But now I know it was because her eyes and Elaine's eyes are the same color…the color of my father's eyes. And Elaine is around the right age, too."

"You mean that Greta made her own niece work for her as a maid?" Susan asked, now looking indignant on Elaine's behalf. "What kind of person does that?"

"A not very nice one, I'm afraid," Randall said. He didn't want to go into any more detail than that; most likely, Susan Latimer had already heard far too much. However, since she'd kept his family's secrets all these years, he had to hope she would hold this one close as well. Even so, he added, "I hope we can keep all this in confidence, Susan."

"Of course," she responded immediately, looking slightly offended that he would even have to ask. "Nothing that's said in here will go beyond these four walls."

He supposed he had to be content with that promise. For now, though, he needed to confront Greta about what she'd done…and to let the sister he didn't even realize existed know a little more about her past.

Randall's hands were so wrapped so tightly around the steering wheel, Joanna could see the knuckles standing out white against his tanned skin. There were so many things she wanted to say to him and wasn't sure she should.

Of course, she understood his anger. She would have been blazingly, furiously outraged to learn that she had a sibling who'd been kept from her. One could possibly argue that Greta hadn't even known Randall had been born until he finally crossed her radar, but even so, there was no reason for her not to tell him that Elaine was his twin sister.

Unless Elaine herself didn't know who her own mother was, and Greta wanted to make sure that little secret remained buried for all time. Joanna had to admit that was the most likely possibility; for whatever reason, she'd probably farmed her inconvenient niece out to another Van Horn to raise and allowed the woman to remain ignorant of her true parentage.

Either way, it seemed like Greta Van Horn had a lot to answer for.

"I'm sorry," Joanna said briefly, and Randall flickered a quick glance at her before returning his attention to the clogged streets around them. By that point, it was nearly seven o'clock, but it looked to her as though New York didn't have any plans to settle down any time soon.

"It's all right," he returned, although the clipped tone in which he delivered those words made her think it was really the opposite of all right. "I got some important information from Susan. Honestly, I'm grateful for what her mother did. Otherwise, I would never have been raised by my parents."

"But you might have gotten to live with the

Winfields," Joanna pointed out, and he gave her a thin-lipped smile that was more of a grimace.

"I honestly don't think Greta would have allowed that. And I don't know how it works when it's a couple of witch clans fighting over a child, but in general, the courts tend to side with the mother's family when it comes to custody battles."

Joanna wasn't really sure how that sort of thing worked, either. Children with parents from two different clans had been virtually nonexistent before the last seven or eight years…at least, in any of the clans she knew of. There hadn't been much opportunity for the sort of custody fights Randall was talking about. When her parents separated, it had been to protect her, and so naturally there hadn't been any discussion about who she'd live with. She'd gone to Kayenta with her mother, and that had been the end of it…at least, until Damon Wilcox passed away and Naomi Wilcox had decided it was safe for her daughter to return to Flagstaff.

But even she knew that Randall was right, and the Winfields probably would have had an uphill battle making a claim for Randall and Elaine, especially since their father was dead and couldn't help by contributing the necessary DNA for a paternity test. These days, that sort of thing could still be determined by testing close family members, but Joanna had no idea whether that sort of technology had existed back in the early 1980s.

It took them nearly forty minutes to battle their way from Susan's office near Soho to the Van Horn mansion on 77th Street, but eventually they made it. Once again, Randall's parking luck seemed to be in play, because he found a spot only half a block away from the house.

They got out of their rented car, Joanna almost unconsciously straightening her jacket and running a quick hand over her hair to smooth it in anticipation of their upcoming audience with Greta Van Horn. It probably didn't matter what she looked like, but she also didn't want to create a bad impression.

This meeting was going to be contentious enough as it was.

The sun had gone down by that point, and the air had a definite bite to it, a damp chill that came off the East River and felt very different from the crisp, fresh breezes that continually moved across the peaks and forests that surrounded Flagstaff.

Or maybe the chill that went down her spine as they mounted the stone front steps to Greta Van Horn's imposing mansion had absolutely nothing to do with the cool air that surrounded Joanna right then.

Randall reached out to push the doorbell. It

clanged within the house, ominous as a bell tolling in a graveyard.

Then again, that might have just been Joanna's imagination playing with her head.

It seemed like a very long time passed before anyone answered the door. When it finally swung inward, an attractive blonde woman, probably around forty, looked out at them. She seemed vaguely familiar, even though Joanna knew she'd never seen her before.

"Hello, Elaine," Randall said smoothly, and Joanna had to keep herself from startling at the name. This was his long-lost twin sister?

Apparently, although they didn't resemble one another very closely. Maybe something about the finely cut lips and the firm chin, but Elaine's features were much more delicate, her eyes a deeper blue.

"Is Greta in?" he went on. "I need to speak to her about something. To the both of you, actually."

"To me?" Elaine responded, looking startled. She gave a quick glance over one shoulder and said, "She's having dinner with the family."

A dinner to which he hadn't been invited, obviously. Joanna didn't know why she should be offended on Randall's behalf, except it seemed strange to her that Greta would go to the trouble of bringing him to New York and then effectively ignore him once he was here.

"Well, I'm sure she won't mind a little interruption," Randall said, and moved toward the door.

Obviously flustered and at a loss as to how she should respond, Elaine stepped out of the way. Joanna followed him inside, mostly because she didn't know what else to do.

The foyer was dimly lit by sconces of amber frosted glass. They cast enough light for her to tell that this house had been built on a much more massive scale than the one Randall had inherited in the West Village, although the dark wood and stained glass of the arched windows told her they were probably around the same vintage.

With both Elaine and Joanna following a few paces behind, he strode down the long central hallway, obviously intent on a particular destination. That became clear enough as Joanne heard the clink of cutlery and the low murmur of voices up ahead, and they entered a large dining room with an enormous table in the center, although only five places were currently occupied.

At the head of the table sat Greta Van Horn. As soon as she caught sight of the newcomers, however, she stood up, glaring at the trio with cold blue eyes that were uncomfortably similar to Randall's.

"What is the meaning of this intrusion?" she demanded. Her gaze rested on Elaine as she added, "Didn't you tell them I was at dinner?"

"That's my fault," Randall said, looking supremely unconcerned that he'd just barged into his aunt's dinner party. "But we need to talk."

Seated to her left, a blond man with equally icy eyes—a man Joanna guessed was probably the son Randall had mentioned in their meeting with Susan Latimer—rose as well. "It couldn't wait?" he asked. "Maybe they don't teach manners where you come from, but around here, it's considered rude to come into someone's house uninvited and interrupt their meal."

One eyebrow lifted. "Actually," Randall drawled, "I was raised right around the corner from here, so I suppose I'd have to say they're New York manners. But we need to talk, Greta, and we need to talk now. Unless you want to talk about me and Elaine in front of your kids."

"'You and Elaine'?" echoed the woman who'd been sitting at Greta's right, probably her daughter. "Mom, what's going on?"

The *prima's* expression had hardened as soon as Randall mentioned Elaine. Without looking at her daughter, Greta said, "We can go in the library. The rest of you"—she paused and glanced at her children and the man and woman who had to be their spouses, all of whom appeared both worried and irritated by the interruption—"please continue your meal. There's no reason for Randall's rudeness to keep you from eating."

After delivering that shot, she stalked from the table, past Elaine and Randall and Joanna, and down the hall, passing several doors before she led them into a large room that looked to be a library of some sort. She shut the doors behind them and crossed her arms, glaring at her nephew.

"There is a time and a place for everything, Randall," she snapped. "And this is not it. You couldn't have waited until tomorrow?"

He faced her, expression cool and utterly unruffled. Watching him then, Joanna could see why he'd made such a good agent. Nothing seemed to faze him. "Because what's a few hours after forty years of lies?"

Elaine glanced at her aunt, expression perplexed. "Greta, what is he talking about?"

"Nothing that concerns you," the *prima* said. "In fact, I think this whole charade is in utterly bad taste. You can go—I'm sure there's something you can do in the dining room."

"Stop treating her like a servant," Randall commanded, eyes narrowing slightly.

"Oh, but that's what I am," Elaine said quickly, even as a faint flush touched her cheeks. "And I don't mind, really. I volunteered to work here for the *prima*."

"I find that hard to believe." He paused for a second, then added, "You never told Elaine she was your niece, did you?"

At once, the woman's blue eyes widened in astonishment, even as Greta said, "You don't know what you're talking about, Randall."

"Oh, I think I do," he replied. His gaze moved to Joanna for just the barest second. Although she couldn't exactly give him a smile, she managed to incline her head ever so slightly, offering encouragement in a subtler way. "You lied when we stood here in this very room and you told me that you'd been looking for me for forty years. The real truth is that you hadn't even known I existed until I came to New York in December to visit my mother. Then you felt the resonance of another Van Horn in the area and put two and two together. That was when you hatched this scheme to bring me here."

"Pure speculation," Greta shot back, but something in the way she couldn't quite meet her nephew's cold gaze told Joanna that the *prima* knew she was on shaky ground.

"Speculation based on solid intelligence," he said calmly. He looked at Elaine, whose flush from a moment earlier had disappeared, and his expression softened ever so slightly. "I know this has to be a complete shock to you, but it's the truth. You're my twin sister, and our mother was Greta's younger sister Alicia. She died only a few hours after we were born. Greta came and took you away, but she hadn't known her sister was pregnant with twins, and so she didn't even think to look for a second child."

Elaine wore the expression of someone whose world had tilted on its foundation. Although she looked as though she would very much have liked to sit down, she remained where she was, arms crossed. Her posture wasn't one of defiance, though, but, Joanna thought, one of protection.

"I can't be, though," Elaine said. "My parents were Lorna and Jonas Van Horn. I'm only distantly related to Greta...aren't I?"

This last was accompanied by a pleading glance in her aunt's direction. Greta's jaw tightened, but she didn't reply.

"That's who she put you with to be raised," Randall said. "At least, that's my best guess. Why, though? Why didn't you raise her as one of your own?"

"Because then I would have had to admit that my little sister was pregnant out of wedlock," Greta replied. Each word was ground out, as though she had to force it past her clenched jaw. "I thought it better to have Lorna and Jonas raise her, and then determine what to do once her powers manifested. Only...they didn't."

That revelation seemed to startle Randall; his

gaze flickered for just a second before he regained control of himself. "You don't have any magic?" he asked his sister.

Her fingers twisted in the plain dark skirt she wore. While her outfit wasn't exactly a maid's uniform, the simple white blouse and straight black skirt were the next thing to one. "Not really," she confessed. "I can unlock doors, and make a candle light if I touch it. But that's about all. I never came into my talent...whatever it was supposed to be."

"You see?" Greta said, now sounding almost triumphant. "She had very little to contribute to the Van Horn clan, but at least she could make some use of herself working here."

"Well, you're certainly a piece of work," Joanna snapped, unable to contain herself any longer. During this whole exchange, she'd tried to keep out of it, since this was Randall's family business and not hers, but even she had her limits.

The Van Horn *prima* eyed her the way she might have eyed a cockroach crawling across her dining room table. "And who are you, anyway?"

"I'm Joanna Wilcox," she replied proudly, chin lifted.

"You don't feel like a witch," Greta remarked, patrician nostrils flaring in dislike.

"But I am. And what you've done is disgraceful."

All that observation earned her was a sniff. "I hardly think," the *prima* said, "that a Wilcox has any right to call anyone else a disgrace."

Damn, had the Wilcox reputation traveled all the way to the East Coast? Joanna tried to think of an effective retort, but was forestalled by Randall saying, "She's right. What you've done is a disgrace. Whether Elaine has any viable magic or not doesn't give you the right to have treated her this way. Besides," he went on as Greta opened her mouth to speak, "I didn't have any magic, either, remember? It took an outside force to wake it up."

This comment didn't appear to convince the *prima,* whose mouth remained set, pale eyes glittering with malice. "Oh, so you're saying that we simply have to 'wake up' Elaine's talent?"

"Yes," Randall replied, and now he did smile a bit as his gaze met Joanna's. "Although probably not the same way mine was woken up. Still, I have an idea."

Before Greta could speak, he went over to his twin sister and took both her hands in his. She startled, almost as if he'd given her an electric shock. But then her eyes grew wide, and she said in a murmur, "Oh, my God."

"What is it?" he asked, then began to pull his fingers from hers.

She clung to him for a moment longer, face pale. Then her expression shifted from surprise to determination, and she let go and hurried over to her aunt, grasping the older woman's hand before she could pull it away.

Although it really wasn't possible for Elaine to go any paler, considering how fair her skin was to begin with, she still looked utterly shocked. "I don't want to believe it," she said, then dropped Greta's hand as if she'd been holding a rattlesnake.

"Believe what, Elaine?" Randall demanded, taking a step closer to her.

"Nothing," Greta said. If possible, her tone sounded even more imperious than it had a moment before. "She's just pretending, trying to make you think that the touch of her twin brother was enough to wake up her powers."

His brows lifted. "Oh, so you admit that we're twins?"

"That's not what I said—" the *prima* began, now almost flustered.

"It doesn't matter," Elaine cut in. She appeared oddly calm, as if her aunt's admission was all she'd needed to come to terms with the situation. "Because that's exactly what happened—Randall took my hand, and suddenly, I could see into his mind. I saw why he'd come here to help me, and I saw what Susan Latimer, the midwife's daughter, told him." A pause, and she went on, "And when I touched your hand, Greta, I saw what you'd been planning."

"I wasn't planning anything—"

"Yes, you were."

Joanna highly doubted that the Elaine who'd opened the door to her and Randall would have had the courage to cut off the Van Horn *prima* not once, but twice during the same conversation. Whatever he'd awoken in his twin, it appeared to have given her an extra helping of bravery at the same time.

Ignoring the evil glare Greta sent in her direction, Elaine said, "The reason she wanted you here was to get her hands on the money in the trust. It could only be released to one of Alicia Van Horn's heirs, and she couldn't allow herself to admit that I was Alicia's child. Having a niece without any powers would have been a real blow to her standing in the clan. But once you claimed your fortune, then she could safely get you out of the way when the time was right. She didn't want that money going to a bastard child—she thought you didn't deserve to have it. The murder would look like an accident—Karl would use his gift to get you to fall asleep, and then he'd smother you. As your closest relative, Greta would inherit the money and the house."

Joanna listened to all this in dawning horror —a horror she guessed showed clearly on her face —but Randall didn't even blink.

"Now, that makes sense," he said. "I did

wonder why you went to all that work to get me to New York and then did basically nothing to get me to be a part of the Van Horn clan."

"This is ridiculous!" Greta sputtered. The pallor of her face gave the lie to the defiance in her words. "She's making all this up in retaliation for how she thinks she's been treated."

Elaine only gave her aunt a sad smile. "I wish I were making it up. But I'm not. And I'm pretty sure my parents had their suspicions about who my mother really was, but of course they didn't dare ask too many questions for fear you'd cut them off." She stopped there and looked over at her brother. "I just don't know what we're supposed to do next."

"There isn't much we can do," Randall told her. "Information gleaned during a mind reading isn't exactly admissible in court."

"Because this is all nonsense," Greta spat, eyes narrowed in fury.

"I wish it were," he returned. "We all know the truth of what really happened…and we'll also keep it to ourselves to spare the family any trouble. But in return, Elaine and Joanna and I will walk out of here, and Elaine and I will split the inheritance between the two of us. And you won't hear from either of us again." He paused to send Elaine a questioning glance, as if to ask whether that was all right with her, and she nodded.

The *prima* crossed her arms and gave them a narrow-eyed glare. "You're members of a witch clan. You can't simply 'walk out.' You're Van Horns."

"Not by choice," Elaine said. "And we have someplace else we can go."

She must have seen in Randall's mind that they were half Winfield, and therefore definitely had a place to land that wasn't in New York. Joanna appreciated that Elaine hadn't given any details about exactly where they were headed. Greta could stew on that.

And maybe at some point she'd figure it out, but by then they'd all be long gone.

As if picking up that very thought from her mind, Elaine added, "And we'll be going now."

She turned then and went to the double doors Greta had closed just a few moments earlier. Her fingers rested on the crystal knob as she looked over her shoulder at her brother and asked, "Coming?"

Randall took Joanna by the hand. His fingers were warm and friendly, telling her that it was all going to be fine. "Yes," he said. "I think it's high time we leave."

They went out, leaving an angry—and impotent—*prima* behind them.

19

"YOU'RE REALLY SURE ABOUT THIS?" RANDALL asked. Yes, he'd asked Joanna the same question roughly five or six times since they returned to Arizona, but he still wasn't quite sure he could believe her when she told him she was ready to make such a radical change.

She looked up from the box she was packing. Her hair was braided away from her face, but a few strands had fallen loose during her exertions, and she looked more beautiful than he'd ever thought possible. "If I weren't sure, I wouldn't be packing my house, Randall."

He couldn't help grinning at the wryness in her tone. "Okay. I just wanted to check."

"Well, stop. I'm fine. It's going to be fine."

Thanks to his gift of luck, he had to believe her. Why Greta Van Horn hadn't retaliated against them and instead allowed them to walk out of her house, he still wasn't sure...although he privately believed she might not have been as strong a witch as she wanted everyone else to think.

Whatever the reason, they'd left without being stopped. Randall had taken Elaine to the house that was once their mother's, just so she could see it for herself and decide what she wanted to do with it.

All she'd done, though, was walk through the ground-floor rooms, as if assessing their size and their contents, before turning to him and asking, "How much do you think we can get for it?"

As it turned out, quite a lot. His twin had been reunited with her Winfield relatives for less than a week when they got the news that the house had sold for a hair under nine million dollars. Once it was out of escrow, they would split that amount between the two of them and add it to the already considerable fortune that was their inheritance. Elaine might have walked out of Greta Van Horn's house with only the clothes on her back, but she'd ended up with a hell of a lot more than that.

And Randall and Joanna had gone back to Flagstaff, after calling Connor and Angela to come pick them up from the alley near the hotel where Joanna had been staying. Their eyes had been full of questions when they arrived, but they saved the full story for when they'd all safely returned to Arizona, with the *prima* and *primus* thoughtfully taking Joanna straight to her house.

"I hope this doesn't mean we're going to have yet another clan gunning for us," Connor remarked after hearing the tale, and Joanna had grinned.

"I doubt it. We made Greta Van Horn look bad, and I have a feeling the last thing she wants to do is broadcast how someone other than her came out ahead."

Privately, Randall thought the Winfields had a lot more to worry about than the Wilcoxes. After all, Joanna had only been peripherally involved in the affair, and the Wilcox clan had pretty much an entire continent separating them from the Van Horns, whereas the Winfields were only a state away.

But he supposed it was possible they had no idea where Elaine had even gone. It wasn't as though Elaine or Randall had told Greta who their father truly was, and so she might still believe he was a civilian. In fact, she probably needed to keep believing that, if only to explain why they'd been such late bloomers when it came to their magical gifts.

Better that than to think her sister had gone behind her back with someone from another clan, he thought with an inner grin.

Once Connor and Angela had left, however, Randall and Joanna faced each other in the living room of her home. For a long moment, neither of them said anything. At last, though, she touched his arm and gave him a funny little smile.

"So," she'd said, and that was all.

He'd understood, however. And he'd realized exactly what he needed to do.

No words at first, just his lips touching hers, so she would know that he couldn't think of anything he wanted more in that moment than the connection that had grown between them over the past week, strengthening it...embracing it... recognizing it for exactly what it was.

And then he'd murmured, "I don't want to go back to my house."

"I don't want you to, either," she'd responded.

They'd gone upstairs and made love, almost feverishly, as if they both needed to reassure the other person that there were no second thoughts involved here. There was still much to be worked out, decisions to be made, but the two of them came first.

Everything else could wait.

After a day or so had gone by, however—and after Elaine had called Randall to check in, and also to let him know that one of the Winfields who was a real estate agent had helped her locate and purchase a home of her own—he realized that he and Joanna couldn't remain in this unsettled state forever, that a choice was looming before them...one which couldn't be avoided.

"I don't have much to offer you," he'd said one morning as the bright sun slanted in through the kitchen windows and he wondered if he could possibly ask Joanna to leave this sheltered, lovely place. His home, his clan, was on the East Coast, but her home was here.

That remark had made her shoot him an incredulous stare. "Not much to offer?" she echoed, now with an amused smile lifting her sensuous lips. "You do realize you're a multimillionaire now, don't you?"

Oh, that. Because it hadn't done much to change his day-to-day life, he hadn't wasted a lot of thought on his half of the inheritance, now waiting for him in various savings and brokerage accounts. "True," he admitted. "But I don't have any kind of a career anymore. My work was something that defined me for almost fifteen years, and now I have to decide if I want to be a man of leisure or whether I want to do something more with my life."

For a few seconds, she was quiet, playing with a long strand of her hair as she wrapped it around her finger. "You don't want to be an alpaca rancher?"

The words could have been spoken in jest, but

he didn't think so. He knew what she was asking...what she hoped for from him.

"I'd love to be an alpaca rancher, as long as I'm ranching alongside you," he replied.

They'd shared another kiss then, one that promised to transition into something more, if he allowed it to. But as much as he wanted nothing more than to take Joanna to bed again, he knew they needed to lay everything out on the table.

"And where would we be ranching?" he asked next.

They were standing in the kitchen, sharing a cup of coffee. She set down her mug so she could reach over and twine her fingers in his.

"Wherever you want to," she said. Her eyes met his, wide and dark, naked in their honesty. "As long as I'm with you, it doesn't matter so much."

Randall didn't answer right away. Inwardly, he knew what he wanted, even as he thought he would be asking so much of her to give up this house, her clan, her mother in Kayenta.

He didn't know if he was worth that.

"Even in Connecticut?"

"Even there," she said, her voice firm. Before he could say anything, she went on, "Or maybe especially there. I know it's going to be strange to start over in a new place, but it's not as though I'd be doing it alone. Besides, you have your clan there—"

"And you have the Wilcoxes here," he cut in.

But Joanna only smiled. "Yes, and it's not like we can't come and visit from time to time. We're not being exiled, after all. But you have a lifetime of catching up with your sister...and all the Winfields. And even though I doubt we'd be welcome back in New York, I'm pretty sure we could convince your mother to come to Connecticut to visit. It's not that far."

No, it wasn't. He'd be much closer even than he'd been when he lived in Virginia. Most likely, Barbara would be thrilled with such an arrangement, even if he might have to go through a few contortions as to why he wouldn't set foot in New York ever again.

"If you're sure," he said.

"I'm sure," Joanna responded. Although she wasn't exactly smiling, the warmth in her gaze told him that she knew she was making the right choice.

"I'll want to marry you soon," Randall said, his voice firm, and that time she did grin at him.

"Oh, you'd better," she replied. "You think I'm going to move all the way across the country just to shack up with someone?"

About the only thing he could do in answer to such a remark was to pull her close to him and give her a strong, coffee-flavored kiss, a response that soon led to them going upstairs to the bedroom so they could seal the deal.

After that, everything seemed to go into overdrive. The same real estate agent who'd found Elaine her house also located a farm on the outskirts of Litchfield, with ten acres and a lovely restored home that had been built in the 1890s. Joanna researched companies that would safely transport her herd of alpacas—including the *crias* —all the way across the country. She fretted that she wouldn't be able to accompany them personally, but since the truck would have to cut across the territories of many, many witch clans, that plan wasn't exactly feasible.

But many reassurances later, it had come down to the two of them packing those of her furnishings she wanted to put in the truck, and which ones she'd determined she would leave in the Flagstaff house. She'd decided not to sell the place for the time being, and instead was renting it out to a couple of Wilcox newlyweds who were having a house built and needed someplace to land until construction was completed.

"I'll decide what to do with it after that," she said. "It's paid for, so it's not like it's a huge money suck. And Jasper already promised to look after the place for me until I make a final decision."

Randall had thought that sounded like a good

plan. If Joanna wanted to keep one foot in Flagstaff, so to speak, he couldn't quite blame her. Besides, it would give them a base of operations for the times they did decide to come back to visit.

Now, though, they were almost done; the truck was coming the next day. They'd told the moving company they'd be flying to Connecticut, although that wasn't the exact truth. No, Connor and Angela had already offered to teleport them to their new place, after being given detailed photos from the real estate listing so they'd know exactly where to go.

"Of course, I have an ulterior motive," Angela had confessed with a grin. "I want to see your new house."

"There won't be any furniture," Joanna warned her, but the *prima* didn't seem too worried by that.

"It's okay," she said. "I'll get to see it all done up when we come back for your wedding, right?"

Randall and Joanna exchanged a glance. They'd already gotten permission from Blair for a few of the Wilcoxes to attend the ceremony, which they planned for late May, partly because it seemed like a nice time of year for such a thing, and partly because that would put almost a month between their wedding and Addie and Jake's nuptials, which had been on the calendar for

much longer and which they didn't want to interfere with. Anyway, that would give Randall and
Joanna enough time to get their house set up
before the true heat of summer descended—
although, as his mother had fretted, not nearly
enough time to plan a *real* wedding.

"It's just going to be a backyard ceremony
with a couple of dozen people," he'd told her
during one of their phone conversations, and she'd
made a tsk-ing sound, as if annoyed that he
wouldn't be having a big church wedding, the sort
of thing that made the society column of the
newspaper.

But he'd never planned that sort of life for
himself, and he wasn't going to start now.

"I thought you'd be glad that I'm getting
married at all," he told her dryly. "Wasn't it only
last Christmas that you said you'd given up
on me?"

"Oh, well, *that*," she replied. Although he
couldn't see her, he guessed she'd made an airy
wave with the hand that wasn't holding the
phone. "All right, I suppose you have a point."

And she hadn't made any more arguments,
seeming to signal that despite her grumbling, she
was more than happy with the situation.

As was he.

They shared a meal of takeout at the dining
room table—one of the pieces Joanna wasn't

taking with them, since she claimed its simple rustic style didn't quite fit with the Victorian fittings of their new home in Connecticut—and toasted new beginnings with a bottle of wine from Connor's winery down in the Verde Valley. Just another little piece of Arizona they'd be leaving behind, although Connor had assured them that he'd be happy to ship them a case whenever they wanted.

It was very quiet, since the livestock transport had come that afternoon and loaded up the alpacas, taking them away on the first leg of their cross-country journey. Sassafras, Joanna's gorgeous calico cat, was curled up on the floor not too far away. Normally, she wasn't the friendliest of creatures—she still hadn't warmed up to the idea of having an interloper like him around at all times —but no doubt she sensed that change was coming, and wanted to keep her mistress nearby.

Randall watched the glow of the single candle at the center of the table reflect in the rich, dark depths of Joanna's eyes and send little flickers of gold along the silky strands of her night-hued hair. He still wasn't sure what he'd done to deserve someone like her, but, as she'd said as they first began to grow close, sometimes it wasn't about what you deserved.

It was what you wanted.

And he wanted this future with her. Even a

few weeks earlier, he could never have imagined such a future was possible. Against all odds, though, she loved him. She knew the worst about him, the things he'd done while working for Homeland Security, and she still loved him anyway.

What more could he ask than that?

"Ready for this?" he asked, and she set down her wine glass so she could reach over and take his hand.

"As long as you're with me," she replied.

His fingers tightened on hers, and he smiled. "Always."

The End

The Witches of Wheeler Park series continues with Laurel's story in *Healing Hands,* which will release on May 19, 2021.

Demon Born

An Ill Wind

Higher Ground

Haunted Hearts

THE WITCHES OF CLEOPATRA HILL*

(Paranormal Romance)

Darkangel

Darknight

Darkmoon

Sympathetic Magic

Protector

Spellbound

A Cleopatra Hill Christmas

Impractical Magic

Strange Magic

The Arrangement

Defender

Bad Blood

Deep Magic

Darktide

THE SEDONA FILES*

(Paranormal Romance)

Bad Vibrations

Desert Hearts

Angel Fire

Star Crossed

Falling Angels

Enemy Mine

TALES OF THE LATTER KINGDOMS*

(Fantasy Romance)

All Fall Down

Dragon Rose

Binding Spell

Ashes of Roses

One Thousand Nights

Threads of Gold

The Wolf of Harrow Hall

Moon Dance

The Song of the Thrush

THE GAIAN CONSORTIUM SERIES*

(Science Fiction Romance)

Beast (free prequel novella)

Blood Will Tell

Breath of Life

The Gaia Gambit

The Mandala Maneuver

The Titan Trap

The Zhore Deception

The Refugee Ruse

STANDALONE TITLES

Hearts on Fire

Taking Dictation

Golden Heart

Night Music: A Modern Reimagining of The Phantom
of the Opera

Ghost Dance: A Sequel to Gaston Leroux's The
Phantom of the Opera

Flight Before Christmas

* Indicates a completed series

ABOUT THE AUTHOR

USA Today bestselling author Christine Pope has been writing stories ever since she commandeered her family's Smith-Corona typewriter back in grade school. Her work includes paranormal romance, fantasy romance, and science fiction/space opera romance. She makes her home in New Mexico.

Don't miss out on any of Christine's new releases —sign up for her newsletter today!

Christine Pope on the Web:
www.christinepope.com